SLEEP WHEN YOU'RE DEAD

A NOVEL
CHRIS HOLLENBACK

Library of Congress Cataloging-in-Publication Data

Hollenback, Chris.
  Sleep when you're dead / by Chris Hollenback. -- First Edition.
      pages cm
  "Distributed by Midpoint Trade Books"--T.p. verso.
  ISBN 978-0-9910699-0-3 (paperback) : alk. paper)
  1. Serial murderers--Fiction. 2. Murder--Investigation--Fiction.
  3. Green Bay (Wis.)--Fiction. I. Title. II. Title: Sleep when you are dead.
  PS3608.O48457S54 2014
  813'.6--dc23
                            2014003242

For information, or to order additional copies, please contact:

TitleTown Publishing, LLC
P.O. Box 12093 Green Bay, WI 54307-12093
920.737.8051 | titletownpublishing.com

Distributed by Midpoint Trade Books
www.midpointtrade.com

Printed in the United States of America

Interior design by Vally Sharpe
Cover Design by Michael Short

In loving memory of John Hollenback, Jr. and Cory Sherling

SLEEP WHEN YOU'RE DEAD

1

Hailangelo watched the vague shape of Tess Miller through her clouded and textured bathroom window. It made her look like a tragic figure in stained glass. From outside her apartment in Green Bay, Wisconsin, he gleaned her basic gestures—brushing her red hair, touching up her lipstick, putting on her coat, and heading toward the door. Hailangelo could watch her for hours, patient as a priest hearing confession after confession. Tess came out of the complex and walked to her car in the parking lot. She wore tight jeans with a revealing top and a black wool coat she would undoubtedly leave in the vehicle once she arrived at the club.

He casually approached. "Going to the convent?"

She noticed him but avoided eye contact, ignored the remark, and used a keypad to unlock the door to her black Civic sedan.

"You look so trite," Hailangelo said.

That got her attention. She opened the door, paused, and sneered at him. "Excuse me?"

"Every girl in every club dresses like you," Hailangelo said. "They're like fruit flies: each time I throw out the compost I think I'm rid of them, but then five more flutter around the sink. But you? You could be so much more, with the right mentor."

She exhaled hard, clearly annoyed, and sat in the driver's seat. She tried to close the door.

He caught it and held it open. In a warm voice he said, "We haven't formally met." He knew her name, knew her schedule—he knew more about her than her own mother did.

"Do I *know you*?" Tess said, giving the door another tug—to no avail.

"Everybody in town knows me."

"Except me, apparently," she said sardonically.

"Ever see the life-like statues of the Hail football players?"

"You mean in the stadium?" She pointed at it, in clear view, next door to her apartment complex. So much for city planning.

"Yes, in the atrium of Hail Stadium." He could tell by the recognition on her face that she knew exactly what he meant. The statues were landmarks, their images used by the chamber of commerce to attract tourists. "I'm the one who created them." Fans called him "Hailangelo" and treated him like a celebrity. The Hail made Green Bay famous across the country by bringing home more championship trophies than any other club in pro football history. The team featured his statues prominently on its website. This made him ubiquitous. He leaned down to her. "I would really like it if you posed for my next sculpture."

Tess sat in the driver's seat and feigned flattery. "You want *me*?" He'd seen her do this to other men before. She was so adept at the routine that anyone would think her sincere.

"You'd be the perfect muse...if you did exactly as I say."

Her face lit up on cue. She knew how to let men down, and could gauge instantly how gentle or harsh she needed to be. "I'd love to, but my mother told me not to pose for strangers."

"This isn't posing." Hailangelo jabbed a hypodermic needle into Tess's carotid artery. The myriad ways she knew how to tell men *no* went out the car door. He pressed the plunger, injecting a high dose of hydrocyanic acid into her bloodstream. He covered her mouth with his other hand and waited about thirty seconds for the poison to disable the part of her brain that controlled oxygenation. He whispered to her. "You see? Now you won't be doomed to wallow in the battle of the clones at the nightclubs. Now you can rise above the bourgeois to the pantheon of elegance."

He lifted her into the passenger seat and extracted the keys from her hand. His dear mother, may she rest in peace, had given him a humble name. How was she to know then that it would never live up to his stature? He got in, drove her car to his art studio, and parked behind the building. From there, he carried Tess inside. He rang out the thousand hours of peace and rang in his love of darkness.

Three days later, he stood on a wooden stool in his studio, Sergei Rachmaninoff's haunting *Piano Concerto No. 2* rolling and roiling from stereo speakers into the air around him. The recording featured the composer himself playing with the Philadelphia Orchestra, and the inflection and phrasing made Hailangelo feel connected to Rachmaninoff's greatness. He drank a Black Russian from a tall glass with one hand, dipped a brush in acrylic paint with the other and lightly stroked the cheek of his latest sculpture. He smudged it with his fingertip, blew on the paint to help it dry; he adored each aspect of her countenance, and longed to kiss his statue's lips.

"*Madame X*, you are my most gorgeous creation," he whispered to Tess. He set down the glass and the brush, put her hair into a bun and spritzed it with perfume. Nothing like working with *real* hair, he thought. He had posed her head turned to one side so she could gaze over her shoulder, wearing a black velvet dress with a sweetheart neckline and skinny silver straps. She stood still with her weight slightly over her right foot.

Hailangelo stepped down from the stool, retreated five steps from Tess and appraised the statue. He glanced at the poster print on the wall, a reproduction of the classic *Portrait of Madame X* by American painter John Singer Sargent. Hailangelo compared *Madame X* to Tess, his eyes shifting from one to the other. He smiled. He had created a three-dimensional *Madame X* with such realism it nearly took his breath away.

Like many artists, he sought recognition for his works, whether he was showering in praise or melting in criticism. His *Madame X* was different. He knew he had hit on something that could not be denied. She belonged in his exhibit in Manhattan—yet he doubted he could ever let her go.

2

Casey Thread entered the locker room of the Green Bay Hail with confidence. He wore a fitted gray Italian blazer with a white pocket square over a white tailored shirt, with slim-fitting jeans. In high school, jocks had mocked him for being a pretty boy who dressed like a *faggot*. He didn't view himself that way; he simply followed sartorial advice in magazines. That interest had eventually led to his career in journalism.

Casey approached the team's superstar player, Todd Narziss, who stood in front of his wooden locker in nothing but a jockstrap. Narziss resembled the statue *David* on steroids as he removed copious lengths of tape from his wrists. Casey turned from the pungent sweat, sniffed less stale air, and held out his recorder in the vicinity of the athlete's mouth. He had known Narziss for years, having covered the team as a beat reporter at the *Green Bay Times*. Casey had long dreamed of writing freelance articles for national magazines, and now he lived it. He didn't relish the idea of spending more quality time with Narziss, but had taken the assignment anyway because it would pay the rent.

He had ample competition. Journalists gathered around the superstar athlete, buzzing a little more than usual with the playoffs looming for one of the most popular teams in football. Narziss mumbled something; everyone laughed, likely relieved to catch him during an amiable moment so they could get their requisite daily quote and move on with their lives.

Camera flashes bounced off the smooth wood lockers; Casey squinted and turned away, thankful they hadn't triggered another of his narcoleptic sleep attacks. He blinked repeatedly and dug the edge of a credit card into his palm to stay awake. Before he could even attempt to wiggle back into the media hoard and ask Narziss questions, Casey's cell phone rang. He stepped toward the exit across the plush carpet, which featured the Hail's logo—a navy H enclosed in a solid white circle. The phone identified the caller as Nell Jenner, a friend Casey had met through Elena Ortega a couple years ago. Ah, Elena, with her generous curves and beautiful long black hair. He exited the locker room to answer the call.

"I'm worried about Elena," Nell said.

Casey had been on dates with Elena and was smitten by her intellect and the descriptions of her native Ecuador and the Andes surrounding her hometown of Quito. Her tales of Colonial architecture, lazy palm trees, old Ecuadorian women in trilby hats, and sculptures by Caspicara had enchanted the reporter from the Midwestern flatlands. At her apartment, she had even made him a bowl of her *mami*'s fanesca, a twelve-bean soup. She had insisted her version didn't do justice to the original, but he found it savory. Elena could be charming, as in the way she would wistfully describe the soup as making her feel at home: "The preparation, tradition, aroma, and taste jettison me back to childhood." Casey had felt for her when she'd wished her *mami* would follow her to the States, rather than stay with her abusive father. "And for what?" Elena had asked Casey. "To clean hotels and fold towels into swans, all for a pittance?"

"Worried?" Casey said now into the phone. "Why?"

"She was supposed to meet me for drinks Saturday night," Nell said. "She never stands me up."

"She'll turn up. You should have called me; I'm a stellar wingman."

"When you don't fall asleep. I had work to do anyway. But I had a hard time concentrating on it."

"Elena didn't answer her phone?"

"No," Nell said, "and you know how she is."

"Yeah. If she doesn't pick up, she at least texts back."

"In seconds."

"Well," Casey said, "if something's wrong, you should know." Nell was Elena's best friend.

She sighed. "I hope she didn't have some sort of family crisis."

"She didn't go back to Quito, did she?"

"Not that I'm aware. I'd think she'd have at least texted me. Or put something on Facebook. I didn't want to overreact, but by Sunday, I was really worried. She has been known to hang out with some shady characters."

"You, for instance," Casey said.

Nell scoffed. "Yeah, I'm shifty all right. Today, I called the Morris family's house."

"Where Elena babysits." Casey rubbed his eyes, fatigued as usual. He could use a cappuccino.

"Right. I spoke to Mrs. Morris, who told me that Elena had been helping her by taking Shantell to daycare every weekday for the last two years. It's a huge deal because Rihanna is a single mom. Today, Elena didn't show up."

Casey thought of a photo Elena had shown him on one of their dates, of a statue called *La Virgen de Quito*, the one that adorned the top of a volcanic hill known as El Panecillo, overlooking her home town. The 141-foot-tall statue depicted a winged Madonna figure stepping on a snake. Elena adored the statue, not just for its beauty, but because she believed it watched over her and her city to keep them safe. Casey wondered if she was safe now.

"I bet you want to find her as much as I do," Nell said.

"Me?" Casey said innocently.

"Come on, Casey. I know you two dated."

"Once or twice." Four times, actually. Casey had been a perfect gentleman. They hadn't even kissed on their initial dates. He had hoped that might change at the party last Friday at the White House, the residence of one of the Hail's office employees, on Pennsylvania Avenue in Green Bay. The employee, LeRoy "Skeeto" DeWillis, had been one of Casey's best friends since kindergarten.

Skeeto was the team's PR director and was supposed to keep the players out of trouble. Except he also wanted to be the players' friend. So, like a father who throws drinking parties in the basement for his underage teenagers, Skeeto had turned the White House into the local hangout for some Hail players, a place they could gather away from public scrutiny. Casey once asked Skeeto why he would take on that risk, and Skeeto said that if the players messed up, at least he'd be there to clean it up before the police or media arrived. No offense to Casey — Skeeto trusted *him*. In fact, Skeeto had offered him the use of a bedroom during the party. That night, dance music had thumped downstairs out of surround sound speakers and subwoofers, and Elena had asked Casey if he wanted to go upstairs so they could have a normal conversation without yelling. On the way, the U2 song "Mysterious Ways" came through the speakers, and Casey said, "Finally, a good song." Elena had said her favorite U2 album was *The Joshua Tree*. Casey liked it, but he preferred *Achtung Baby*.

As they arrived at the top of the stairs and walked down the hallway, she'd said, "I've always wanted to see U2 live."

"I saw them once."

"Recently?"

"Actually my mother took me, back when I was 15, when they were supporting their album *Pop*."

"Extraordinary. That album's underrated."

"I know. Bono and The Edge did an acoustic version of 'Staring at the Sun' that I'll never forget."

She had bitten her lower lip. "It would be great to see them together."

Casey had resisted the urge to frantically take out his phone and search for their tour schedule. *Breathe. Your most important breath is your next one.*

They had entered the bedroom and he had turned on a lamp.

She'd smiled and said the light reminded her of home.

"Your parents have a lamp like this?" There was nothing fancy about it; it was a simple silver stem with an off-white shade.

"A long time ago, Quito earned the nickname *Luz de America*," she'd said, "Light of America—because it was the first city to declare independence from Spain. So when I see a light like this, yes, it reminds me to be brave, aggressive, and to insist on taking what's rightfully mine." She'd leaned in and kissed him, her tongue soft in his mouth. They had started breathing heavier and heavier, holding each other closer and closer. She'd removed his shirt. What Casey lacked in bulk he made up for in toned abdominals. His entire body had tingled when she pushed him back on the bed, removed her blouse and gave him a "come hither" look.

As she'd unfastened her brassiere, the cups barely clinging to her breasts, most men would have been ready for liftoff, and become overzealous puppies licking and pawing at her. Casey? He'd had a narcoleptic attack.

Now he snapped out of his reverie, walked down the hallway to distance him from the Hail locker room, and asked, "Did you call the police?"

"I just did," Nell said. "They're going to check out her apartment. I figured I'd stop by to see if I can tell what's going on, or answer questions they might have. Care to join me?"

"Yes, I'm at Hail Stadium now," he said. Elena's apartment was a block away. Nell lived on the other side of town, so Casey would have time to get a few more quotes from Narziss before walking to Elena's place. He'd catch up with the athlete later during their scheduled one-on-one interview.

"Great," Nell said. "See you in fifteen."

Casey re-entered the locker room. He could barely keep his eyes open, but had no time for a nap. Narziss held court, answering questions and mugging for the video cameras. Casey wriggled through the mob to hold out his recorder close to Narziss's face. Instead, he fumbled it to the ground. The cassette ejected, bounced, and landed on Narziss's size-twenty Reebok. Embarrassed, Casey reached for the tape.

But the superstar grabbed it first. "Nice hands," Narziss said, tapping the cassette on Casey's forehead. Journalists held their highlighter-sized digital recorders and laughed like bar patrons at happy hour. Most of them wore jogging suits or golf garb. Narziss grinned at his own cleverness. "Ever hear of a digital recorder, Thread?"

Casey snatched the tape, rewound the spool with his pinky, and inserted it back into the recorder. "Can't trust digital."

Narziss guffawed. "Yeah, like the Internet: just a fad."

Reporters chuckled. Awfully charitable of them. Casey hit the record button, sniffed, shuffled his shoulders and held the recorder for a quote. "*A fad*, like how those co-eds say you fondled them at the bars?"

The journalists chortled.

Narziss opened his mouth but nothing came out. He glanced side to side and ran a hand through his flat-top haircut.

Casey's confidence swelled. The room went silent, except for a few snickers. Beat reporters couldn't afford to tell off a Hail player—access to interviews meant everything. If they crossed a player, the Hail Public Relations Department could ban them from the locker room. For Casey, being a freelancer granted freedom. He didn't burn many bridges but, since his job spanned a cornucopia of cities and topics, he could afford to stand up to jerks. Narziss was the kind of testosterone bomb who wouldn't respect Casey unless he challenged the dominant lion like an upstart hyena.

Narziss scowled—he'd learned it from his father, a first-generation German who taught math and coached football, and his Austrian mother, who worked at a Chicago canning plant. Casey had met them once at a post-game reception. They didn't like him either. Narziss made fists. "Get out of my face, Thread!"

The sudden aggression startled Casey, and he swore he saw a mustached reporter sprout purple wings and flutter across the locker room. It was only a hallucination, resulting from a narcoleptic sleep attack. Next thing he knew, he absorbed blows to both shoulders.

Narziss had pushed him. "Thread! What the hell?"

Casey's head and shoulders slumped, his entire body still as a statue. He felt incredibly embarrassed, with the entire room looking at him, Narziss towering over him.

Narziss toyed with Casey, loving the audience. "Thread, you freak, my son wants to bring you in for Show and Tell." More chuckles.

Casey suffered from a rare form of narcolepsy, a neurological disorder, wherein his head drooped in partial cataplexy—or loss of muscle control—while the rest of his body froze in sleep paralysis. Since he couldn't move any part of his body other than his eyes, he often envisioned news articles to pass the time and maintain sanity:

JOCK SO FUNNY, REPORTER FORGOT TO MOVE

GREEN BAY, Wis. — A local man, Casey Thread, suffered a narcoleptic attack today in the Hail locker room. Reporters laughed, adding credence to a new poll showing that most think narcolepsy is hilarious. Thread said that in middle school, boys

ran to him with garden snakes they knew would scare him into
a narcoleptic episode, all while an older bully filmed it with a
camcorder. "How clever!" Thread said.

Now Casey heard what sounded like water draining from his ears after swimming. He snapped out of the sleep attack and, for a moment, couldn't distinguish reality from hallucination. He said what came to mind. "Why would your son want me for Show and Tell, when his dad could demonstrate how to have an affair perfectly well?"

Narziss's eyes bulged and muscles flared as he grabbed Casey by his blazer and tossed him against a nearby locker. Pain shot through Casey's body, especially the back of his head, which bumped a metal clothes hook. The room became a blur. The media throng stepped back.

Hail quarterback Johnny Oakley yelled to Narziss from across the locker room: "Beat up the big reporter, Narzy! You're such a tough guy." Oakley flashed his go-to smoldering look—the one from the underwear ads, and gave Narziss an upward head nod. Oakley made millions and dated models and some jealous reporters didn't like him. Casey did, because Oakley took the time to treat others like human beings. Casey's height and slender build were dead giveaways that he had never played college football, much less pro, so he instantly lost most players' respect. Not Johnny Oakley's. He shared Casey's view that a little respect for others went a long way.

Narziss chuckled, released Casey, and made a feeble attempt to smooth the reporter's pocket square. Some onlookers laughed with Narziss, undoubtedly to curry favor; the rest returned to business, interviewing other players.

Narziss removed his jock strap. He closed his eyes and, with forefinger and thumb, dropped it to the floor with a satisfied grin, even though he stood five feet from the trainers' laundry bin. He knew they'd pick it up for him. He sauntered naked toward the showers like a crooner on stage, singing "I've Got You Under My Skin" surprisingly well.

Casey rolled his eyes and left.

3

Casey crossed the stadium parking lot on foot and headed toward Elena's apartment, where two squad cars were already parked outside.

Nell appeared, approaching the complex from the parking lot, her long blonde hair looking particularly luminescent. She met Casey in front.

"I don't suppose Elena has been playing Wii in her apartment this whole time." Casey felt drowsy, so he took a caffeine tablet from his pocket and swallowed it.

Nell pulled her large curls to one side of her neck. "You probably enjoy picturing her in her underwear doing Wii yoga."

"Tennis," Casey said, "but I'm flexible." They both walked up the external cement stairs of the apartment complex, sliding their hands along the iron railing toward the second floor. The temperature hovered around thirty degrees, and Casey cursed himself for forgetting his gloves. "My hand is liable to stick to this metal."

"Just don't put your tongue on it," Nell said.

The steps led to an outdoor walkway with entrances to each apartment. The doors were navy blue with big white numbers, all corresponding to the digits of the most legendary Hail players—guys like Herb Davis, Billy Kronski, Johnny Oakley, and Todd Narziss. Elena lived in apartment 55, labeled after Kronski, the best linebacker the Hail had ever had. Two cops stood outside Elena's door. One was short, white, young, and slim. The other—older, taller, thicker, and Native American—knocked on the door.

"Excuse me, Officer," Nell said. The cops turned to face her.

"I'm Nell Jenner, I called you about my missing friend, Elena Ortega," she said.

"Yes, ma'am," the fit young officer said.

"Have you found her?" Nell said.

"There's no answer here," the older cop responded.

"Can't you enter under exigent circumstances?" Casey asked, having covered crime for the *Green Bay Times* in the past. He hoped to someday get back to writing more crime and feature stories for magazines. For now, though, sports was his niche and he couldn't work for free.

"There's no sign your friend is in danger," said the older cop. "Unless you know of evidence to the contrary."

"I know she never stands me up on a Friday night," Nell said. "And in two years she has never *not* shown up to walk her friend's kid to school."

"People leave town unexpectedly," the young officer said. "Did Ms. Ortega say or do anything out of the ordinary in the last few days?"

Nell shook her head. "No. But I've got a really bad feeling about this. Please, is there anything you can do?"

The older officer frowned. "We'll err on the side of caution and generate a missing-person file on your friend. I'll have her cell company put a watch on her phone number in case there's activity on it." The officer turned to leave. "Let us know if you hear anything else."

"You're not going to look for her?" Casey said.

The younger cop stopped, swiveled, and smirked. "Who are you?"

"Casey Thread. I'm a friend of Elena's."

"Well, Mr. Thread, more than 2,300 Americans are reported missing every day."

"Yikes," Casey said and glanced at Nell, avoiding the officer's glare.

The cop stepped closer to Casey. "Most of them are children who have either run away or disappeared with a family member, but hundreds are adults. Very few are abducted." He leaned even further toward Casey, his face flushed, his breath smelling of coffee. "We don't have the resources to look for all of them, okay? So we prioritize the ones who are *actually* in imminent danger."

What an insolent conclusion sans evidence, thought Casey. "Nobody knows what has become of Elena," he said.

"Hrmf," the younger officer said.

"Let us know if you hear anything else," the older cop said, in a tone fit for talking to toddlers. "Okay?"

Casey raised his brows and squinted.

With that, the officers left.

This had already been quite a day for confrontations, and Casey hoped it wouldn't be one of those days that snowballed from bad to worse. He glanced at Nell and said, "I should have read *How to Deal With Difficult People* before I accepted this assignment." Nell smirked as they moseyed down the steps outside Elena's apartment and back to the parking lot. He had an empty feeling. "Is there anything we can do to help?"

"Other than annoy the uniforms?" Nell said.

"Got that covered." He hadn't meant to alienate the police. But if they weren't on the case, someone had to do something.

Nell nodded in the direction of the gas station. "When I last spoke to her on her phone, she had stopped for gas across from the stadium. We could ask the clerk about it."

Casey gently grabbed her wrist. "That's a good lead. I'm parked in the stadium lot. Want a ride?"

"Yeah."

"I'll drop you back at your car after." They strode to his Ford sedan and got in. Casey drove through the stadium lot, towards the gas station. He wondered whether Elena was in a hospital. Or a ditch. He suddenly fell into a narcoleptic fit, motionless with eyes open.

The car drifted into the path of an oncoming car, each vehicle traveling about twenty miles per hour. Casey panicked, but could do nothing to stop it. *Crap crap CRAP!*

Nell grabbed the steering wheel. "Casey! Watch out!"

They smashed head-on into the oncoming silver Prius. The collision jolted his entire body, leaving him with a numbing sensation.

The airbags inflated, which was fortunate for Casey, since sleep paralysis prevented him from bracing himself. His body swelled, pulsing in raw pain.

"Casey, are you okay?" Nell said.

He couldn't move, couldn't breathe, his face nestled in the air bag. Great, just wonderful. Was this how he would go out: death by giant ball of air?

Nell pulled him back into an upright position in the driver's seat and shook his shoulder. "Casey? Case!"

He snapped out of it and took a deep breath to recover. He coughed, and took several more desperate breaths to regain his equilibrium. Lightheaded, his pain receded and his gratitude for Nell grew.

"Good to see your narcolepsy is under control," she said.

"The lid's down tight on it." Casey staggered out of the Ford like an elderly man. "I'm so sorry, Nell." His doctor had warned him not to drive for longer than fifteen-minute stretches, for fear of having an attack. But this had come much more quickly. "Are *you* okay?"

"Yes, I'm fine," she said. "Are you?"

"Yeah, yeah." The frigid, dry air nipped at his skin, slowly turning it into sandpaper. "Let's check on the other driver."

The airbags had deployed in the Prius, and an elderly woman gingerly got out of the vehicle.

"Are you okay, ma'am?" Casey said.

"I'm fine, other than my glasses." The lady presented the gnarled remnants. She checked her short white hair. "And here I just got a perm."

"Sorry about that," Casey said sincerely. He could see his breath in the frigid air. "Glad you're okay." Pedestrians stopped and asked if anyone was hurt. This would put points on his driving record, jack up his insurance rates, and become a royal pain of a project when all he wanted to do was find his friend and ensure her safety.

Casey called the police to report the accident. In minutes, a squad car pulled up. The same younger officer they had met at Elena's apartment appeared and asked if everyone involved was all right. The cop gave Casey a glance as if to say, "You again?" then spoke with the elderly woman.

For now, Casey couldn't go anywhere, but he could regroup with Nell and strategize. So he whispered to her, "Did you know Elena was having an affair with Todd Narziss?"

Nell rolled her eyes. "Yes, of course I knew. How did you find out?"

"She told me at the party the other night. It was…kind of weird."

Nell shrugged. "Maybe she wanted you to be jealous."

His heart panged. "Don't get me wrong, I like Elena and all, but sleeping with Narziss? That's worse than gargling toilet water."

"You think she's off at his vacation home?" Nell said.

Casey knew Narziss had one in the Virgin Islands. "She said she had broken it off, that she was single." While he had been shocked that night to learn of the affair, he had been heartened to learn that she was interested in him and, even more so, to discover that she was available. He'd never asked when she had broken it off with Narziss, and a part of him didn't want to know. Now he hunched with Nell near the accident, sharing body heat and wishing he could teleport to Quito for a subtropical vacation.

"She could be back home now," Nell said. "But then she would have canceled our plans, I know it. It just…doesn't feel right."

Something gnawed at Casey's stomach. "Maybe Mrs. Narziss found out about his affair and hired someone to get rid of her husband's mistress."

"Don't even say that," Nell said. But her expression signaled that she had thought of the same scenario.

Casey gesticulated. "Great, I'm scheduled to have dinner tomorrow night with the happy Narziss family."

"Good luck with that."

Casey reached into his crunched car and extracted a canteen of cappuccino. He took it nearly everywhere he went. Caffeine didn't prevent his sleep attacks but it did counteract his constant drowsiness. While waiting for the tow truck, he used his smartphone to locate the numbers for both Green Bay hospitals and called them to see if Elena Ortega had been admitted that morning. Both receptionists said no. Next, he called a free clinic downtown that served many immigrants. There was no one by the name Elena there either, not even a woman fitting her description.

Nell looked hopeful as he ended the call.

Casey frowned and shook his head. He gazed forward and his shoulders slouched.

Nell dipped her head to look in his eyes. "Casey? Case."

He imagined another headline:

LOCAL MAN WISHES TANTRIC SLEEP ATTACKS WOULD CLIMAX, ALREADY

Nell shook his shoulder. "Wake up, sleepyhead."

Casey snapped out of it. "Thanks."

"Do you just…fall asleep?"

"Not exactly. I sort of freeze. During a sleep attack, I can see you and hear you, but I can't move."

"You fall asleep like that a lot?" Nell said.

"What's a lot?"

"More than you pee?"

He proffered his cappuccino. "I pee a lot. I'm the town narcoleptic."

"You shouldn't be driving," Nell said.

"Statistically, it's safer to fly."

She whacked his shoulder. "Let me drive you around, at least for a while."

Casey turned serious. "I can't ask you to do that."

"I insist. Being the top sales consultant in my Baciare Cosmetics district means I drive a company car."

"Seriously? You're number one in your district?"

"Yes."

"Well done, you."

"Thank you."

Casey smiled. "I appreciate you giving me a ride for a while. At least until we find Elena." He paused a moment, returning to thoughts of his last encounter with her, and where she might be now. He wanted to learn more about her country, her family, her culture. At the same time, he couldn't get past her affair with a certain athlete. "What does she see in Narziss?"

Nell smirked. "The fame, the money, the statue, the—"

Casey raised his palm and patted the air. "Okay, I get it, thanks."

Nell lifted a shoulder. "My mom always says, 'Girls pack a special wallop—it's how we get men to marry us.'"

Casey shook his head. "Elena's not the marrying type."

Nell folded her arms. "But you're wondering if she's into you."

Casey glanced at her. "Do you think she is?"

"You sure were into her."

Regardless who she was or what she had done, Casey knew Elena, respected her, and he couldn't just assume she would be fine. If only she had wings like the *Virgen* statue in Quito, then she could fly to safety. He paced. "What if someone took her? We've got to find her."

4

Nell glanced at the car accident, then at Casey. "Hey, Elena's my best friend. I want to find her as fast as you. But panicking won't help."

Casey didn't respond but kept pacing until the officer returned. A flatbed tow truck arrived to transport the damaged Ford.

The police officer approached Casey, pulling on a black winter hat with GBPD sewn on the front. He asked what had happened.

Casey admitted blame and surrendered his driver's license. The officer took it back to his squad car, wrote a ticket, and gave it to Casey. The reporter let out a long, frustrated breath that he could see in the cold air.

"At least we weren't on the Interstate," Nell said. Once the officer dismissed them, they walked through the stadium parking lot, crossed the street, and entered the gas station. The middle-aged white woman behind the counter kept scanning Ding-Dongs and Cokes. Three customers stood in line.

Casey noticed her name tag and said, "Hi, Sandy."

The cashier fluffed her long dishwater-blonde hair. "How can I help you?" She appeared to be in her late thirties and smelled like cigarettes, even from across the counter. Casey had never realized the strength of that odor until he quit smoking. Not that he blamed her for puffing away. He had long viewed cigarettes as his best friend, and quitting his nicotine addiction had been like burying that loyal pal. Still, it was that, or he'd be the one getting buried prematurely.

A teenager in line said, "Hey, there's a line, and it starts back there." He thumbed over his own shoulder.

Casey cleared his throat and held up an index finger. "One moment, please," then turned back to Sandy. "Our friend is missing. Her name is Elena Ortega. She worked at the Hail Pro Shop."

Nell went with it. "When I last spoke to her Saturday late afternoon, she was here."

"What did she look like?" Sandy said, scanning another item.

"She's Latina," Nell said, "about five feet, nine inches, with long black hair."

"Are you two cops?" Sandy said.

"No," Casey said. "Just friends of Elena."

"If she's such a good friend, why don't you call her?"

"Tried that." Casey flashed a photo of Elena he'd taken on his phone during Skeeto's party.

Sandy raised her brows and stepped backward. "Oh, *her*."

Casey felt a surge of excitement. "You recognize her?"

"Todd Narziss came in here an hour ago asking about the same woman."

Narziss?

"That's *right,*" Nell said, as if having an epiphany. "Last Friday night, Elena got another call while she was on the phone with me. She clicked over, and it turned out to be Narziss."

Sandy smiled, revealing yellow teeth. "I'd have worked for free, had I known Todd Narziss would be in here. God, he's hot." She cackled, snorted, fanned herself, and glanced at Nell. "Am I right?"

Nell raised her brows, tilted her head, and cringed.

The teenager in line exhaled his disgust at the delay.

Casey scribbled Sandy's quote in his notepad. "May I quote you on that?"

"Huh?"

"I'm a reporter with *Sports Scene* magazine. I'm writing about Narziss."

"Lucky!" Sandy placed the backs of her wrists on her hips and pouted.

"So I can quote you?"

Sandy shrugged. "Go ahead. It's true. And I'm single." She laughed heartily.

"Do you remember Elena?"

"Yes, she bought an Arizona iced tea. I remember because I told her that was my favorite and she agreed." Sandy scanned the teenager's Mountain Dew and Funyuns. The teen wore a gray hoodie and had piercings in his tongue, lips, and nose.

Casey and Nell glanced at each other. "After she bought the tea, do you know where she went?" Nell said.

The teenager paid and left.

"That's none of our business," Sandy said. *Beep. Beep.*

"Look," Casey said. "I've interviewed Narziss many times. He wouldn't come here unless he wanted something from you."

She guffawed. "He can use me all he wants."

Casey couldn't take any more. "Listen, Sandy, we happen to know our friend had something going on with Narziss, who is married with two kids."

Sandy paused and looked at Casey. *"Going on* going on?"

All the customers in the gas station turned and stared as if Casey were a pink alien.

He swallowed. "He might know more about her disappearance than he has let on. Please. What did you see?"

Sandy scanned a case of Miller Lite and lowered her voice. "Okay. I already told Todd this, so what the hell. She called a cab."

Casey felt deflated. That was her big secret?

"A yellow cab?" Nell said.

Sandy nodded. "Your friend walked here on foot from the stadium. The driver pulled up near Pump 4, didn't buy anything, just got out of the cab and went over to her. A few seconds later, they got into his cab."

"Got surveillance?" Nell said.

"I'm not allowed to give that to anyone but the police, and only if they have one of those …whatcha-jiggers."

"A warrant?" Nell said.

"Yeah, a *warrant.*" She shrugged and protruded her lips. "Sorry."

An old man dressed in Hail gear handed Sandy whiskey, peanuts, and Tums. Sandy continued. "The cabbie was white, had a bad comb-over. It wasn't Frugal Taxi…" She tapped the scanner with her long, pink fingernail. "Maybe Northwoods Taxi?"

"You mean North*Star* Taxi," said the oldtimer in a hoarse voice.

"That's it!" Sandy exclaimed. "Knew there was a 'North' in there."

"Remember which way the taxi went?" Casey said. Now they were getting somewhere.

"Down to Mancinni Ave.," Sandy said. The street was named for the team's famous coach. "He turned left. That's all I know, Mister…"

"Frog," Casey said.

Sandy stared at him without expression. "What's your first name, Mr. Frog?"

"Kermit. Thanks for everything." He headed for the door.

Nell leaned toward Sandy. "Don't mind him." She pointed a finger at her own head and made circles with her hand. "He's a little…"

Sandy rose to her toes and called after Casey. "Hey! You ain't gonna buy nuthin'? Not even a Miss Piggy Pez dispenser?" Casey turned just enough to see that she actually held one.

Casey shook his head. Nell followed him.

Sandy shrugged and ate a Pez.

5

How could one improve on a classic? The answer, to Hailangelo, was to begin with the right materials. The moment he had seen Tess walking on the University of Wisconsin-Green Bay campus, he knew she was the perfect choice. Yes, she had the requisite slender frame, long hair, and angular bone structure. More than that, it was her body carriage, the confidence and intelligence she exuded. He knew full well, though, that he couldn't just take her. No human hunter simply chased down an elk, tackled it, and mounted it on his wall. Acquiring material required patience to learn the prey's habits, dupe it closer with a ruse, select the right moment to attack, and remain calm during capture. The last measure carried particular importance, given the danger of the target fleeing or, worse, bruising and breaking in a way that even he couldn't repair with putty or disguise with paint.

In art school he had studied the great hyperrealist sculptors George Segal, John De Andrea and, most closely, his idol Duane Hanson. He realized he owed them a great debt, and vowed not to let their brilliance be wasted. Like the masters, Hailangelo had learned to use plaster and polyvinyl to make statues from scratch appear impeccably real.

While Hailangelo's most famous statues depicted Hail football players, he preferred his other polyvinyl statues—those depicting the common person in everyday settings. But fame amongst the team's fans led to lucrative orders that paid for his lifestyle. Praise from football fans and New York art critics doused his brain with dopamine, but eventually those spikes waned. Besides, polyvinyl could be toxic and might have caused the cancerous death of Hanson. Hailangelo preferred to live. His new technique involved taking his statues to an entirely new level of hyperrealism. All life came to an end eventually, even his, but he could fix this phenomenon for a chosen few. He'd made it his life's work to capture the most beautiful women he could find and immortalize them forever through a blend of taxidermy and sculpture. Thanks to a machine that sped up the taxidermy process, his dream could become reality in a matter of hours, rather than weeks.

Now he sniffed the paint on Tess's cheek and could tell it was dry. Her ambivalence beckoned him, so he slid onto the oak box, held her, and kissed her. She still felt cold from refrigeration. He hated having to do that but, without it, rigor mortis would set in much faster and malleability of the skin would have been lost. Hailangelo couldn't allow this, as the pose meant everything to him. After all, he knew his artistic limits. He was no Sargent, no Jean-Léon Gérôme, no

Michelangelo. But if he adapted their talents and gave them new life, ah, now *this* would be a way to take the most beautiful women and improve them for all time.

Jealous peers had criticized Hailangelo for "selling out" to America's most popular sport, for not truly creating anything new with his polyvinyl "avatars," for aping Hanson and selling it to the masses. How wrong they were. Yes, he enjoyed commercial popularity and had amassed resources. But he had given back to the community—by leaving his new, human art creations on college campuses in Colorado Springs, Colorado; Galesburg, Illinois; and Ames, Iowa. For these sculptures he'd sought no buyers, no critics, no fame, and no credit. He'd just covered them with a gray tarp in his studio, removed the seats from his minivan, and carefully loaded each statue face-up. Hailangelo had then driven to a place he felt would accentuate the statue, waited for the right moment when nobody would witness the unveiling, and left the sculpture for all to see.

What could be more selfless? Hailangelo knew most geniuses were underappreciated by their peers. It had taken weeks for observers to realize that the statues were made from human material. Even the FBI had scoffed at a young woman named Tess Miller, who brought to their attention the resemblance of the statue in Colorado Springs to a photo she had seen on a missing-persons website. The local TV news stations lined up to interview the photogenic Tess. They wanted to know: *How did it feel to out-fox the FBI?* She had shrugged it off and said the FBI was busy, and that she'd gotten lucky. Hailangelo had wanted to shake that young woman's hand—among other things. He knew he could because, based on the newsclips, he could tell that her personality defaulted to please and submit.

His good deeds had not gone unpunished, as he'd had to suffer through public speculation about who could have created the human statues. As if any hack taxidermist could pull it off! *Please.* Journalists speculated whether the statue in Ames was the work of a copycat or the same person.

It wasn't that he wanted credit. It was the disregard for his talent that bothered him. This was one of many reasons why it pained him to set free his beloved doves, despite the media attention they eventually garnered, and the high he got from the attention. He kept their hearts close to him — in pickle jars on a shelf in his studio. Perhaps he'd leave one more statue, *Madame X*, as a parting gift to the public.

He felt melancholy to think that this statue could be the last made from a real person that he'd ever leave in public. He knew he had to stop. After all, Hailangelo was a student of history: the BTK Strangler, alias Dennis Lynn Rader, had taken ten victims, ceased his work, and blended into society as a deacon, father, and scout leader. Rader had known how to count the proverbial cards and leave the casino while he was still ahead. He had lived undetected for years, and may never have been caught had he not foolishly taunted the police, who'd eventually used a floppy disk he'd sent them to track him down. Hailangelo would not make that mistake, as doing so would take him away from his *Madame X* and prevent him from ever bringing the *Pygmalion and Galatea* to life.

Regardless, he had to make this final public exhibition count. To him, placing the statues was like playing hide and seek. It titillated him to the point of euphoria that passersby would get "warmer" and "warmer" and not even realize his statue had been hiding in plain sight.

It was 3:30 a.m. on the Tuesday he left Green Bay, driving his minivan nine hours to Columbridge University in Columbia, Missouri. Fortunately, despite winter temperatures, the highways were mostly free of snow and ice, and had been thoroughly plowed and salted. In Columbia, he turned left on South 97th Street, and then hung a right on Columbridge Way. He swiveled his head around, searching the campus for the proper location. He had scouted for ideas online, but always kept an open mind in case inspiration struck. When he spotted the ten Ionic columns that stood vanguard in front of Jamesville Hall, he instantly knew he had found the perfect place. He illegally turned off the road and drove the minivan over walkways and lawn, moving toward the columns. He wouldn't have dared to try this with his old Caravan but his new model had better shocks. He knew that the Ionic columns had survived the fire at Columbridge Hall in 1873. The school board had planned to tear down the pillars, but students, faculty, alumni, and citizens had rallied to prove the columns were safe, historic, and deserving of protection. In cases like these, Hailangelo adored the proletariat.

He hoped his statues would last as long as the columns, which formed the centerpiece of a roundabout in front of the stately Jamesville Hall, with red bricks and Roman columns of its own. With nobody in sight, Hailangelo parked and unloaded his *Madame X* statue. He used a dolly to wheel her between the center columns. Hailangelo glanced around again to be sure no insomniacs, college drunks, or third-shift employees watched him. Like a magician, he tore off the tarp in one swoop, folded it crisply and set it in the back of the minivan.

She looked radiant. He blew *Madame X* one last kiss and climbed into the minivan. He flashed back to the moment he had plunged the syringe into Tess's neck and become aroused. He grinned and thought, *hydrocyanic acid works every time*. With that, he drew in a deep breath, catching one final waft of her perfume, and drove home. As he left campus and pulled onto the highway, the emotional high began to wane ever so slightly, melancholy cradling him. This triggered the plans for his next creation.

He would definitely recreate the *Pygmalion and Galatea*. He already had the perfect material in mind, and he would keep her all for himself.

6

As they left the gas station, an alarm sounded on Casey's phone. "Crap, I have an interview with Narziss in five minutes. It's for *Sports Scene* magazine."

"Oh sure, you get a woman in your car, have your fun, then just leave her behind," Nell teased.

"I don't have time to cuddle."

"That's all right. I have work to do, anyway."

"I'll call you," Casey said, and jogged through the parking lot to the stadium atrium entrance, past Hailangelo's polyvinyl replica statues of tight end Todd Narziss and quarterback Johnny Oakley. The statues included details like arm hair, sweat, grass stains on the uniforms and real Hail helmets, which were navy blue with the team logo. Fans often mistook them for the real players, and parents would become angry when the statues ignored their kids' autograph requests. The expansive atrium had been built with exposed steel rods—painted navy blue, of course—to reinforce the unfinished ceilings, giving it a look similar to a restaurant converted from an old warehouse. Casey took the glass elevator to the third floor and approached the PR reception desk, a curved wood-and-steel concoction. On the walls hung life-sized, black-and-white framed photo prints of Hail stars: Oakley held the football cocked behind his head in perfect form; linebacker Billy Kronski hulked over a crumpled defender he'd just flattened. In the image, Kronski flashed the sinister smile and wide eyes of a psychopath pleased with his work.

"Hi, Delores," Casey said.

Delores Tyme's business cards read Public Relations Receptionist but should have said Inside Dirt Queen. "Casey Thread," Delores replied with a smile, radishes for cheeks. Poor Delores still wore too much blush. "What brings you back?"

"I'm writing a *Sports Scene* article on Todd Narziss."

Delores looked at her computer. "Oh, yes. A one o'clock." She spoke in a tone overly sweet and appropriate, like a kindergarten teacher. "Bruce will be right out to show you to the interview room."

Casey nodded and placed his hands in his jeans pockets. "Thanks."

Delores poked her tongue out of one corner of her mouth and slowly turned her head from the computer screen—a telltale sign she had dirt to dish. "Did you hear about Elena?"

"Yes. You know her well?"

She touched her fingertips to her cheek. "Of course. She works at the Hail Pro Shop."

"What can you tell me about her?"

Delores tilted her head. "Casey, why should I share such details with a magazine writer?"

He turned away, toward the Kronski poster. "Just making conversation…"

"Well, I guess I could share a little." She chortled. "Yes, of course I know Elena well. Sweet little thing. She belongs to our book club."

"Book club?" He hadn't realized Elena was well-read.

Delores refocused. "Why yes, we read romance novels." She adjusted her snug, polka-dotted dress over her plump frame. "The group includes the ladies around the office. We have coffee and talk about the hunks in the books. I can't believe Elena's missing, the poor thing. Hope the baby's okay."

Casey froze. "Baby? Whose baby?"

Delores turned in her chair to face Casey and made an innocent face like a kid on a 1950s sitcom. "Elena is pregnant, you know."

Casey coughed, almost choked. They didn't call Delores "Prime Time" for nothing. "Pregnant?" he said. "That's…great." He swallowed. "How far along?"

"Aren't *we* nosey?"

He covered. "I'm just concerned on account of her disappearing."

Delores dipped her head slightly and peered up at him. In a rather loud voice she said, "I heard you two had a little…float on passion's waves." She twiddled her fingers.

Casey squinted. "We met. She's…nice." It couldn't be his baby, right? He'd fallen asleep before they had consummated the relationship.

Delores continued. "It was last Thursday night, at Skeeto's party over at the White House." She rested her chin on the backs of her hands. "You two found a bedroom upstairs and had a good time. Until you took a nappy."

Casey wondered how the hell she knew that. Narcolepsy or not, he still couldn't believe he had had an attack while kissing Elena. Although he did have an excuse: Elena's skin had felt so soft and warm that his heart began pounding—triggering his disorder. Most people yearn to sleep more often. Casey felt drowsy nearly all day; his peers had no idea. It was almost enough to make him wish he could give up sleep entirely. "Who told you that?"

Delores giggled. "Oh, I have my sources."

"The baby…can't be mine."

"Of course not, dear."

After an awkward silence, he said, "Can I quote you on the pregnancy tip?"

"Only if you refer to me as a 'league source.'"

"Done," he said. Perhaps something positive could come out of his humiliation.

"I'm not sure how far along Elena is. She barely showed." Delores inspected her nails. "Of course, Elena's skinny. She could afford to gain weight. I *look* at a brownie and put on ten pounds."

Casey's attention drifted to wondering who had fathered Elena's baby. Suddenly, the narcoleptic attack that had truncated his romantic night with her seemed less embarrassing and more serendipitous. He had always thought he'd be a good dad when the time came—after all, he had great role models in his father and grandfather—but he certainly didn't feel prepared for that responsibility now. He could barely stay awake long enough to take out the garbage. What would happen if he had an attack while changing a diaper? Perish the thought.

Bruce Waters from the PR staff appeared in the hallway. "Casey, Todd's ready for your interview. Right this way."

"Thanks, Delores," Casey said.

"Anytime." She flashed a sly grin.

Bruce led Casey down the hallway. "How's life on the Bay?" Bruce said, referring to Casey's apartment on the shoreline of Green Bay.

"I love it," Casey yawned. "It is a great place to play guitar and collect my thoughts. How are the kids?"

"Good." Bruce was amiable but had the personality of a graham cracker.

Casey tried a different tack to get Bruce talking. "Must be exciting around here with the Hail hosting a playoff game…"

"Sure," Bruce said.

"Lot of interview requests?"

"Yeah."

"What are you up to these days?"

"Working."

"You don't say? Bruce, Narziss has had a great year. But he's… distracted."

Bruce opened the door to the small interview room and flipped on the light. The walls were white, the ceiling and carpet navy blue, with a maple table and two chairs. "*Distracted?*"

"Right. Maybe he's acting a bit funny off the field?"

"He has been moody," Bruce admitted, "but…"

"That's nothing new."

He curled his lips to one side. "You said it." There was an awkward pause.

A few seconds later, Narziss stood in the doorway, eclipsing the hall light with his six-foot-five-inch frame. Narziss exhaled hard and said, "Our PR director said Todd Narziss better come do this or he'll get slammed in the article."

Way to go, Skeeto, Casey thought. Narziss had nicknamed LeRoy "Mosquito" because he stood not much taller than Gary Coleman. Oakley had shortened the moniker to "Skeeto" and it stuck.

Now Narziss sat in a huff and didn't look at Casey. "Don't expect pleasantries."

"I'll get right to it then." He hit record.

Bruce leaned against the wall by the door.

Casey faced him. "Bruce, you mind?"

"Oh, right." Bruce stepped out. PR people had every right to stay in the interview room, but most of them respected requests from reporters to ask the players questions one-on-one, especially if the subject was uncontroversial.

Casey sat about two feet from Narziss. The superstar's muscular thighs were as thick as the reporter's slim waist. Casey liked to toss interviewees a softball question as an icebreaker. "You're having your best year as a Hail player," Casey said. "How much of that is thanks to the emergence of Marshon Cummings at running back?"

"MC's having a great year," Narziss said. "It certainly has helped Todd Narziss to get a clean release from the defenders at the line of scrimmage. When Oakley fakes the handoff to MC, he's got Todd Narziss wide open downfield."

Casey hated when players referred to themselves in the third person. People who did that invariably had life-sized portraits of themselves hanging in their homes. If Casey wanted to keep a superstar like Narziss happy, he knew to stick to football. He needed Narziss for this story and might need him again. Still, he couldn't shake the thought of Elena lying in a ditch or the woods. "You know Elena, right?"

"Excuse me?"

"Elena Ortega."

"Never met her."

Interesting. "I already know you know her."

"Then why ask me?" Narziss said.

"She works at the Pro Shop, and told me the other night that you had an affair with her."

"This for your story?"

"Just curious."

"You're a terrible liar," Narziss said.

"You offering pointers?"

Narziss forced a laugh. "I thought we were talking sports."

"I took this assignment for *Sports Scene* to talk about your playoff run. But when a pro-shop employee, who happens to be my friend, tells me she's involved with you and then disappears, things change."

Narziss finally made eye contact. "If she disappeared, how do you know she didn't just leave town on vacation?"

"Sources. So you *do* know her, then."

"Off the record?"

He knew damn well it wasn't, Casey thought, glancing down to make sure the red light on his recorder still illuminated, and that the cassette reels rolled.

"Yeah, I knew her. I bought a big order of Hail gear for the kids at the local hospital on behalf of the Narziss Foundation. Elena filled the order."

41

"You *knew* her?"

"Listen to Narziss when he speaks," Narziss said.

Casey scratched his head. *I am listening, you ass-clown.* "But you said it in the past tense."

"Are you my English teacher now?" Narziss said. "Go weave a scarf."

"There's a correlation between English and weaving?"

Narziss waved at Casey. "Whatever. The point is the kids. I really feel for these little peeps cooped up in the hospital when they should be out playing ball."

Narziss bragged about practically everything, but it didn't surprise Casey that he was coy about his affair with Elena. Casey tried baiting the player with something chauvinistic he'd otherwise never say. "I bet the boys at the hospital wanted to jump Elena's bones."

Narziss saw through it and sat up. "This is a non-story."

Casey leaned forward in his chair. "Come on, Todd, people will love you when they read about your gentle side, helping sick kids."

"They already love Todd Narziss."

Casey wondered how much they'd love him if they knew he had been banging the Hail Pro Shop girl while Mrs. Narziss took care of the kids. "So you're saying there's nothing more to your relationship with Elena?"

His smile evaporated. Then it reappeared. "You're fishing for drama for your story. You think every pro athlete is a womanizer."

"No, I don't. But I think one athlete is."

Narziss leaned back and laughed. "You know, Thread, I give you props. Most reporters are kiss-asses, but you give it right back."

"I also won't let you wiggle out of dinner tomorrow night," Casey said, half joking but, like most quips, grounding it in more truth than he'd readily admit.

"You're lucky you're writing for *Sports Scene* magazine, or I'd tell you where to go."

These were the realities of sports reporting. Casey had scheduled the dinner in addition to the formal interview so he could get a sense of Narziss's life away from football. The editors of *Sports Scene* would have it no other way. "Need me to pick up a pizza on the way?"

"Samantha said she's making chicken curry." The superstar grinned. "Narziss loves things that taste like chicken."

Casey rolled his eyes. "So we're still on?"

Narziss held out his hands. "I've got nothing to hide."

Pressing the affair risked losing access to Narziss for this article and forever into the future. On the other hand, this exposé could make his career. "*Nothing to hide.* So you've told your wife about the Elena rumors?"

Narziss leaned toward Casey, pointed a bratwurst-sized finger and whispered, "If you bring that up to Samantha, Narziss will kill you."

Casey certainly enjoyed living, so for the moment he dropped it. Then the image of Elena lying dead reappeared in his imagination, soon followed by a hollow feeling. He wondered if Elena had asked Todd to leave his wife. Casey heard himself speaking before the words left his mouth yet he couldn't pull them back. "So you had nothing to do with Elena's disappearance?"

The star stood up. "What's wrong with you? Todd Narziss has been here, at the stadium, preparing for the playoffs. I don't have time for anything else."

Like a bastard child? Casey looked up at him and smirked. "Just because you were here doesn't necessarily mean you didn't know she would vanish."

Narziss made an incredulous spitting noise. He looked toward the hallway. "Bruce?"

Casey remained seated and said, "Come on, Todd, just a few more questions."

He pointed at Casey. "Don't push it, Thread. We're done." Narziss walked toward the door, rolling his right shoulder with machismo, cracking his knuckles and stretching his head to each side, clearly wishing he could use the reporter to knock out the drywall.

"Well, this is an amazing start," Casey said. "I have a feeling we'll make more progress tomorrow night."

Narziss paused in the doorway and gave Casey a look like, *You've got to be kidding.*

Casey thought for sure Narziss would call off the dinner interview. So he said, "You know I'll write this article whether you participate or not. Do you really want Mrs. Narziss to read about this in *Sports Scene* magazine? Hear it from all her friends? On the other hand, if you deny the affair, tell your wife about the rumors now, then you have nothing to worry about in having me over. I'll behave. I promise."

Narziss glowered. "Fine." With that, he left.

A moment later, Bruce appeared in the doorway, watching Narziss stride away. Bruce looked at Casey and asked his pat question, "Interview go okay?"

7

After the interview, Casey called Nell. "Can I buy you coffee at Fixate Factory?"

"Twist my arm," Nell said. "I love that place."

"My sister Leila works there," Casey yawned, "and I need a caffeine infusion, stat."

Fifteen minutes later, she pulled up in a lipstick-red BMW Z4 Roadster convertible.

Casey laughed. "Seriously? Nice wheels!"

"Thanks, I just earned it from Baciare Cosmetics."

Of course she did. "You make real money selling cosmetics?"

"I make enough to convince people that I'm a robber baron."

Casey envisioned a pyramid scheme as he got into the car.

"Of course, that's not true," she continued, pulling away from the stadium. "But we are independent contractors, so we call our

45

own shots. My current national director lives down the street from Oprah."

As he rode, Casey periodically pinched his own arm to stay alert.

Fixate Factory lacked square footage but had character. Olive walls featured hand-painted cream paisley flourishes in the corners. The stereo played mellow bossa nova music with sultry singers set to electronica dance beats. Periodically, live musicians or poets would take the mic. The toffee-flavored coffee smelled rich. Leila Thread dispensed whipped cream on a customer's mocha.

"Hey Case, what's up?" Leila said, sounding somewhat ambivalent. She fiddled with a strand of blue hair that had fallen astray from her bun and pushed up her black glasses. The siblings hugged awkwardly across the counter. Casey introduced Leila and Nell.

Leila invited them to sit at the counter.

"What can I get you?" she asked them.

Nell and Casey ordered cappuccinos and scones to go.

"You have a nice complexion," Nell said to Leila.

"Yeah, riiiight," Leila said, half-asleep and pointing with a pen at a zit on her nose. Actually, Leila did have fair skin, which she got from her mother. But she never wore makeup and, ever since the attack, had cared little about her appearance.

Nell motioned at Leila. "Easy to fix, even easier to prevent. Ever try Baciare Cosmetics? We have an in-CRED-ible four-in-one facial cleanser."

Leila folded her lips into her mouth and rubbed her temple, where Casey could still see the scar from the cigarette burn. These were the same nervous tics she'd done since high school whenever she felt intimidated or infuriated by another female. "Um, makeup's so not my thing." Leila glanced down and saw she had chowder on her shirt. She wiped it with a white towel.

"I used to feel the same way," Nell said. "But after I tried Baciare skin-care products, I was hooked. Now I'm a sales consultant!"

Leila stared blankly. "Oh goodie." She handed them their drinks.

Casey chugged half his cappuccino and wished for a flask.

"I like the blue hair," Nell said to Leila. "I bet we could find a lip color to complement it perfectly." Nell handed Leila a business card depicting lipstick that resembled candy. "Well, call me, I'd love to give you a free facial. You deserve to be pampered."

Leila handed them a paper bag with scones, narrowed her eyes, folded her lips in again then smacked them. "Anything else?"

"Check, please," Casey chimed. They followed her to the cash register, where a man was paying for his takeout order.

Casey could have sworn he looked familiar. He nudged Nell and whispered, "Isn't that the sculptor who made the stadium statues?"

"Hey, yeah, I think it is. Ask for his autograph."

Casey introduced himself to the sculptor. "I'm writing about Todd Narziss and the Hail for *Sports Scene* magazine." They shook hands.

"Hailangelo," he said, accepting Casey's business card.

"Yes, I interviewed you once before for the *Green Bay Times*."

"Oh right," Hailangelo read the card. "I thought you looked familiar. Hey, are you related to Leila?"

"Yeah, she's my sister."

"Small world." Hailangelo smiled at Leila. She raised one brow skeptically and wiped the counter.

"I'd really like to interview you about your Narziss statue for my story. Since it's part of the local lore."

Hailangelo was in his late twenties or early thirties and had clean-cut brown hair parted on the side. He was a guy a girl could bring home to Mom. "It would be my pleasure. I'll call you."

"Terrific. Nice to see you again. Keep up the stellar work."

Hailangelo grinned. "Oh, I will." He took his food and coffee and left the shop.

Casey handed Leila his Visa card. "I'll see you later this week, okay?"

"Yep, call my cell," Leila said, running his card and handing it back along with the receipt. "Good to see you, Case." Her voice lacked emotion.

It wasn't that they didn't get along. It was more that they had grown into such different people. At times in their lives, Casey had figured it was the age difference. After all, five years could be an eternity when one kid is in ninth grade and the other in college. Though now it meant less. It had more to do with a certain night, and their general lack of things in common beyond their parents and genetics. Sometimes it felt like Leila had grown tired of continuing to make the effort. "Thanks, sis." He signed the receipt and handed it back to her. "Good to see you, too."

Nell and Casey returned to her Beemer and she gave him a ride to his mother's house. "Got any big plans with your mom?"

"Not really. It's Bridge Night and I promised to give her a ride."

"She doesn't drive?"

"She has early-onset glaucoma from smoking."

Nell stared at him a moment and he waited for the inevitable question. "How will you drive her without a car?"

Casey shrugged. "Call a cab. Maybe I'll try the same taxi service Elena used."

"Yeah, great, then you could disappear, too." She took a bite of her scone. "By the way, you know Skeeto's dog, right?"

Casey felt grateful for a change of subject. "Who could forget a doggie named Bag?"

"The morning after Skeeto's party, Elena was passed out in the hallway of the White House. Doggie Bag sniffed her face, then her back and butt, paused and made an 'ew' face."

Casey laughed. "No way."

"It's true. I got her up and dressed."

Casey appreciated knowing that he wasn't the only one who fell asleep at inopportune times and, in an odd way, he related to Elena. While that image of her wasn't exactly alluring, it didn't change his overall opinion of her when she was awake; she was sharp, gentle, and drop-dead gorgeous. She never paid for drinks and, like many girls who enjoyed this status, was prone to getting drunk. Then again, Nell and Leila would never pass out on the floor, would never even give a dog a *chance* to sniff them. Plus, Elena had slept with Narziss. Narziss! Somehow, the sheen of Elena faded. Regardless, she was missing and pregnant. He had to find her.

"You may want to think twice before you fall for Elena," Nell said.

"I'm not falling for Elena," Casey said. Technically, he had already fallen for her.

"You sure about that?" Nell pulled the car up in front of his mother's house, a white ranch with black shutters and a matching front door.

Casey smirked. "Only woman on my mind right now is my mother."

"Sure you don't want me to just give you both a ride?"

"Thanks, but Bridge Night isn't for a few hours. I'm sure you have better things to do."

"I do have a Baciare appointment. Have fun with your mom."

Later that night, his mother, Elzbieta Thread, sat next to him in the cab, her long gray hair up in a bun. Her skin had wrinkled from decades of smoking; Nell could have made a killing selling anti-aging creams just to her. Elzbieta did have decent cheekbones and a triangular nose that she had passed on to her son. She was sixty-three years old and stood five-foot-three, but carried a big verbal stick and didn't hesitate to use it. Casey respected that. She got things done. Hell, she'd raised two little kids on her own after her husband died. He owed her the world for that.

"I'm making pot roast for dinner tomorrow."

"You don't have to do that, Ma. I could bring home takeout."

"Takeout? I don't go for that. You live in town, yet you only have one night a week for your mother."

He knew that, tough as she seemed, she really did miss him. "Ma, I'm sorry, I'd really like to spend all week with you." His proverbial pants were on fire. "But you know I'm writing my first major feature story for *Sports Scene* magazine."

"Aren't we big in our britches." She shuffled her shoulders and looked out the passenger-side window.

"It's my job, Ma."

She shook her head. "That's your job—with the Church's shortage of priests!"

Casey sighed. What was it with so many mothers from her generation wanting their children to become priests, rabbis, or ministers? Perhaps they wanted to approach other moms and say, "In your face! My son is holier than yours!" Or maybe it blossomed from a Freudian yearning to preserve their sons' purity. What else could be such a surefire ticket to heaven?

"Well, you won't be a writer for long, anyway," Elzbieta said. "You never finish anything. You're always falling asleep before you can."

Typical mother. Casey figured her beefs with her kids stemmed from her own insecurity. She'd convinced herself she was the All-American Mother. To Elzbieta, that jibed neither with her daughter's rape nor her son's mediocre accomplishments in all parts of life, so she'd decided the problem had to be her children's attitudes, and that it was her task to fix them.

"Actually, Ma, I think I might be on to something with the disappearance of a Pro Shop worker who was having an affair with the team's best player."

"An affair?" Elzbieta exclaimed. "That's worse than murder!"

Here we go. "Actually, I think murder is far worse."

Elzbieta crossed herself. "I was just telling my neighbor about the violent wave of crime."

"Mom, this would be the first murder in Green Bay in eight months. And don't be scaring Mrs. Van Klooster like that."

"What about that rape and murder a week ago?"

Unbelievable. "You mean the one in Milwaukee, two hours away?"

"Maybe the killer's got a car. Don't be a *dummkopf*." She nodded her head as if to say, So there. "A lot of girls have been disappearing around here."

They're probably all hiding from their mothers, he thought. "Doesn't mean that's what happened to Elena."

"You, of all people, should know about women being attacked."

"Really, Mother?" His fingers tightened into a fist. She had to go there. He closed his eyes, took a deep breath, and relaxed.

The cab turned into the parking lot at the Sunset Shores Recreation Center. The cab driver glanced over his shoulder and smiled. "We're here, ma'am."

Elzbieta learned forward. "Thanks. You want a cookie?"

The cabbie frowned. "Payment will do."

Casey apologized for her and asked the driver to wait and keep the meter running.

"Oh, it's running," the cabbie said.

Elzbieta got out of the car.

Casey followed and tried not to show his displeasure. "Mrs. Peterson is hosting tonight?"

"Yes," Elzbieta said. "She always cheats."

They walked toward the door of the recreation center. "Cheats? How?"

"She passes her dish of mints to distract us while she corners the cards. I may be going blind, but I wasn't born yesterday."

Casey thought, *Can't get anything past my mother. In your face!* "Have a good time, Ma."

"I'll try." She took a step inside the doorway and turned back to her son. "See you, kid."

The curve on her face looked strangely like a smile. The front door shut and he pivoted, smacked his lips, and walked back to the cab.

"Where to?" the taxi driver said.

Casey wanted to ask him to drive fast off the Tower Bridge. Between Elena, Narziss, his mother, and narcolepsy, he had just about had it. Instead, he gave the cabbie the address for his apartment. The *Virgen* statue in Quito had been constructed from more than seven thousand pieces of aluminum. He hoped Elena was still in one piece.

8

Hailangelo sat in his house in Green Bay, using his laptop to log onto the website for ABC 27 News in Columbia, Missouri. The site had been streaming a video of the mysterious *Madame X* statue that had caused quite a stir, and the reactions of those who saw it. Students had discovered it on their way to early morning classes. "I thought she was some kind of performer," a coed said. "But like, then she didn't move." The coed said frat boys sent cat calls toward *Madame X* before they realized it was "just a statue." They wrote it off as funny at first.

This drew the sculptor's ire. *Just* a statue?

On video, a school administrator told News 27 she noticed stitching along the back of the statue's foot. It was then she reported the incident to campus police, who eventually realized that the statue was the work of a taxidermist. The reporter appeared on camera in front of the columns, police snapping pictures of the statue behind her. "Police have not identified the victim, and would not confirm a connection to similar bodies left in Colorado, Iowa, and Illinois during the last year. However, News 27 has identified a pattern of precisely three months between the appearances of each of the four human statues."

A tanned male news anchor asked, "What does the FBI have to say about it?"

The reporter, a young woman, answered, "The Bureau is in fact assisting police in determining whether the statues are connected. If they are, the FBI would surely take over this case, since it crosses state lines and involves more than two homicides."

The anchor asked, "Do police have any idea who could pull off this display?"

"They wouldn't say, but News 27 has learned that campus police officers have already interviewed art professors and students on campus, and have taken DNA samples they hope to compare to any found on the body. Forensics experts swabbed the body this morning for further analysis. Reporting from campus, Wendy Lee, ABC 27 News."

Hailangelo giggled as he cleared his internet browser's history. He knew he couldn't have pulled off this stunt back when he was an art student in college. Perhaps he could have used polyvinyl replica statues, but not the real thing. He had used surgeon's gloves throughout the process of creating *Madame X*. He had kept her dress in a sealed plastic bag until the trip to Columbia. Neither would carry his DNA.

Three months ago, he had been questioned in Green Bay shortly after the third human statue, a lifelike rendering of *Mona Lisa*, appeared in Galesburg. The FBI had originally sought out hyperrealist sculptors and talented taxidermists living in Colorado, Iowa, and Illinois, but had since expanded the search nationwide. Hailangelo, known for his polyvinyl exhibits in Manhattan, Chicago, and Hail Stadium, had drawn the interest of Special Agent Antonio Torres from the Milwaukee FBI Field Office, who one day knocked on Hailangelo's door in Green Bay and asked if he would answer a few questions.

Took them long enough, Hailangelo thought, but invited him in anyway and cooperated completely.

When Agent Torres, a dapper Latino in his thirties, asked if Hailangelo had any experience in taxidermy, he paused and admitted he did. After all, his shop had been no secret. "Surely, if taxidermy automatically made someone a serial killer, the FBI would be awfully busy," he said. Hailangelo had prepared for this day by studying FBI journals, videos, and podcasts.

Agent Torres asked to see Hailangelo's shop, and got the full tour of the one-room store on Green Bay's east side. The agent thanked him for his compliance, left his business card and asked Hailangelo to call him if he thought of anyone else who might be behind the creation of these statues. After all, he probably knew most of the people capable of such a feat.

"Will do, Agent," Hailangelo promised. After Torres left, Hailangelo thought about how Milwaukee police had stood at the door of serial killer Jeffrey Dahmer, even returning to Dahmer a delirious victim who had escaped from his apartment. Left free in society, Dahmer killed a total of 17 victims before his capture.

Hailangelo knew he had passed a major milestone—his first encounter with authorities. It was time to bring his *Galatea* to life.

9

Nell dropped off Casey at NorthStar Taxi on the way to a Baciare Cosmetics party with wives of Hail players—her best customers. The lot had been plowed, brushed, and salted to the point that he could see the pavement.

Casey wrapped his red scarf around his neck to protect himself from the chill and counted the NorthStar parking stalls, twelve in all. There were taxis in all but four spaces.

An African-American gentleman in his sixties came out to meet him. "Can I help you?"

"Hi, I'm Casey Thread, a reporter with *Sports Scene* magazine investigating the disappearance of a Hail Pro Shop employee." Casey handed him a business card.

The gentleman took the card, glanced at it, placed it in his pocket and said, "I'm Tyrese."

Casey shook his hand. "A pleasure."

"Likewise."

"You work here?"

"Yes, I'm the manager." Tyrese wore a plaid wool skicap. "Do you need a ride?"

"Not at the moment. The missing young woman is a friend of mine, Elena Ortega."

"A friend of yours? How so?"

"I dated her for, oh, a night."

Tyrese grinned. "Well, take it from an old-timer: you were a lucky man for a night."

Casey raised his brows.

"What?" Tyrese said. "I may be old, but I'm still breathing."

Casey nodded and smiled. He could hardly blame the man. "Do you know Elena?"

"I do. She is a regular customer."

Wait a second. Tyrese had access to the taxis and he knew Elena. "Do you ever drive a cab?"

"Haven't in years. I'm like air-traffic control, but for our ground units. Do you work with her?"

Casey shook his head. "No, why?"

The man didn't answer. Curious. What did he know about Elena's co-workers? Did he suspect someone at the Pro Shop?

Tyrese hiked up his pants, nodded and said, "Okay, I'll help you."

"Do you have anything against the Pro Shop workers?"

"Pro Shop? No, of course not."

Strange. "Are all your cabs accounted for?"

"Well, funny you should say that." Tyrese looked toward the office, probably to confirm that his boss couldn't hear him.

Casey knew from his research that Oscar Oleysniak owned the place. "Why is that funny?"

Tyrese turned back toward the row of cabs and lowered his voice. "Units one, four, and five are serving customers right now. But there should be a cab in slot twelve." Tyrese peered over his silver reading glasses, a flat toothpick hanging out of the corner of his mouth.

"How long has Cab Twelve been missing?" Casey said.

"Since Friday night." He firmed his lips and nodded.

"That's the same day she disappeared," Casey said, looking at stall number twelve. "What about the driver?"

Tyrese leaned in and muttered, "Haven't heard from him since."

A pit formed in Casey's stomach. He glanced at the parking stall marked "12," then back to Tyrese. "Did the cabbie report picking up a woman near the stadium Friday night?"

"No," Tyrese said. "But we have a GPS tracking device in the trunk of every taxi. Our computer displays the location of the cabs in real time as they move, for security of course, but really more so I know which cab to send where."

"And where was Number Twelve?"

Tyrese exhaled, as if he had expected that question from the moment Casey arrived. "I was working Friday night. By watching the electronic command board, I could tell Cab Twelve idled about a block from Hail Stadium for twenty minutes, waiting for the next assignment."

"Are the trips recorded?"

"Not by us." Tyrese blew out his hot breath, which materialized in the cold air between them. "It's expensive and not necessary."

"Are you recorded in the office?"

Tyrese gave him a look of surprise mixed with humor. "Actually, yes. Surveillance is on in the office twenty-four seven in the event of a break-in. I can assure you I was not driving that cab, Mr. Thread."

Casey swallowed and raised his chin a bit. "Just…covering all bases."

Tyrese cleared his throat. "Anyway, most of our traffic goes to and from either the airport or Hail Stadium. So, that much was normal."

"What wasn't normal?" Casey said.

"Well, at one point Friday night, he turned onto Edge Road and stopped."

"For how long?"

"A minute, two maybe," Tyrese said. "Getting gas, I thought. Though…it was weird."

"What?"

Tyrese grabbed his toothpick and worked it between his teeth. "Ed usually calls in his gas stops. I have to remind some drivers, but never Eddie. He was by-the-book."

"He didn't call in?"

"Nope. Just took off." Tyrese shrugged. "I suppose it's possible he might have forgotten to call in about the stop. But he wouldn't have just taken off and never called."

Adrenaline pulsed through Casey. "Do you know where he went?"

"Yes, he took Mancinni Avenue to Highway 41," Tyrese said, pointing in the direction of the stadium, as if they could see it. "Headed north, stopped along the shoulder of the highway, about a mile up, from what I could tell. Then the GPS tracking went dead. Hasn't come back online since."

Casey scribbled notes as he said, "The cabbies know where the GPS box is located?"

"The veteran drivers do, yeah."

"How long has that driver—"

"Ten years," Tyrese said.

Casey paused a moment. Had that driver dislocated the GPS so he could take Elena somewhere nobody would find them? Goosebumps covered Casey's skin. "What did the police say?"

"We haven't contacted them. The boss didn't want to."

"Doesn't your boss want his cab back?"

Tyrese grinned. "My boss doesn't like cops."

"That's right, police have been leaning on him for drug trafficking, right?" It had been in the news.

"Yep. Haven't found anything, though. The boss simply said Cab Twelve was out on duty. Which, I suppose, *could* be true."

"But you don't buy that."

Tyrese shook his head. "Hell no. Eddie, the driver of Cab Twelve, is the bossman's go-to guy for delivering packages."

"Is it normal to have a go-to guy?"

"Well, we've got some drivers who are better than others. But the odd part was Ed delivered *all* of the boss's packages. Mr. Oleysniak never uses the mail, and he never delivers them himself. Elena would talk to the boss often."

"Elena? About what?"

"I don't know. But I can tell you she was responsible for a boom in our business."

Couldn't be. Not Elena. "What are you implying, sir?"

Tyrese shrugged. "We delivered a lot of packages on her behalf, multiple times a day. She'd call us from random locations and we'd send the cabs there to pick up her boxes and deliver them to whomever."

"Listen, Elena wasn't a vestal virgin, but she's my friend, and I don't like what you're insinuating."

"I'm not insinuating anything, Mr. Thread. You wanted the facts. I'm giving them."

Casey sighed and wrote on his pad. "She have a problem with the post office?"

"Unlike the post office," Tyrese said with a sly smile, "we don't scan packages or ask what's inside." He raised his brows at Casey.

"Her shipping costs must have been through the roof." Of course, if she made enough off the packages, shipping wouldn't be a big deal. "You don't think…"

Tyrese tilted his head. "Drugs? I have never seen the inside of those packages, but it's possible. She'd drop off larger boxes when she'd visit Mr. Oleysniak."

Sleeping with Narziss was one thing. But dealing drugs? "No, no. She was seeing a rich guy. Didn't need the money. Why take the risk?"

"Well I don't know for sure, Mr. Thread. But consider who could afford to buy the drugs."

Professional athletes. Could that be how Elena met Narziss? Selling him drugs?

"When Elena scheduled deliveries, did she call you, or go through your boss?"

"Lately, she would call Ed directly on his cell."

Casey's hand quivered. "Did she order any pickups the day she disappeared?"

Tyrese thought for a moment. "Yes. Yes, she did. She told our cabbie to pick it up from her at the stadium."

Casey had almost had sex with Narziss's drug-dealing mistress. Nausea swelled. He placed a fist to his mouth until it subsided. "Who was assigned to pick it up?"

Tyrese cleared his throat and glanced back at the office. "Oleysniak personally assigned Ed to Cab Twelve."

Through the glass front wall of the building, Casey saw Oleysniak stick his head in Tyrese's office, turn around, spot them and raise an eyebrow. Casey's flight instinct was aroused, but he couldn't leave now. Not this close to getting a real lead on finding Elena.

Casey wondered if Elena had for some reason changed the drop spot to the gas station. "Why do you think Elena didn't drop the packages herself?"

"She didn't have a car. No driver's license. She was a foreigner without a green card. More importantly, she also wanted to keep herself removed from the actual exchange of money."

"If she didn't have a car, what was she doing at the gas station last Friday?"

Tyrese shrugged. "Buying something to drink?"

That jibed with Sandy's recollection of Elena buying tea. "Is it possible Cab Twelve was loitering in the area, waiting for either a call to come in or for Elena's pickup?"

"That would be my guess."

"Any idea where Ed could be now?"

Tyrese turned his back toward his boss, who neared. Tyrese whispered, "He always talked about how much he loved fishing and hunting at his cottage up north."

"How could he afford a cottage?"

"Inherited it, if memory serves," Tyrese mumbled.

Oleysniak came closer.

"Eddie's last name?" Casey whispered.

"Plasky," Tyrese answered. "With a *y*."

"Any idea where this cottage is?"

Tyrese leaned in and whispered. "It's on Blue Lake Road in Minocqua. I remember because it was the same name as the lake."

Casey scribbled.

Oleysniak's shoes crunched on snow. His hair was white, his neck thick, and his skin looked like raw ham. Oleysniak said, "Can I help you?"

Casey shook Tyrese's hand and said, "Thanks for your help."

Tyrese glanced at Oleysniak. "He didn't know we already had a vendor for a tracking system."

Oleysniak sneered at Casey. "No solicitors."

Casey saw Nell's red BMW pull into the lot. She rolled down the window. "Hey, sleepyhead. Need a ride?"

10

Nell drove Casey to Narziss's house for their scheduled interview and dinner. On the way there, Casey asked about the cosmetics party.

"It was stellar," she said. "I met my monthly goals in one day."

"Nice." He filled her in on what he had learned from Tyrese. "How in the world did Elena get mixed up in selling drugs?"

Nell shrugged. "Because her father runs them in Ecuador."

"You knew?"

"You didn't? How do you think she afforded the European furniture and designer shoes?"

"I had wondered about it, but never got around to asking. Once I heard about the affair, I figured Narziss paid for them."

He yawned. He reached into his pocket and swallowed a caffeine tablet and a Provigil capsule.

"Her father's a dangerous man," Nell said. "He'd mail you your mother's fingers to send a message."

"How do you know that?"

"Elena told me. That's why she's in America—as his drug mule."

"What? Oh, great. Just great. I was making out with the Godfather's daughter."

"Relax. He's not going to come after you for that. Unless he thinks you knocked her up."

The blood drained from Casey's face.

Nell tittered. "I'm kidding."

"Could Señor Ortega have something to do with her disappearance?"

"Wouldn't surprise me. Then again, I've been thinking she could have 'vanished' this week as a way to get out of the drug trade." Nell took her hands off the wheel just long enough to pantomime quotation marks.

They arrived at Narziss's address: 8383 Hickory Drive, Green Bay. Narziss had an enormous brick mansion on the outskirts of town. It featured a turret over the foyer. The redwood door stood at least ten feet high, no doubt custom-built for the altitudinous athlete. Casey thanked her and Nell drove off. As he approached the house, Casey wondered if he'd get the oversized door slammed in his face. Or worse. Nevertheless, he knocked and heard footsteps approach. Casey swallowed, bracing for impact from the Hail's hulk.

Samantha opened the door. She was his age, brunette, his height in heels, and slender with curves. "Casey?"

"Mrs. Narziss?"

She smiled warmly. "Call me Samantha. Come in."

"Thank you." The circular foyer, with its gray marble floor, had more square footage than Casey's entire apartment. Inset into the center was a black marble star. The wide, spiral staircase featured a redwood railing. The place looked gorgeous.

Two little kids collided with Samantha's legs. She called to them with remarkable softness, "Kids, I'd really like it if you settled down." She glanced at Casey. "They react better to whispers than screams."

He respected her methods. "You're an excellent mother."

"I don't know about that."

"Beautiful house."

"Thank you."

"It's huge."

"Six-thousand."

"Square feet?"

"That's right."

Casey couldn't imagine cleaning or heating it. "With that much space, you could lose the kids."

"Wouldn't that be nice?" she quipped, bending down and gently grabbing her son by the chin, wiggling it and making a cutesy face. "Can you say hi to Mr. Thread?"

The boy meekly said "Hi," then buried his head in his mom's embrace.

She addressed her guest. "Todd said he's going to be a few minutes. Can I get you anything to drink?"

His throat had dried. "Water would be great."

"Certainly." She went into the kitchen.

Casey wondered if Todd Narziss had told his wife about the incident with him in the locker room, or about their previous interview. Probably not. Why go there?

"Here you are," she said, handing him a glass.

He drank the entire thing.

"Wow, thirsty," she said. "Allow me." She took his glass and returned it to the kitchen. When she returned she said, "Would you like the tour?"

"Thanks. Is that a…waterfall?" Casey squatted and peered around the staircase toward the kitchen, where lannon stones lined an indoor lagoon. He could hear the water cascading and pooling.

"Oh, that's hardly a *waterfall*. It's just a decoration."

Casey guffawed. "A decoration is a wreath your mother makes from twigs with a homemade snowman hot-glued inside. *That* is definitely a waterfall."

"Todd's upstairs, watching game film in the theater," she said to Casey, then called to the kids, "Brent, get off your sister!" She apologized to Casey. "I feel like a zookeeper."

"My sister and I gave our mother a workout at that age." He flashed back to playing Kick the Can with Leila and the neighborhood kids, and how invariably someone would end up crying to mom. And yet, those games were some of the best times of his life.

He and Samantha scaled the spiral staircase. "On the left is the restroom if you need it. Next is Todd's workout room."

It looked like an infomercial for Bowflex and Gold's Gym. Mirrors covered the walls. Large flat screens perched in each corner near the ceiling. A digital camera sat on a tripod wired to a cable coming out of the wall.

"Todd's office is next door," Samantha continued, strolling down the hardwood hallway. "I'll see if he's ready for dinner. The theater room is at the end of the hall."

"May I use the restroom while you check?"

"Of course." She turned and walked down the hallway.

Casey entered the bathroom, paused, then snuck into Todd's office. Hail memorabilia hung everywhere on the walls and shelves — jerseys, game balls, photos with teammates. Some items were from the early 1900s. Two walls were navy blue and the other two white, reflecting the team colors. On the ceiling was a life-size poster of Narziss running with a football and "TODD NARZISS, #83" in huge blue lettering. Also on the wall was an electronic picture frame, the kind that refreshes periodically with different digital photos. It was wired to the wall with a cable similar to the one attached to the camera in the workout room. A family picture appeared on the fifty-inch screen when Casey walked in, but it soon turned to a picture of Narziss with Oakley on the field after a game, then a shot of Narziss flexing for the camera in his weight room. Casey laughed and shook his head.

Normally, he wouldn't snoop through someone's private belongings without asking permission. After all, an ethical journalist gets information from first-hand knowledge, reliable sources, the library, or the Internet. If a reporter can't find the information there, there's no story. But in this case, Casey could envision Elena huddled in an alley downtown, bleeding. The odds of finding her alive decreased exponentially every hour. He owed it to himself and Elena to check if Narziss had a role in her disappearance. At least, that was his rationale. After all, pinning a superstar athlete with the murder of his mistress and unborn baby would put the "me" in "career advancement."

Casey glanced out the office door; the hallway was empty. He rifled through Narziss's desk drawers but found nothing helpful. There was a filing cabinet in the corner—locked. He opened a desk drawer and inside hung three keys. He found it amazing how so many people hid keys so close to the corresponding locks—putting house keys under door mats or in potted plants a mere foot away, or placing a spare car key behind the license plate. Why bother locking up?

He tried the first key in the cabinet. No luck. He tried the second. Nope. His hands quivered. The third worked. He exhaled relief, glanced at the door to the hallway, then opened the drawer and flipped through folders until he found Narziss's cell-phone bills.

Casey had witnessed Narziss taking a call on his cell in the Hail Locker Room the night Elena disappeared. The fact that Narziss had taken the call stood out as odd to Casey—most players didn't talk on phones in the locker room due to lack of privacy. At the time, Casey had figured the caller to be Samantha Narziss, or perhaps Todd Narziss's agent.

Now he had other hypotheses. Casey used his phone to snap a picture of Narziss's cell phone account number. With that, he could check to see who'd called Narziss Friday night around the time Elena disappeared and possibly connect him to her disappearance.

The hallway light dimmed. "Looking for something?" Narziss stood in the doorway.

Casey flinched, but purposely didn't look at him. Instead, he pretended to appreciate the décor. "Cool memorabilia, man, you should totally get Todd Narziss to sign everything."

Narziss wasn't amused. "Thread, what the f—"

"Todd!" Samantha interrupted, entering the room. "The kids?" Sure enough, their progeny careened into Daddy's legs a half-second later, giggling.

"Sorry," Todd said to her. "Thread, tell us what y—"

Casey's heart felt as if it were ricocheting inside him like a Super Ball. "Would you like the Hail coaches to call more plays for you?"

The football question seemed to surprise and disarm Narziss. "Hell, yeah. Todd Narziss always wants the ball. But what were you doing in my office?"

Samantha said, "Oh, Todd, don't take yourself so seriously. He was just doing research for his story. Right, Casey?"

Little Brent chased his sister down the hallway, then back toward the adults. The boy jumped onto his dad's waist, hugging him and sliding down Todd's legs like a firefighter answering the bell and taking his father's sweatpants with him to the floor.

"Brent!" Todd shouted, bending down to pull them back up. But the kids didn't stop wiggling or laughing until Samantha softly said, "Settle down, kids."

Todd hastily hiked up his pants. Casey couldn't help but smile. "I'm flattered, but you probably greet all your guests like this."

Narziss's eyes bulged and his chin jutted as he leaned toward Casey. He whispered what sounded like it should have been shouted. "Get. Out."

"But what about our interview?"

"OUT!"

11

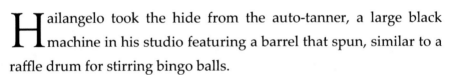

Hailangelo took the hide from the auto-tanner, a large black machine in his studio featuring a barrel that spun, similar to a raffle drum for stirring bingo balls.

The mold for the *Pygmalion* was nearly complete. Somehow, the arms still fought him a bit—they looked forced, artificial. True, this often appeared to be the case until he covered and painted the statue, but he realized he couldn't rely on those accoutrements to pull it off. The pose had to be natural, and look alive.

In his studio, he walked around the mannequin-mold he would use to immortalize Galatea. As he stared at the plaster, the solution came to him. The sculptor rolled his right shoulder twice, dipped it below the height of the left shoulder, assumed the pose of the woman in the famous painting, and realized he needed a bit more plaster along the top of the shoulder on the right side.

73

Of course. It had been there all along, taunting him, waiting for him to find it. Just as his other statues had taunted the public. He supposed it qualified as poetic justice. Still, while other self-absorbed sculptors had walked past their wounded statues, he viewed himself as the Good Samaritan who took the time to nurture the mold for the statue and ensure its perfection for the final product. His artwork's beauty went much further than skin-deep.

Later, he carried the hide to the polyvinyl mannequin. It fit perfectly over the mold. He secured it. Eventually, he glued glass eyes in place, fitted clay around the sockets and painted details. He had a steady hand, superb concentration, and rare patience. He viewed these traits as the keys to success in any part of life, and the most critical of them was patience.

When he had finished, he stepped off the stool and took his usual five steps back so he could view the entire human sculpture. The statue clearly yearned for him, he thought, as she bent back and down, her right arm prepared for his embrace. Her left arm, bent at the elbow, had been flexed upward at the shoulder joint, positioned as if for balance. Taken together, the contour of her arms mimicked the pose of Cupid aiming his bow, though she needed no implement to seize his affection.

He glanced at a framed print of the classic painting *Pygmalion and Galatea* by Jean-Léon Gérôme, featuring the bearded sculptor named Pygmalion kissing his female statue, Galatea, as she supposedly came to life. Hailangelo's statue mimicked Galatea down to every last detail, except that his creation had a darker skin tone while the original's was alabaster. That, and he had left her hair down.

Long hair excited him. It stimulated his blood flow and filled his brain receptors with pleasure. He spritzed perfume on her hair, closed his eyes, and inhaled deeply. "We're all alone now," he said to her, embracing his Galatea and giving her a passionate kiss.

§

Casey went to his sister's apartment. Leila had three new canvases on the wall above her couch in the living room, all originals she had painted. The first was a profile of her staring face to face with a Bengal tiger, the feline's jaws slightly ajar. The second was an image of a mother hawk perched over two baby birds, its wings outstretched, and Casey couldn't quite tell if the matron wanted to feed the chicks…or eat them. The third featured trees along an everglade, ominous like something out of *The Heart of Darkness.*

Casey wasn't sure what to make of them, aside from wondering if they reflected Leila's life experiences. Regardless, they were well done. "Your paintings are stunning." He complimented her despite her propensity to not take it very well.

"Thanks." She lay on the couch, flipping through a magazine. "Is Fairytopia Barbie your girlfriend now?"

"Who, Nell? No. Known her a long time."

"How long?"

"Couple years. She's a friend of Elena's."

"Who's Elena?"

"My friend from the Hail Pro Shop who went missing over the weekend."

Leila looked up from her magazine. "You mean the one you made out with...until you had a sleep attack?"

Great, even my sister knows. Had Skeeto told her? The Hail players, coaches, and the media agreed that playing pro football in Green Bay was like swimming in a small aquarium. In Green Bay, even Casey couldn't keep his kissing *faux pas* a secret. "Anyway, Nell just earned her first car from Baciare Cosmetics."

Leila looked up. "A car? Or a Pepto-Bismol boat on wheels?"

"A Beemer Z4 convertible."

Leila let that sink in, then turned a page. "Good for her."

"She could hook you up." Casey thought a career change could spark her into a more positive outlook.

Leila gave her brother a toxic stare. "To sell makeup?" Her apathetic persona worked at age twenty-three, but in a few years it wouldn't. They both knew it. She pointed at her blue hair. "Duh."

"She said it's decent money," Casey said.

Annoyed, she flipped shut her magazine—*Rolling Stone*—and frowned. "Who are you? Mom? Jesus."

"Neither. Did you call Dr. Stepnowski?"

"Here we go." She reopened her magazine and resumed reading it.

Casey wanted to write for a big-time monthly magazine someday. Some days, he wanted it so much he furiously shook his head so he would no longer think about it, like a drenched dog after swimming in a lake. *Remain calm. Your most important breath is your next one.*

"Come on, Lei," he stepped toward her. "He really helped Fiona, that reporter from the *Green Bay Times*."

"Why don't *you* see a shrink, Narcolepsy Boy?"

"I did see a psychiatrist."

SLEEP WHEN YOU'RE DEAD

"Once?"

"Twice. Anyway, Dr. Stepnowski helped Fiona get past her social anxiety."

Leila slapped the magazine on the couch. "Fiona's an anorexic who thinks she's Gene Simmons. And you think I'm crazy?"

"Fiona's not that crazy," Casey said.

"You do think I'm crazy!"

"Of course I do—I'm your brother. I just want the best for you."

"Then quit reminding me of it just because you feel guilty it happened outside your college apartment." She scoffed. "Leave me alone. Between you and Mother, I can't stand it!"

"I thought Mother refused to discuss it."

"She won't directly," Leila said. "But she itches around it like it's the pox. The other day she says, 'Leila, you have no health insurance. You need a real job with benefits.' Can you believe that?"

"Health insurance helps. I know that first-hand." He yawned and pressed the end of the triangular piece of old credit card into his palm.

"Whose side are you on?"

"Nobody's." Casey made the peace sign. "I'm Switzerland."

Leila flopped back on the couch. "It's not like I list *raped* as a bullet point on my resume. Besides, I don't want to take some lame-ass job and spend my whole life in a cubicle being a tool for the Man."

"I hear you," Casey said. "On the other hand, you're not going to work at Fixate Factory forever." She could afford to be a waitress for the foreseeable future because of the low cost of living in Green Bay. But she couldn't go on like that forever, could she?

She didn't respond.

"So what is your plan, Lei?"

"I have no idea. But hell, why can't Mother let me figure that out?"

Leila had a point. "What did Ma say exactly?"

"She said, 'That unfortunate event has been holding you back.' I'm like, 'Mom, Uncle Marty leaving a stench in your bathroom is an unfortunate event. I was *raped*; you can say it.'"

"What'd she say then?"

"Nothing. Just lit a cigarette."

"Of course she did."

"I'm like, 'We're not doing this. Either accept me for who I am and let me live my life, or back off.'"

"She's just trying to look out for you," Casey said. "She can't undo what happened, but she can try to lessen the pain." He could relate.

"I need something for the pain in my ass known as Motheritis."

Casey remembered a run-in he and Leila had had with the town bully during Casey's freshman year at Green Bay Southwest High School. "Do you remember when Bobbie Chintzy threw his football and hit you right on your glasses?"

"Who could forget stuff like that?" Leila said, staring up at the ceiling.

"I punched him, tackled him, and warned him never to go near you again, so Bobbie's mom brought him over to show his shiner to Mother, who promptly called me over and whacked me upside the head with her *Reader's Digest*."

A smile burst below Leila's blue bangs and between the long strands of her hair. "Ma with the subtlety. Wish I could have seen her give you that whuppin'."

"The reason I survived is I told her Bobbie broke your glasses. That's when she called you down from your room. Once she saw you with your bruised face…"

Leila perked, like a dog waiting for her owner to throw a tennis ball. She said, "Mother started whacking Bobbie upside his head with her magazine—chased him half-way to Hail Stadium."

Casey chuckled. "I thought Bobbie would leap into the stadium stands to save his life."

"Wouldn't you, with Mother chasing?"

They laughed together, harder than at any time since childhood, until it ached in a way they didn't mind, like muscle cramps after a satisfying workout.

Casey said, "The thing about Mother: she's insufferable to her own children."

"Like a baboon that eats its young," Leila agreed.

"But give her credit," he said. "If a leopard tries to attack a baby baboon, boy, does the mother baboon make the big kitty regret it."

"I'm done letting Mother fight my battles." Leila lay on the couch, staring at the ceiling. "Ever wonder what it would have been like if Dad had lived?"

"Of course," he said. "They have these computer programs that project how people would look in forty years, or how a pro-football game is supposed to play out."

"You try one with dad's picture or something?"

"No. I don't trust those computer simulations. In real life, predictions rarely materialize. So what if there's a seventy-five percent chance of something? That means nothing unless it actually happens. That's why you play the game, that's why you live your life. There's too much chance to consistently predict the future. So, you just experience it."

"You think Dad died from chance?"

"Dad died of cancer."

"What was it like, knowing?" Leila said.

"*Knowing?*"

"That he was dying."

"You don't want to know."

"Yes. I do."

Casey folded his arms, shifted his weight and stared at his sister. "You may think you want to know about Dad, but you don't. Trust me."

"But—"

"Well…since I know you won't drop it…it wasn't *knowing he was dying* that was hard. The cancer was easy to deny. The hard part was watching him starve to death because the nausea prevented him from keeping food or drink down. Ever see someone starve to death?"

"No."

Casey remembered his father's gaunt face, chapped lips, and cracked skin. Every time he thought of it, he had an urge to scrub his forehead, as if that of all things would erase those memories. "That scared me stiff."

"Literally?" Leila said.

"Yeah, at times. Dad's breath smelled metallic from all the medications. As he died, in his final moments, he gulped for air like a fish in a net."

"You were right." Leila placed her palms on her cheeks. "I didn't want to know. Thanks a lot."

"Sometimes, I wished I had been a baby like you."

"Did Mother sugar-coat it?"

"You mean like, 'Daddy went to sleep in Heaven'?"

"Yeah."

"Hell no. You know Mother. She believes in Heaven, but wanted me to toughen up, so she said, 'Your father's dead and he's never coming back.'"

Leila paused for a few seconds. "I grew up trying to envision him."

"You've seen pictures."

"But no video. No personality. He's like imagining a song I've never heard. At least you were five at the time. You knew him."

"I know, Lei. I wish you could have known him, too. He loved you so much, he'd rock you in his arms, hold you over his head, sing to you."

"I'm sorry you had to watch Dad go through that, Case."

Outside Leila's apartment window, a bare tree branch wagged in the winter gust. His father had died in the living room, lying in a hospice bed. A few hours later, two big men from the funeral parlor came into their house, didn't even knock, just came in like drones programmed to cart away the dead. Casey would never forget sitting on the kitchen floor, hearing the zipper on the body bag. Crazy as it might have seemed, he had hoped his dad would recover, even from stage-four cancer. The hope he had back then was about making more memories, holding on for one more. "That zipper on the body bag. I heard it coming. Then it just…stopped."

Leila slouched back into her couch, again staring at the ceiling. She appeared uninterested but Casey knew better.

"That's why all my clothes were button-down until high school," he said.

"You've got issues, Casey."

"Thanks for calling me black, Dr. Pot."

Leila turned her head toward her brother. "I'm a little teapot, short and stout. Here are my neuroses, here is my spout. Maybe you should see Dr. Step-dad-ski."

He sat cross-legged on her floor, resting his chin on his fists. "Stepnowski. When they wheeled Dad's body out of our house, I couldn't feel God. I just felt alone."

"So you don't believe in God."

"Maybe the real question isn't whether God does or doesn't exist. Maybe the real question is, how do we act? If we all *act* like God doesn't exist—being selfish and vicious to each other—then for all intents and purposes God *doesn't* exist, or might as well not. But if we act like God does exist, then in essence, She does. Does it matter whether God created the earth and all life, or the other way around? Either way, the waves you send out bounce back to you from all directions."

"You're such a dork. Go back to finding Elena."

"You haven't heard anything about where she is, have you?"

"Why would I know anything?"

"People talk. You work at a coffee house."

"I haven't heard a word."

Casey walked over to her.

She looked up at him. "What?"

He took off a silver necklace and handed it out to her.

She sat up. "What is this?"

"They're Dad's dog tags."

"From Vietnam?"

Casey nodded. "He was there early on, in the 60's, when LBJ escalated the war."

"Don't you want them?"

"Of course I do. I remember him wearing them on Veteran's Day and the Fourth of July. But I know you didn't get the chance to see that. So I want you to have them, so you feel a part of Dad close to your heart. His last words before he died were, 'Breathe. Your most important breath is your next one.' Maybe he can protect you better than I can."

Leila put the necklace over her head, pulled her hair out the back and kissed the dog tags bearing her father's name. She held them close to her heart and hugged her brother.

12

The Green Bay Hail players took the field for pre-game warm-ups before a playoff game at Hail Stadium against St. Louis.

Meanwhile, in the press box high above the field, Casey grabbed a weenie on a toothpick, popped it in his mouth, and strolled across the room to his seat. He opened his laptop, logged on to the website of the *Green Bay Times*, and read an article about the disappearance of Elena Ortega, 24, a Hail Pro Shop employee, written by Mai Tao. She quoted Hail CEO Dan Stone, who said: "The Hail are doing everything we can to assist the police in their search." Casey continued reading.

Authorities traced a signal from Ortega's cell phone to a grassy patch at Heritage Hill in Green Bay, the 48-acre state park famous for its old log cabins and annual Civil War reenactments.

Twenty officers and five canines combed the park, located the Ortega's phone, called the most recent phone numbers saved in the call history and ran prints. Detectives learned that the person who had placed the recent calls had found the phone outside the gas station near the stadium shortly after Ortega disappeared Friday night. A police spokesman said, "We know who found it. His story checks out."

Police secured a search warrant for Ortega's apartment, based on evidence that her disappearance was coerced. The department, however, did not release any details on what evidence they may have found.

Casey took the elevator from the press box down to the field level and used his media pass to get on the sidelines. He missed the smell of the spring turf, but even in the winter the field looked lush. The heating coils underneath the surface kept the hybrid grass-turf alive, and lamps helped it to grow.

He liked to see the players up close before the game, remember their true stature, and gauge their intensity and focus. The thirty-five-degree temperature was balmy for a January game in Green Bay. The crowd was jubilant, drunk on the high of alcohol, grilled meat, national media attention, and the promise of what their team could accomplish for posterity.

Casey found Skeeto walking off the field near the end zone. "Skeet, I got some leads on how to find Elena."

"For real?"

"She hopped a cab."

Skeeto raised his brows and laughed. "Come on, man."

Casey would have argued the point, but he noticed a security guard named Big Mikey leading two men in suits along the sideline, heading in their direction. Big Mikey pointed at Casey.

Casey's adrenaline spiked and he leaned toward Skeeto. "What the—"

Skeeto raised a hand. "Let me handle it." Skeeto gave Big Mikey a half "high-five," half-handshake.

About ten yards away, Narziss jogged to warm up for the game. He glared at Casey.

Casey fell into sleep paralysis standing up; his shoulders and head slouched into partial cataplexy. Stress had taken its toll.

Narziss saw that, grinned, grabbed a football from the ground and hurled it as hard as he could at Casey's chest. The ball bounced off his pectoral, knocking him off-balance enough so that he fell to the ground. Narziss shook his head, laughing along with a couple of offensive linemen. A coach blew his whistle and called the players into a warm-up drill.

LOCAL NARCOLEPTIC MAN
BECOMES TACKLING DUMMY

The next thing he knew, Big Mikey, Skeeto, and the two men in suits stood over him.

"You okay?" Skeeto said.

Casey wanted to respond but couldn't.

"Come on, Mr. Thread, get up," one of the men said. As Casey peered at the men huddled over him, he felt as if he had fallen down a mine shaft and the rescuers had no way to reach him. "I'm Detective

Meyer," the tall man said, flashing his badge. He waved toward his shorter counterpart. "This is my partner, Detective Tony Gioli."

"Get up," Gioli said. "We need to talk."

Casey didn't move.

"I said get up."

"Come on Casey," Big Mikey said. "This ain't funny."

Casey hoped Skeeto would explain that it was the narcolepsy. No such luck.

Detective Meyer reached down and pulled back Casey's eyelids. He poked Casey under the ribs. Gioli leaned over and pinched Casey's wrist to excruciation. Still, Casey couldn't react.

Meyer seemed genuinely surprised, and he glanced at Skeeto. "What's your friend's problem?"

"He falls asleep a lot," Skeeto said, grabbing Casey's shoulder and shaking it until Casey finally snapped out of it. For Casey, it was the constant shaking—not pain—that brought him out of an episode. He sat up and peered at Skeeto.

"I'll handle it," Casey murmured incredulously.

"Mr. Thread," Gioli said, flipping open a notebook. "You okay?"

"Yeah, happens all the time. I have narcolepsy."

Gioli said, "So you won't mind a few questions?"

Casey stood and dusted himself. "What about?" His head hurt from the fall.

"You were the last to see Elena Ortega the night before she disappeared, correct?"

"Where'd you hear that?" Casey said, glaring at Skeeto, who flared his eyes and shrugged like he knew nothing about it.

"We have our sources," Meyer said.

"I did see her the night before she disappeared," Casey admitted.

Gioli smirked. "Oh, really?"

"Yeah, at Skeeto's party at the White House. But I wasn't the last to see Elena that night."

"How do you know?" Gioli rocked from heels to toes.

"Because I had a sleep attack, went home the next morning, and haven't seen her since."

"Did Ms. Ortega say anything that seemed strange?" Gioli said.

"She bragged about sleeping with Todd Narziss." Now *that* qualified for strange.

Gioli looked up from his notepad. "*The* Todd Narziss?"

"Right there." Casey thumbed toward the player wearing the number "83."

Gioli shook his pen to get ink flowing and took more notes.

"You and Ms. Ortega argue?" Meyer said.

"No," Casey said. "Why would we?"

"You had a romantic relationship with Ms. Ortega," Gioli shrugged a shoulder. "But you argued. I understand—I quarrel with my wife from time to time."

"Who said I argued?"

"Answer the question," Meyer said.

"I kissed her once. That's it. We went out a few times." He stuck his hands in his black wool coat and hopped to stay warm. "I really should be getting up to the press box. My fingers are numb and I'm supposed to be using them to cover Narziss for *Sports Scene*."

Gioli pursed his lips and raised his brows. "Well, well, the kid's a big shot, Meyer."

"Mmm-hmm," Meyer said, acting like he was impressed. "Wait until I tell the wife."

"Problem is," Gioli said, "we need to take you downtown."

"Downtown?" Casey said.

Meyer and Gioli nodded. They looked like a hot dog and hamburger standing together. "We found a syringe in your wrecked car, Mr. Thread," said Meyer, the hot dog.

"Wrecked car?" Skeeto said.

"I had a little accident," Casey said.

Meyer nodded. "It's at the body shop. The needle contains hydrocyanic acid, the same substance found in trace amounts in the bodies of female statues recovered on college campuses across the Midwest."

"That's impossible," Casey said. "I've never owned a syringe in my life. Right, Skeeto?"

"Uh, right," Skeeto said, not convincing in the least.

Gioli leaned in to Casey. "So tell me, Mr. Thread, how is it that a car is supposedly empty at the time of the accident, yet at the body shop it has a syringe with a highly lethal substance at a time when your recent flame disappeared?"

"I have no idea," Casey said. "Somebody must have planted it in the car."

"Who would do that?" Meyer said.

"Someone who wants me out of the way," Casey said.

"Do you have any enemies?" Gioli said.

"Other than Narziss?"

"We need you to come with us," Meyer said.

"Why?" Casey said.

"We can do this casually if you cooperate," Meyer said. "Or seventy-thousand spectators can watch us drag you out."

"I told you—someone planted it."

"Right," Gioli said. "Santa's elves. Come with us."

"Am I under arrest?" Casey asked.

"No," Meyer said. "We're just curious about a few things. We want to be sure we have an understanding."

"Skeeto," Casey said over his shoulder as the cops led him out of the stadium. "Please tell Nell I'm downtown."

Skeeto pointed toward Casey. "You got it."

The detectives led Casey up the ramp, where a rabid fan known as Hail Mary stood in her usual spot near the tunnel. Her garb made her look like a cross between the Virgin Mother and a typical football fan. The cops led him through the concourse and out the stadium. They arrived at the detectives' unmarked car. Meyer directed Casey into the back seat and shut the door.

§

At the station, they deposited Casey in Interrogation Room 3. Gioli sat across the table from him while Meyer paced behind his partner. "You know about Ms. Ortega's condition, right?"

Casey frowned. "Condition?"

"She's pregnant," Gioli said.

Casey wondered how they knew that. Maybe they had spoken to Prime Time. "Yes, actually. I knew that. Why?"

Both detectives frowned and shared another glance.

"We know you slept with her," Meyer said.

"Who told you that?"

"Lots of witnesses from the party at the so-called White House," Gioli said. "They saw you go into a bedroom with Ms. Ortega, and they said that it ended prematurely and you weren't happy about it."

"Elena and I went up there to make out and it ended there. I fell asleep kissing her. It was the narcolepsy."

"Okay, that's a new one," Gioli admitted, glancing at his partner. *"It was the narcolepsy."*

The detectives laughed.

Casey said, "So, yeah, I was frustrated, but not with her. Embarrassed, actually."

Gioli said, "Where were you last Friday?"

"I have fifty people who saw me in the Hail locker room, and an editor who can corroborate that I'm working on a freelance assignment for him."

"Who?" Gioli asked.

Casey gave him the editor's information.

"People lose consciousness when narcolepsy hits, right?" Gioli said.

"No," Casey said. "In fact, in my case, I'm temporarily paralyzed but quite aware."

"We interviewed some Hail staffers," Gioli said. "They all have alibis that check out. When we asked them for suspicious characters, a few mentioned you."

Of course they did. When in doubt, blame the freak who turns to stone for no apparent reason. They'd never understood Casey and probably never would. "Me? Why?"

"Well, they mentioned the narcolepsy."

There it was, the Narcolepsy Card.

Gioli pulled his chair closer to Casey's. "I understand where you're coming from, bud. You sleep with this girl who's way out of your league."

"I didn't sleep—"

"You hope to score with her again, right? But you hear she's pregnant and you have this split second when you're not thinking. You have to get rid of the baby."

"*What?*" The entire conversation seemed to freeze, like an over-exposed Polaroid picture, and no amount of shaking it would bring it into better focus.

"Don't worry about it," Gioli said, chuckling casually. "This was a one-time thing, right?"

"What was a one-time thing?"

"Disposing of Elena Ortega. You normally wouldn't do this. You just slipped, right?"

Where did he get this craziness? "I told you, she's my friend. I care about her. I've been looking for her because I'm concerned about her."

A middle-aged brunette entered the room, wearing a black business suit and matching glasses. "This interview's over."

"Are you my attorney?" Casey said.

"That's right," she said, turning to the cops. "What do you two think you have on my client?"

Her presence relieved Casey. But from where had she come? Who had summoned her?

"Nice to see you again, Rebecca," Gioli said. "We don't have much—just a syringe with poison, motive, and opportunity."

"What about a body?" Rebecca said.

Meyer smirked. "We're looking. Maybe your client can lead us to it."

"No body, no murder," she said. "Do you even have prints on the needle?"

Gioli said, "We don't have them back yet."

"So you have no body, no prints, just evidence recovered *after* my client relinquished custody of a wrecked car at an unsecured location?"

Gioli started, "The body shop assures us—"

"Come on, Detective." She placed her hands on her hips and shifted weight. "Every body shop leaves the doors open and most leave the keys in the ignition, for Pete's sake. Do you have any physical evidence?" She looked exasperated.

The cops said nothing.

"Well, do you?" She looked back and forth at the two detectives, who both glanced at their feet. "You're throwing spaghetti in the dark, hoping it'll hit a wall." She guffawed. "Come on, Casey, it's time to go home."

Casey sprang to his feet, smiled at the detectives and followed her out the door. "Thank you, Counselor."

Rebecca kept walking. "Don't thank me yet."

Casey caught up to her. "They can't possibly charge me, right?"

She glanced at him. "Did you have anything to do with the disappearance of that woman?"

"Hell no."

"Then don't worry."

"How'd you get here so fast?"

"Nell called me." She opened the door to the lobby and waited for him. "You're a free man."

He entered the lobby, and there Nell waited. She rose, smiled, and hugged him. She felt soft and warm and smelled like mangoes. Instinct urged him to press her against the wall and kiss her. Then he remembered they were looking for Elena, and he mentally scolded himself. Still, a guy could be grateful. "Thank you."

"Of course. Skeeto called, I relayed the news to Rebecca, and came straight here."

"How do you know Rebecca?"

Nell checked her lipstick in a compact and winked. "She's one of my best customers."

The detectives caught up to them in the lobby. "Thanks for your time, Mr. Thread," Meyer said.

Gioli folded his arms. "Don't be leaving town."

Casey and Nell walked out.

13

Hailangelo sat in a red leather chair, gazing up at his Galatea, tracing with his eyes the contour of her hips. He drank another Black Russian, set it down, the ice clinking. The sculptor held out his hands to frame her.

She stood perfectly still on her pedestal, leaning toward him, entreating his embrace, but he would not give it. Could not. "You are looking particularly radiant tonight, my *amor*," he said. Was that a faint grin on her face? Yes. Yes, it was. Her concupiscence for him had no bounds; he had convinced himself of it. "I desire to ravage you this very minute," he said. "But I mustn't. I am bound to protect you."

He stood and made a fist. "I cannot rest until all threats to you are eliminated." He finished his vodka and coffee liqueur and knelt before her, raising his palm at an angle toward her face. "I worked so hard to create you, love, I could not bear to lose you."

Nearly in tears, he stood on a wooden crate and gently kissed her lips, cupping her cheeks in his hands. He ripped himself away from her magnetism and went to his desk where, on a mannequin head, hung his latex mask he had created. He put it on, covering his entire head and creating the appearance of a real skull, like one might see at an event on *Dia de Los Muertos*. He had painted the angles to create the illusion of concaved bones.

He turned back to Galatea and pondered what would happen to their love upon death. Hailangelo believed his thoughts and emotions would short circuit. But hers? He giggled. One day, patrons would pay money to see her. Security guards would remove anyone who tried to photograph her. Collectors would covet her. The museum would charge a fee to reproduce her image. She would live forever. He had given their love immortality.

He removed the mask, placed it in his black Calvin Klein briefcase. Hailangelo lifted his needle to the light, tapped it with his fingernail, and squirted a bit of its contents into the air. He placed it in a hard cylindrical container, closed it in the briefcase next to the mask and walked to the door with it. As he left, he blew a kiss to Galatea.

§

Casey left the police station, called a cab, and rushed back to the football game. He returned just before halftime. In the press box, he sat next to Skeeto and said, "They couldn't hold up the game for me?"

"The refs asked," Skeeto said, "but we said you wouldn't want to impose. How'd you get out so fast?"

"Nell called a lawyer."

"So you're clear?"

"I'm innocent. Whether they believe me or not, they have no prints, no evidence whatsoever. Thanks for giving Nell the heads up."

"No problem."

On the other side of Casey sat Kenny, who had spotted game stats and interesting tidbits for Casey and the Hail PR staff over the past three years. Kenny was an enthusiastic man in his late forties who had developmental disabilities. He had met Casey and Skeeto a few years prior, when Casey had been a reporter at the *Green Bay Times*.

Kenny had approached the two at Bay Beach Amusement Park in Green Bay while they sat on a park bench playing music for passersby. They called themselves "The Filing Cabinets," the squarest name they could imagine, and sang mostly covers of songs written by the Beatles or Bob Dylan. Casey played the guitar and sang while Skeeto laid down funky grooves on his conga. Kenny had heard them play "Zombie Girl," a bluesy, whimsical song about an ex-girlfriend who happened to be a zombie. Casey sang:

My date for the prom:
Well, she strangled my mom,
She's a zombie girl
Loves me for my brains.
She's seven-foot-three
And she's coming for me,
She's a zombie girl

She's a bit insane.
Ooooooooooooooooo,
Zom-bie Girl!"

Despite Casey's slightly off-key performance, Kenny had loved it and had become The Filing Cabinets' number-one fan. In fact, upon meeting Casey after the gig, Kenny recited all of the lyrics to "Zombie Girl."

When Casey discovered Kenny had a photographic memory and loved the Hail, he convinced Skeeto to give Kenny a press pass so he could assist with statistics. On more than one occasion, Kenny had calculated player stats and milestones well before the Hail PR team.

Between plays, he would often rock forward and backward, staring into his hands and muttering what he thought the Hail would do next. He occasionally nailed it.

Now, Kenny and Casey watched intently as the Hail battled St. Louis with a minute left in the half. It was the first game in which Narziss had dropped more than one pass, and already he had dropped three.

"Casey?" Kenny said.

"Yeah."

"Narziss is having a bad game."

"You're right. I think he's distracted."

"By the cold?"

"No, I don't think it's the cold," Casey said.

Kenny rocked in his chair. "That's bad for your article. Very bad."

"Well, not necessarily. Could be interesting to write about how the mighty have fallen."

"People don't like to read about the losers. Don't write about losers, Casey."

§

The teams competed hard in the second half. The clock in Hail Stadium read two minutes remaining in regulation. Narziss knelt on the opponents' forty-five-yard line, head down. Casey couldn't believe he hadn't come down with that previous pass. Actually, it was fortunate for the Hail, because it had appeared that he had caught it and fumbled. But the referee ruled him down, no fumble. The fans didn't seem to mind that the ref blew the call. The faint chorus of boos from some of the vexed fans surprised Casey. Still, Narziss could live down a few drops. Had he literally fumbled the season away, fans would never have forgotten, and might never have forgiven him.

Oakley hurried his Hail teammates to the line of scrimmage so he could hike the ball before the replay officials had a chance to look at the play. The crowd chanted, "Go Hail, go! Go Hail, go!" The cheers energized the home team.

Casey wondered if Narziss had trouble concentrating on the football because his thoughts focused on Elena. Was she dead? Alive in Ecuador? Still carrying the baby?

"Hike!" The center snapped the ball into Oakley's hands. Fortunately for Narziss, Oakley handed the ball to Marshon Cummings, who ran over the St. Louis defense for a key first down to extend the drive.

On the next play, Hail wide receiver Terrell Sims caught a short pass for a gain of five yards. There were ninety seconds left and the Hail were ahead by six points. Still, if Green Bay didn't keep the ball, St. Louis would have the chance to score a last-second touchdown, win, and eliminate the Hail from the playoffs.

Hail Mary, the team's most loyal fan, sat in her usual end-zone seat. Some fans believed that she gave the home team good luck. Casey didn't; he believed in actions, reactions, talent, skill, and chance. On third down, Oakley handed the ball to Cummings for a sweep run right. A St. Louis linebacker ran through unblocked and tackled Cummings in the backfield for a loss of three yards. St. Louis called time-out.

With seventy seconds left in the game, the Hail needed a first down to seal the victory and advance to the conference championship. As they huddled on fourth down with nine yards to go, Narziss looked at his quarterback. Casey had no doubt the tight end wanted the ball thrown to him.

A streaker ran across the field. In the press box, a burly reporter declared, "I hope *he* doesn't drop any balls." Big Mikey tackled the streaker and landed on him, and the crowd and reporters groaned.

Oakley called the play in the huddle. The Green Bay players lined up. Through binoculars, Casey could see a St. Louis linebacker jawing with Narziss, probably heckling him.

The center snapped the ball and Narziss slipped past the linebacker. Oakley threw the ball to him and with the defender draped on his right arm, Narziss tipped the ball with his left hand and caught it one-handed against his chest.

First down, game over. The crowd erupted. The Hail would advance to the conference championship game. Narziss glared at the dejected linebacker and tossed the ball in his face.

§

After the game, Hail Coach Bobby Druthers addressed the media. He wasn't thrilled with the close game after his team had dominated St. Louis earlier in the season.

"Were you surprised to see Narziss drop those passes?" Casey asked.

"No," Druthers said coolly.

"No?" A national reporter said. "Narziss is your best player."

"Right," Druthers said. "And when your best player is distracted during practice all week, it's predictable that he'd have a lackluster game, too." Coach Druthers rarely called out a star player in a news conference. When he did, though, it invariably motivated the slumping athlete. It was an unconventional move because most coaches tried to be bosom buddies with all their stars and, unfortunately, it worked as well for coaches as it did for parents.

"Why was Narziss distracted?" Casey doubted Druthers would talk about Narziss's affair with Elena, but his reaction to the question could indicate how much the coach knew about it.

Druthers shrugged. "Coming out of the bye week can be tough because you gotta get back into the swing of things."

Coach speak. "Was it something off the field, in his personal life?"

"You'd have to ask him that," Druthers said. "What I know is what happens in team meetings, practices, and games. He's a player we need to step up next week in the conference championship game. I'm confident he'll do that."

When Narziss arrived at the podium in the media center, he pointed first at the attractive female reporter with long blonde hair and curves.

"Todd," she said, "Coach Druthers said you had a 'lackluster' game. Do you agree?"

Narziss's grin evaporated. "I certainly didn't play to my normal standards. But something tells me if you look at the play-by-play recap, you'll see Todd Narziss made the game-sealing catch for a first down. One-handed. Why don't you ask me about that?"

None of them did.

A reporter said, "Coach also said you were distracted all week in practice."

"Coach said that?" Narziss said.

The video of Narziss tossing Casey into the locker had saturated YouTube, and Narziss couldn't afford any more bad publicity or he'd risk a suspension from the next playoff game. "Todd Narziss's focus was on the St. Louis defense. We'll enjoy this victory until we walk out of here—then it's time to focus on the conference championship game."

"What do you have to do between now and next weekend to ensure you won't drop any more passes?" a reporter asked.

"Look, that wasn't Todd Narziss out there," Narziss said. "The real Todd Narziss doesn't drop passes. Remember my last four all-star seasons? Todd Narziss had never, ever dropped more than one pass in a game, not even in high school. And he won't ever again."

After Narziss finished, most of the reporters remained in the media room to hear Johnny Oakley's thoughts on the game. Meanwhile, Casey snuck out and walked down the hallway in the Hail headquarters. He followed an office staffer until she entered the door to the next corridor. Casey caught it before it closed and locked.

He knew from his time at the *Green Bay Times* that Jane Mota from the Hail's finance department had all the social security numbers for all the players and team personnel. Casey already had Narziss's cell-phone account number. If he could get Narziss's social security number, he could call the wireless provider, pass through the security screen, and find out to whom Narziss had talked the night Elena disappeared.

Security was so tight to get into the building that most Hail staff left their office doors and drawers unlocked. The computers were password-protected, of course. Casey perused Jane's desk drawers and two filing cabinets, but found nothing pertinent.

He heard a door open at the far end of the hallway. A deep male voice called, "Jane, you in there?"

Casey cleared his throat and, in falsetto, said, "Yep."

"Go home," the man said, and the hall light extinguished. "You sound terrible."

Casey didn't move. He heard footsteps and knew he had nowhere to hide. The footsteps grew louder and louder and Casey fell into cataplexy. His head lolled enough that he fell out of the chair and onto the floor. He imagined the headline:

IDIOT FORGETS TO TAKE HIS MEDS
FALLS ASLEEP WHILE TRESPASSING

GREEN BAY, Wis. -- Reporter Casey Thread had a sleep attack inside Hail corporate offices after he forgot to take the Vivactil that had previously helped him avoid complete cataplexy, a league source reports.

Lying behind the desk, Casey could see the shadow of someone standing in the doorway. He wished it were Nell.

"Jane?" the voice called. "Jane?" Casey couldn't see the person's face. Was it Jane's boss? The call for Jane grew louder and louder. Casey finally broke free from the narcoleptic trance and shook his head to clear his mind. He peeked around the desk.

The office was empty. Casey slunk to the doorway, looked to the right then the left: empty. The person standing in the doorway had been a hallucination brought on by the sleep attack.

Casey went back into Jane's office and noticed a manila folder and papers scattered around the floor. He must have knocked them off the desk when he fell. He picked up a stack. One of the pages read: *Paid Bonuses*. It listed names of Hail employees, their individual bonus payments and the last four digits of their social security numbers.

Bingo.

14

Casey sat across a table from Nell at Oakley's Steakhouse, the restaurant owned by quarterback Johnny Oakley. A beef-and-fries aroma filled the air. Most patrons wore jeans. Yet a white-haired gentleman in the booth next to them said to his wife, "It's not every day we get to come to a fancy restaurant."

"Especially after a big playoff victory!" she chirped. Other than Cheffeta's, a truly gourmet restaurant, Oakley's was about as elegant as any eatery in Green Bay.

Casey bit into his chicken wrap. "Aw, man."

"Onions?" Nell said.

"Exactly. I told the waitress I'm allergic to them." Casey showed Nell the purple onion rings hanging out the end of the wrap.

The waitress, a college student dressed in a Hail cheerleader uniform, apologized. "I'll get you a new one."

"Thanks, that's very kind of you," Casey said, and meant it.

She took the wrap back to the kitchen.

"That'll leave a bad taste in your mouth," Nell said.

Casey nodded. "Like Elena being pregnant."

"That's about right."

"You know more than you've told me. Don't you?"

"I don't know the father's identity, if that's what you mean."

Casey smirked. "Narziss thinks it's his."

"Of course he does," Nell said. "I'm surprised he admitted it."

"Actually, he didn't say anything."

"He knows full well it's his," Nell said. She paused. "What kind of woman marries him?"

"The kind who relishes three-story foyers and indoor waterfalls. I think it's Narziss's baby and he wanted to get rid of it. He wants to be governor after he hangs up his cleats, so he can't have a bastard child."

Nell leaned back from the table and cocked her head. "Interesting. You're still hot for Elena, aren't you?"

Casey copied her by leaning back. He knew the instant he'd done it that Nell would interpret his body language as guilt. "Why are you so interested?"

Nell shrugged, gave him a coy grin, and used her fork to play with her pasta. "Not a lot to do in Green Bay."

Casey smiled. "Elena's a friend, and I want to find her to make sure she's okay. Plus, I'd like to know more about what happened to her so that the next time our friends Meyer and Gioli come calling, I'll be ready." He watched their waitress serve people at a table across the room. An elderly woman picked up a chicken wrap and took a bite. "Nell, check that out."

Nell's eyes turned into saucers. "Oh my God." Nell covered her mouth with her hand. They could see Casey's teeth marks in the other end of the lady's chicken wrap.

He walked over to the poor patron and warned her about it. He snickered on his way back to their table. He and Nell broke into laughs, not because the Chicken Wrap Incident was that hilarious, but because they had been so emotionally worn down that, at this point, all they could do was laugh. About Elena. About narcolepsy. About getting falsely accused. About incompetent wait staff. They laughed so hard their stomachs hurt. For a second, Casey feared wetting his pants. After it subsided, they sighed in relief, and eventually resumed eating and talking about anything but Elena's disappearance—if only for a few moments.

Nell regaled Casey with the tale of a recent client she had met with on a farm—the customer wore coveralls for cow milking and boots for manure pitching, but also bought Baciare makeup. "I tell customers that if they sign up to sell our products, they could really supplement their farming income. Rural folks deal with cold, dry air— not to mention wicked wind burn. It screams 'daily skin care.' Baciare moisturizers contain botanical extracts and nourishing antioxidants for fast absorption. And what farm woman doesn't deserve to draw a warm bath at the end of a long day milking udders and tossing feed? I should know; I grew up on a farm. Our quintessential spa cleansers contain eucalyptus, kiwi seeds and bamboo powder to tame the toughest skin."

Casey opened a photo on his phone. "But does it get manure out from under nails?"

"Yes! We have a nail treatment that—are you making fun of me?"

"No." Casey glanced down at the photo of Narziss's social security number. Then he opened the photo he'd taken of Narziss's cell records. He dialed the phone company, and followed the automated prompts to access Narziss's account. He eventually found the records for incoming phone numbers. Narziss had received multiple calls from the same phone number the night Elena had disappeared.

Casey typed the relevant phone number into Google. No results—unlisted. He searched for a private-eye website that offered background checks on people for a fee. Using that site, it only cost fifty bucks to get the name and address attached to the person who had repeatedly called Narziss: LeRoy DeWillis, alias "Skeeto," 1400 Pennsylvania Avenue, Green Bay—the Hail players' White House. Casey felt ill.

"What?" Nell said.

He swallowed. "Let's go." They ran out of the restaurant to her BMW, careful not to slip on the snow and ice. They got in, Casey filled her in, and they drove off. He didn't want to think about how his best friend since kindergarten could be in cahoots with Todd Narziss, or that he could have anything to do with Elena's disappearance. So he changed the subject. "Still has that new-car smell."

"I know, right? And the black leather seats. How 'bout it?"

Casey ran his hands over the cushy leather, soft as a baby's bottom. "Perfection. Bummer that studies show the new-car smell is actually toxic fumes off-gassing."

Nell pretended to waft the smell into her nose. "I better enjoy it while I can." She giggled and cracked the windows.

Casey didn't know much about Nell, but he couldn't help liking her.

A few minutes later, Nell turned onto Pennsylvania Avenue and parked along the curb in front of the White House. As they approached the door, they noticed that the handle lay on the ground a foot away. Nell pulled a tissue from her pocket and used it to grab the hole in the door left by the broken handle. They crept into the house and peeked in the living room where they had partied the previous Thursday, before Elena had disappeared. Casey recalled standing in that very same spot during the party, with Elena next to him.

Now he motioned to Nell, as if to suggest they leave before being discovered.

Nell whispered, "What if Elena's in here?" She stepped toward the couch.

Casey exhaled and followed her.

A man in a skeleton mask stood up behind the couch and swung a cinder block. Casey managed to defend himself with his forearm, avoiding a direct hit to the cranium, but the blow knocked him to the ground next to the couch, where Skeeto lay, eyes frozen up in their sockets.

Before Casey could react, he suffered a sleep attack. *Skeeto?* Was he dead? Casey's mind felt as numb as his limbs. *No, no, no.* Even from the floor, Casey saw Nell throw a roundhouse kick into the masked man's chin, toppling him. He dropped a syringe to the floor. Was this another narcoleptic hallucination?

The masked man hustled to retrieve the needle, tossed a dining chair at Nell, and fled out the front door.

Nell dodged the chair, followed the man to the door, then came back for Casey. She shook his shoulders and asked, "Your arm okay?"

He snapped out of it. "It's still attached. Go after him."

Nell frowned. "He's gone." She helped him to his feet and called 911, reported the intrusion, and requested an ambulance for a probable DOA.

Casey looked down at Skeeto, crouched near his friend, and wept.

"Don't touch him!" Nell cried, but it was too late.

Casey checked for a pulse, but felt nothing. He held his friend in his arms. "No, no, no, no. My best friend. *My best friend!*" He flashed back to playing football in the back yard with Skeeto, jamming as The Filing Cabinets, covering the Hail, high-fiving, hugging. He sobbed.

Gas and fluids gurgled in Skeeto's body.

Nell placed her hand on his shoulder. "He's gone, Case. He's gone. I'm so sorry." She gave him some space and stepped outside for a few moments. When she returned, Casey had settled a bit.

He wiped tears and sniffled. "Why didn't you chase him?"

"And do what if I caught him? Give him a facial?"

Maybe her combat moves *were* a hallucination. One thing certainly wasn't: what had happened to Skeeto. Casey hoped he would wake out of a sleep attack—but deep down knew this wasn't narcolepsy. This was really happening. *Breathe. Your most important breath is your next one.*

"Besides," Nell said, "I wanted to make sure you were okay."

Casey, standing near the corpse, turned away, covered his nose and mouth with his hand. He felt nauseous.

Resigned, Nell put her hands on his shoulders. "Skeletor poisoned your friend."

Casey looked from Nell to Skeeto, stunned, tears streaming down his cheeks. He put his hands to his head. "Was I hallucinating, or did you go all Bruce Lee on that guy?"

Nell shrugged. "I don't know what you mean."

"I saw you pull a roundhouse. At least, I think I did…"

"Don't you have hallucinations?"

"Yeah, during sleep attacks."

She folded her arms. "Well, there you go."

Elena was missing. Skeeto was dead. Casey was flabbergasted. "What the *hell* is going on here?"

"Skeeto lived here." Nell paced. "So the killer knew where to find him. As the director of public relations for the Hail, Skeeto had access to the team's secrets. Maybe he knew something about Elena's disappearance, and someone decided that his knowledge was too volatile."

Casey sniffled, took a deep breath, and tried to compose himself. Not a bad deduction for a cosmetics saleswoman. "Okay, let's roll with that. Who in the Hail organization would have reason to get rid of Elena?"

They stared at each other a moment then said in unison: "Todd Narziss."

"He had a bastard child to cover up," Nell said.

"We have records of the phone calls between Narziss and Skeeto."

"Those are circumstantial. And fruit from a poisoned tree. No pun intended."

Casey had no concern at the moment for court procedures. Would Narziss actually kill Skeeto during a playoff run? It would create a media circus. Something didn't fit.

Two uniformed officers and two paramedics entered the living room. "Police," one of the cops said. "I'm Officer Bickersly. What happened?"

Casey said, "We came here to see my friend, Skeeto, and found an intruder in a mask."

"Field Agent Nell Jenner." She showed her badge to the cops.

"*What?*" Casey had another sleep attack.

Nell reached over and shook Casey's shoulder. She smiled at the cops. "Everyone has their quirks." She turned serious and cleared her throat. "We heard trouble, found the door open, entered to see if Mr. DeWillis was all right, and found him in here. Deceased. The intruder had a syringe."

"How do we know *you* didn't drug him?" Bickersly said to Casey.

"Because a guy in a mask tried to knock off my head." He held up his scraped and bruised forearm as evidence. "The cinder block is over there. I managed to block it."

"I see that," Bickersly said then glanced at Nell. "That all true?"

She nodded. "Sure as I'm standing before you."

"Besides, Skeeto was my best friend." More tears welled. "I loved him, man." He wiped his eyes and tried to wrap his thoughts around the fact his boyhood friend was gone. Forever. He placed his hands on each side of his head, as if it were necessary to keep all his thoughts from leaking out.

"Where is this man now?" Bickersly said.

"He fled," Nell said.

Bickersly raised his brows at Nell. "Description?"

"Skeleton mask, black leather coat," Casey said. "Jeans. That's about it. He was sort of a blur."

Bickersly squinted at Casey. "*Skeleton mask?*"

"Yep," Nell and Casey said in unison.

"Might be hard to pick him out in a crowd," Nell said, trying to lighten the mood.

Casey kept hearing the music of The Filing Cabinets in his head. He bent at the waist, mouth open, crying silently.

Bickersly asked Nell a few follow-up questions as she comforted Casey. After she answered, Bickersly dismissed them. The cop moved closer to the couch to examine the crime scene.

Casey and Nell went outside to get fresh air. She held him, didn't say a word for five minutes. Then she said, "I'm here, and I'm sorry."

Casey wiped tears, blew his nose, and thanked her. After a few more minutes, his mind jumped back to Skeeto's killer, and how Nell had fended him off. "You're a federal *agent*?"

Nell winced. "Um, maybe a little."

She had lied to him. "I don't know how to feel right now," Casey said. "I'm already numb from Skeeto. And Elena sleeping with Narziss. Now this."

"I'm sorry, sleepyhead. I'm undercover. So I only reveal my identity when necessary. It's for your own—"

"Then why reveal it to the cops?"

"I needed them to trust us, not suspect us."

"But we're innocent."

"Of course we are. Even if they came to that same conclusion, it would have taken time to sort out—time Elena doesn't have."

Casey sighed and ran his hand through his hair. "Skeeto was my best friend since kindergarten. We grew apart in recent years, but we still had that history. Now I find out he may have hurt Elena at Narziss's request..." He clenched his fists.

Nell grabbed his upper arms. "Whoa—look at me. We don't know what he did or didn't do. All we know is he's gone." Nell held and comforted him. He felt bad for getting her shoulder wet.

Casey's cell phone rang: unlisted number. He awkwardly broke off the embrace and pointed at the phone. "May I?" He didn't feel like talking—at all—but he couldn't risk missing a call from Elena.

"Please," Nell said.

He walked away, sniffed, wiped tears, and answered. "Casey here."

"I don't know what you were trying to pull at the White House." It was a man's voice and, while it sounded familiar, Casey couldn't place it. "But you'll get your comeuppance," the voice said. "Right now, I'm on my way to your mother's house."

"Who is this?"

"You don't remember me?" the voice said, perturbed. "I remember you."

"My mother's not home this weekend." That was true. She had been shopping in Chicago with her neighbor, Evelyn Van Klooster. Of course, Mother had conveniently forgotten about that trip while deriding Casey for not spending enough time with her.

"You don't say," the voice continued. Now he suddenly sounded smooth and calm. "Never fear, Casey. I'll pay my respects."

"You'll what?" His mind raced like Usain Bolt with his shorts on fire. How did the caller know his name? How did he get his cell number? How did he know about the incident at the White House? Casey looked around the yard, the neighbors' yards—no sign of onlookers. "Come on. Who is this?"

The voice on the other line snapped: "Your family is next if you don't knock it off!"

"Knock what off?"

"Your little investigation. Let it go, or I'll take it out on your *mother*." The caller hung up.

Casey swallowed and signaled to Nell. "Come on."

Nell followed. "Who was it?"

He ran toward the Z4 and she followed him into the car. "I think it was the guy in the skeleton mask," Casey said. "He threatened my mother. He's going to her house!"

15

Nell drove toward Elzbieta Thread's house. Casey was practically hyperventilating. He expected to freeze at any moment.

"Calm down," Nell said. "How do you know it was him?"

"He referenced our little impromptu meeting."

"How would he get your phone number?"

"Hell if I know."

"He must know you. Is your mom home?"

"No. But she's going to return any minute."

"Call her."

Casey groaned and held up his hands in frustration. "She doesn't have a cell phone. I've tried and tried and tried to convince her to get one, but she refuses." He pounded the dash board.

"How far is her house?"

"About twelve minutes away, if we hit all the lights."

Nell called 911, and the operator dispatched a squad car to Elzbieta Thread's residence.

On the way, Casey could have sworn he saw a school of fish floating in front of the car, right in the middle of the street, as if they were under water. A squid swam over the windshield, then a sea cow.

By now Nell knew narcolepsy when she saw it. She reached over and shook his arm. "Casey, wake up. Cas-ey!"

He came to, shook his head. No more sea cow. As they neared his mother's house, he felt anxious, like he had guzzled a pot of coffee. *Breathe. Your most important breath is your next one.* He stared out the window, watching street lights pass by, trying to will them to move faster. Casey really wasn't close with his mother. At all. But she was still his ma.

Nell turned a corner a bit too fast, tires searching for pavement amidst snowy patches. "Who do you think the man in the skeleton mask was? Narziss?"

"No, Narziss is much bigger—like he's on steroids or HGH. Skeleton Guy was slight in comparison."

"That narrows it down."

Casey didn't have a response.

Nell pulled to the curb in front of the house, near a squad car. They got out and ran toward his mother's house. The front door was open, cold air rushing in. When Casey gently pushed the door wider, it clanged against something hard. Nell and Casey froze when they realized that picture frames, books, and other household items were scattered on the floor.

Casey heard his mother crying in the kitchen. "Ma?" He sprinted to her, dodging objects. "You okay?"

She held her face in her hands, leaning against the stainless steel dishwasher. "It's terrible, terrible." Mother sobbed.

He rubbed her back. "We'll clean up everything, Ma. Not much is broken."

"I don't care about things. It's Susan B. Anthony!" His mother had named her cat after the women's suffrage champion because she thought they looked alike; they didn't.

"What about her, Ma?"

Elzbieta Thread sniffled, pointed toward the living room with her left hand, still covering her face with her right. "In there." She resumed crying.

Nell beat him there and gasped.

Casey hurried down the hall and into the living room. He stopped in front of the couch as if it were the edge of a cliff.

Susan B. lay face down on the couch, dead. Mrs. Van Klooster's greyhound, Eli Whitney, was dead too. The killer had laid the pets in a sexually suggestive manner. There were no signs of choking, blunt-force trauma, or other apparent causes of death. Had he drugged them?

A police officer snapped pictures of the animals.

Casey figured the pets had been easy prey for the masked man. Casey returned to his mother, shocked by all that had happened. "Ma, I'm so, so sorry." He half-hugged her while she sobbed for a minute or two. It was the first hug he'd given her in longer than he remembered. Her arms were at her sides, but he squeezed her firmly.

"Who could do this?" Elzbieta said.

"The guy who did this called me from inside your house, just before you arrived home."

Elzbieta's eyes widened and she glared at Casey. "Is he still here?"

"I doubt it," Nell said, "but the police are checking the premises, just to be sure."

"I'm sorry," Elzbieta addressed Nell, "who are you?"

"This is Nell," Casey said. "She's a friend of Elena's, the woman who's missing."

Nell smiled meekly. "I'm sorry about your cat."

"Thank you, dear. She gave affection on her own terms, but who wants it all the time anyway? And what do you do?"

"I sell cosmetics."

"What kind?" Mother said.

"Baciare."

"Oooh, pretty *and* successful," Elzbieta said, elbowing her son. "You wouldn't want to bring someone like that home to me."

So much for wanting me to become a priest, Casey thought. *Or mourning her cat.* Some mothers never miss an opportunity to point out their children's deficiencies—no matter how happy or sad they happen to be at the moment.

More police officers arrived, as did the Animal Control Unit, which ran tests on the pets' bodies then bagged and loaded them into the Animal Control truck. Casey was grateful that he didn't have to carry Eli into the backyard or try to bury him in frozen ground.

Elzbieta wiped tears and shook her head. "Why would the killer call you, Casey?"

"We think it's because of the story I'm researching for *Sports Scene* magazine."

"What?" Elzbieta said.

Casey regretted saying those words the instant they left his mouth. He scratched his head. "He said he'd hurt you if I didn't stop looking into the disappearance of my friend from the Hail Pro Shop."

"Well, stop covering it!" Elzbieta snapped.

Mrs. Van Klooster entered the kitchen. She stood about five-foot-five and resembled Betty White with glasses. "I'm back, Elzy, and I have the tissues," she said. Her makeup had been smeared from crying.

Elzbieta hugged Mrs. Van Klooster and said, "Thank you. If I had known this was going to happen, I would have bought more."

"Don't be ridiculous, dear," Mrs. Van Klooster said. "None of us saw this coming."

That comment tore at Casey's chest, as he *had* seen it coming but hadn't been able to impede it. Nell scribbled something on a pad of paper, ripped it off and handed it to Elzbieta. "I'd really like it if you went to this hotel. Take Mrs. Van Klooster with you. You'll be safe there."

Elzbieta looked skeptically at Nell. "Who are you, Harriet Tubman?"

"I'm a federal agent, ma'am. Trust me."

"CIA," Mrs. Van Klooster whispered to Casey with a wink and a definitive nod. Casey squinted at her.

"Trust you?" Elzbieta frowned. "You just lied to me about your job."

Casey rolled his eyes. "Ma, please."

"I'm FBI Special Agent Nell Jenner." She produced her ID. "I'm staying at that hotel."

"Well," Elzbieta said, "if you're FBI you'll catch this bastard, right?"

"That's the plan," Nell said.

Casey knew he should feel better knowing he had the feds on his side. But the shock of the information was like splashed water on jeans—the deed had been done, but it was taking a while to saturate.

"Don't you have a big FBI team to hunt him down?" Elzbieta asked.

"There are multitudes of ongoing cases," Nell said. "Most situations don't get the resources dedicated to them like you might see on TV."

"Won't he be able to find us if he checks all the hotels?" Elzbieta said.

"It's on my credit card under my name," Nell said.

A female cop told Elzbieta that there were no suspects on the premises, and no sign of forced entry. "Is it possible you left your door open, Mrs. Thread?"

"I suppose it's possible…"

"Ma, how many times have I reminded you—"

"Oh, nobody's perfect," she said with a scowl.

"Leaving your door open doesn't make what he did legal," the officer said.

"We'll get through this," Casey said to Elzbieta. "We'll find the jerk-off who did this."

Elzbieta scoffed. "Such language. He didn't steal the dish soap, you know." It wouldn't be the first time she had "washed" her son's mouth out, although it had been twenty-four years, two months, and a week since the last time. Not that Casey kept count.

She turned to Mrs. Van Klooster and said, "Come on, dear, let's go."

Casey wiped his palm over his face. Mother had hang-ups that he knew might never change. So when her tidal wave washed toward him, he tried to surf on top of it. He and Nell left the house, returned to the Z4, got in and closed the doors. Nell exhaled. "Your mother can be a challenge."

"A challenge is riding a bike uphill." Casey gave her a grave look, letting his hand flop to his thigh in exhaustion. They stared at each other a moment, then chuckled. "She's a piece of work, but I love her."

"I know you do." Nell started the car.

Casey scratched his temple. "If you hadn't had to, would you have ever told me your were a federal agent?"

Nell answered the question she thought he was really asking. "Casey, I really *am* Elena's friend. We want the same thing."

He raised his hands to his head as if to fend off a migraine. "I never questioned your commitment to find her. I asked if you'd planned to level with me."

"Does it matter?" Nell said, exasperated. "Or is the real question whether your chest swelled when you thought you could heroically lead the cosmetics princess to the damsel in distress, Sir Thread the Gallant?"

He took a deep breath and looked out the front windshield. "Look, we both want to find Elena. It's time to hail her cab."

16

When Hailangelo returned to his studio, he set his briefcase on the antique desk, grabbed a tall glass and mixed another Black Russian on the rocks. He drank half of it, the ice slipping to his lips, and then approached Galatea from behind and kissed her on the shoulder. He removed an ice cube from the drink and ran it down her back. He held her closely and became aroused. "It is done, my *amor.*" The alcohol and homicides combined to stimulate his mesolimbic dopamine system, flooding his brain with pleasure. He had become addicted to such stimuli and knew it wouldn't last, so he closed his eyes, inhaled deeply, and savored it.

Urges beckoned him to place Galatea in public, to showcase his greatness again to the world. He imagined the news reports on it, and a museum buying it for display. He wouldn't be credited by name, of course, but would bask in the glory of the attention from the safety of his hiding spot, right under their noses. But that would require giving her away. He couldn't do that—he loved her far too much.

While stalking the woman who would become Galatea, Hailangelo had spotted LeRoy "Skeeto" DeWillis and Todd Narziss with her. This had infuriated Hailangelo, who'd contemplated for days how to deal with it.

Eventually, he'd spoken to Narziss about it before a political rally at East High School. Narziss had been scheduled to introduce the governor to the audience in the school auditorium, and Hailangelo had pulled him aside backstage:

"But she's a good time," Narziss had whispered to Hailangelo.

"I don't care if she's the concubine of the century, you'll stop seeing her."

Hailangelo stood six feet tall, but Narziss still hulked in comparison. "What are you, my father?"

Hailangelo pointed a finger at Narziss's neck as if it were a needle. "I launder the payments for your drugs. If you want that to continue, you'll do as I say."

Narziss laughed at him and folded his python-sized arms. "I'll just get them from Elena. Pay cash and cut out the middle man."

"Not if you want your affair to stay a secret from your adoring fans, deluded into thinking you're the football man of the year and a wholesome candidate for office."

The smile evaporated from Narziss's face. "You wouldn't."

Hailangelo raised a brow and said, "Oh Todd, you know I gladly would."

Narziss held out his hands as if to clutch Hailangelo's neck. "I'll strangle you."

"Tut-tut. Not in the same room as the governor and a packed auditorium. Besides, we wouldn't want Elena to disappear, would we?"

Narziss glowered. "What do you mean?"

"I mean, if you don't stop seeing her, you'll never see her again."

"That doesn't make sense. Either way, I won't see her."

Hailangelo smiled. "Now you're catching up." The sound of the crowd in the auditorium swelled. "I think you'd better get on stage, Todd."

The master of ceremonies announced over the auditorium speakers, "Ladies and gentlemen, all-star tight end for the Green Bay Hail, Todd Narziss!" Without hesitation, the athlete ducked through the curtains and went onstage. Hailangelo listened from behind the curtains.

The crowd chanted, "Go Hail, go! Go Hail, go!"

Todd Narziss waved to his fans and waited for them to calm down. "This year, our team has proven we're winners. We have home-field advantage, we've advanced to the conference championship, but our job isn't done yet, right?"

The audience burst into ecstatic applause.

"It won't be until we win the championship," he said. "Everyone loves a winner. If you want to be an all-star, you'll make sure he gets four more years."

"Four more years!" the crowd chanted. "Four more years!"

Narziss grinned. "Ladies and gentlemen: the Governor of Wisconsin, Lance Moeller!"

Now, in the safety of his studio, Hailangelo snapped out of his reverie and smiled at his statue of Galatea. "They'll never mess with you again, love." He guzzled the rest of the Black Russian and kissed her hand.

17

Casey ran an online search for addresses on Blue Lake Road, then used those to search for the phone numbers registered to those addresses, and quickly had a phone list to call to see if the property owners knew Ed Plasky, the cab driver. Casey claimed to be Ed's fishing buddy, and that he had accidentally deleted Ed's address from his phone. After five rejections, Casey found an old lady who gave him Plasky's location. When soliciting anything, Casey turned to multiplicity: if he had confidence and asked enough people, eventually someone would say yes. The key was not to care that a dozen or a hundred-dozen would say "no" before getting that "yes." After all, why would he care about the opinions of strangers who turned him down? If he didn't ask, it would be guaranteed he wouldn't get what he wanted. He had nothing to lose.

Even though he had an address for the cabin, he couldn't leave right away. First, he needed a ride from Nell and she had other FBI commitments. Second, he had promised his mother that he'd meet her at Leila's apartment. He knew he had to find Elena, but he also couldn't blow off his mother all week, especially after the home invasion. Elzbieta was now staying with Leila until things settled—she preferred that to the hotel. Casey helped Elzbieta bring in groceries. They took a few bags into the complex while Leila remained at the car. In the elevator for the apartment complex, Casey said, "How are you holding up, Ma?"

"Oh, I'm still here," Elzbieta said. "I wish my Susan B. was, too."

"I'm really sorry that happened, Ma."

"I know, kid."

Back in Leila's apartment, it took Elzbieta about three seconds to light a cigarette.

He hesitated at first to say anything, but then remembered Leila could lose her apartment if she allowed smoking. "Ma, you can't smoke in here."

Elzbieta glared at him in disbelief. "What, are you the Board of Health now? You're a smoker!"

"I quit, Ma."

"Eh." She waved at him. "You never finish anything."

Casey swallowed. Mother had said similar things before but this hit him below the belt. "Yeah? Well, I am finishing this. I'm on this new pill, and it zaps my cravings."

"Look, your father died on me with two kids." She held up two fingers, as if he didn't know what she meant. "That left me to raise a five-year-old and an infant on my own." She puffed on the cancer stick. "Did you expect me to be Mother Teresa? So I need a little pick-me-up once in a while. Sue me." She took a long drag, opened the window, and held her cigarette near it. *Strange,* he thought, *how smoke rising from the end of such a lethal product could be so beautiful as it drifts.*

"Look, Ma, the landlord will evict Leila if the smoke alarms go off."

Mother grunted. "I haven't been this oppressed since Hitler."

"Ma, we've been over this: you didn't live in Poland during the war."

"The hell I didn't. I was born in Kraków." She closed her eyes and touched her fingertips to her chest. "I am a child of the War Era."

"You were born after the Germans surrendered."

"By eight months. Technically, I was conceived during the war! My poor Jewish neighbors."

Casey put the milk in the fridge. "With all due respect, you were an infant, Ma—you had no idea what was going on." When she resorted to revisionist history, he felt a responsibility to anthropology and humanity to correct her.

"There you go with the manipulating." Mother gesticulated. "Like I can't read the history books or see the documentaries and feel a connection or a...a...*kindred spirit* with those who suffered next door?" She hastily inhaled nicotine. "Whether I was a month or a hundred years old, I was living right down the street. Now I'm just a widow who worked her *dupa* off to provide for two kids, and you want to flush it all down the toilet. *Woo-kiish!*"

Casey sighed.

Leila entered through the front door, holding a paper bag of groceries up to her chin.

"Oh thank God." Elzbieta crossed herself as she approached Leila, arms outstretched.

Casey took the groceries off Leila's hands and set them on the kitchen counter.

Elzbieta dramatically embraced her daughter.

Casey rolled his eyes. "It has been a whole two minutes since you last saw her."

"What?" Elzbieta said. "Can't a mother thank the Divine Savior for returning her daughter safely? The world is a dangerous place, Casey Jerome Thread, even when you're just walking to your car. You of all people should know that."

Leila intervened. "Ma, lay off him."

That surprised Casey. Leila hadn't done that since, when, tenth grade?

Elzbieta waved again, as if shooing a fly. "Eh. Casey, you should be helping your sister."

He squinted. "Excuse me? I'm the one who's been unloading the groceries while you—"

"I love my dear Leila, but all the self-*loathing*." Elzbieta waved the cigarette in a circle, the smoke trailing. "Her hate for her attacker consumes her, holds her back, which depresses her further."

Leila folded her arms. "Um, I'm right here."

Elzbieta glanced at Casey and held out her palm toward Leila, as if her daughter was Exhibit A. "See? She lets it out on her mother. They talked all about this on Dr. Phil."

Leila's face crumpled. "What?"

Elzbieta looked at both her kids and blew smoke. "It's a vicious cycle, really. And what do you do, Casey? Nothing."

"Stop it, Ma," Leila said, leaning against the door as if her mother had physically pushed her.

Casey folded his arms. "No, it's okay, Lei. What am I supposed to do about it, Ma?"

Elzbieta started sniffling. "You were supposed to watch her! She was fifteen when it happened! *Fif-teen!*" Tears streamed down her cheeks.

His stomach churned.

Elzbieta covered her face with her hands. "Oh! Oh, dear Lord." She crossed herself again. "That terrible event."

"Jesus H. Christ, Mom," Leila said. "I was raped. *R-a-p-e-d.* You can say it."

Her mother howled, covering her ears with her hands, her voice climbing in pitch like a choral warm-up: "We're not doing this..."

"Whatever." Leila said. "Gawd! This is Groundhog Day." She stormed into her bedroom, slamming the door behind her.

Casey glowered at his mother.

She took another drag on her cigarette. "What?"

Casey checked on his sister. "You okay?" Leila's tears made black streamers from her eyeliner. She looked in the mirror. "I'm a hot mess."

He placed a hand on her shoulder. "Want to talk about it?"

"No."

Casey said nothing.

Leila sniffed. "For months, maybe years, I wondered what people would do if I killed myself. I never took physical steps to do it; just pictured hanging from black pantyhose. If I stopped showing up to Fixate Factory, would my boss notice? Care?"

"I'd care," he said.

"Do spirits hang around after death to observe their mother's reaction?"

Casey tilted his head. "I...I don't know, Lei."

"If Satan exists, and he has a sense of humor, that would be my version of hell."

Mother would always be Mother. But the rape? Elzbieta had a point: Leila had to stop letting it define her.

"Every day, I wake up and hope I don't relive it," she said. "The hairline fracture in my windshield reminds me of the crack in the sidewalk where my rapist pounced. I remember the cloth smelled like syrup mixed with chemicals."

Casey nodded. "Chloroform."

Leila dropped her hands and exhaled in exasperation. "I don't want to talk about this." Her auto insurance only paid half the cost of a new windshield, so she couldn't afford to replace it. And since the crack didn't require a fix, she just left it. Casey would have offered to pay to fix it, but he knew she wanted it there to remind her to check the back seat before getting in. Some people were too proud to take handouts from siblings. Leila was loath to admit weakness.

Casey recalled hearing about how the rapist tackled her behind the shrubbery, and seeing how wickedly gnarled the branches had looked. There had been only one light illuminating the off-campus apartment complex and everything had been dark. Where were all the pedestrians? Where were the SAFEWalk people? The police?

The night after the attack, she would tell her rape counselor, her friend Amelia, and Casey that the perpetrator had whispered in her ear, "Just relax and it will hurt less. In fact, it'll feel goooood." At the time, Leila's entire sexual experience had amounted to kissing Bobby Lowenstein at a middle school dance. Casey wished he could go back in time, use what he knew now to avoid a narcoleptic attack, ask someone else to hang out with them in case he had an attack, and protect his sister. That night, they had both lost their innocence.

Leila grabbed a duffle bag and shoved clothes in it.

"What are you doing?" Casey said.

"I'm going to Madison. I'm getting the hell out of here. I miss Amelia."

"Take it easy. It's getting late and you're in no—"

"I'm going, Case. If you want to stay here, fine. But get the hell out of my way."

He stepped aside, and she left without another word.

18

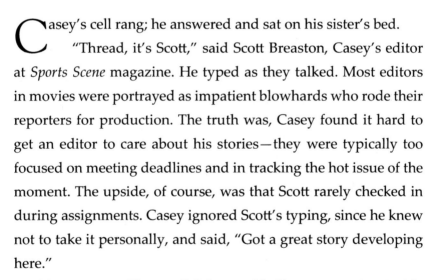

Casey's cell rang; he answered and sat on his sister's bed.

"Thread, it's Scott," said Scott Breaston, Casey's editor at *Sports Scene* magazine. He typed as they talked. Most editors in movies were portrayed as impatient blowhards who rode their reporters for production. The truth was, Casey found it hard to get an editor to care about his stories—they were typically too focused on meeting deadlines and in tracking the hot issue of the moment. The upside, of course, was that Scott rarely checked in during assignments. Casey ignored Scott's typing, since he knew not to take it personally, and said, "Got a great story developing here."

More typing. "Stars sell," Scott said. "Are you getting inside Narziss's world?"

"Intimately. He may be responsible for the disappearance of a young woman who worked at the Hail Pro Shop."

Scott stopped typing. His chair squeaked. "From last week? You're kidding me."

"Nope. Narziss had been playing 'prom night' with the missing woman."

"Anyone go on record about that yet?"

"No. I think his wife might at some point, though. Word is the missing victim is preggos."

"I hear you," Scott said. "You're following it?"

"Like pilot fish to a shark. Might miss a few days of practice."

"Do you need me to assign someone to cover the championship game?"

"I'll be there; I pretty much have the football angle covered already. By the way, I have a sidebar on how the community is cuckoo for Hail puffs. The priests and ministers pray for the team in church."

Scott started typing again. "Sources need to go on record."

"You said that already."

"Hear Cummings broke his leg?" Scott said, referring to the Hail's star running back.

"What?"

"You didn't hear?"

Casey felt instant heartburn. "I didn't see—"

"Relax. It happened during a motorcycle accident after practice. He's in the hospital. The Associated Press just tweeted the story."

Casey had Twitter on his phone, but hadn't checked the updates lately. He knew that, with Cummings out, Green Bay would have a hard time beating New York. Without the threat of Cummings running the ball, the New York defenders could chase Green Bay's quarterback with reckless abandon. Maybe even knock Johnny Oakley out of the game. "I was about to follow up on this disappearance lead out of town."

"Go ahead. But Cummings might have something to say about Narziss. You're tight with Cummings, right?"

"I have his cell number from my days at the newspaper."

"Great. We need something for the magazine that won't be on all the blogs and sports sites across the country."

Casey reassured him, ended the call, and dialed Cummings. His smartphone felt hot on his ear. "Marshon, you okay?"

"Yeah dawg, I'm a-ight," Cummings said, "for being in the hospital."

"Sorry that happened, man, but glad you're okay. Did the doctor say anything about resuming your career?"

Cummings half-laughed. "I'm comin' back. No doubt about it. My leg is confetti but, damn, how can I not? Doc said there's a five-percent chance to resume my career. That's all I need."

"If anyone can, it's you."

"Damn straight. I came back from the broken collarbone, so I can come back from this."

"Nice," Casey said. "Listen, we go way back, right?" Casey had written an article during his last year with the *Green Bay Times* about how the team had strong-armed Cummings behind the scenes, refusing to pay him the going rate unless he agreed to insert a clause in his contract to void everything in the event of a career-threatening injury. Cummings couldn't negotiate with another team because he was a "restricted" free agent, meaning the Green Bay Hail had the right to match contract overtures from other teams. After Casey had written the article, Hail fans lit up blogs and talk radio, outraged that Cummings wasn't getting his due and worried that the team would one day lose their star ball carrier. Johnny Oakley spoke out to the media about his desire for the team to keep Cummings. A week after Casey's article, Cummings got a stellar contract from the Hail without the dubious clause. At the time, Cummings had told Casey he'd never forget it.

Now Cummings said, "We're boys. I'd be screwed right now if you hadn't written that article. Come with it."

"Ever see Narziss with a Latina?"

Without hesitation, Cummings said, "You mean Elena?"

"Yeah." Casey tried not to sound too geeked.

"Damn, she's fiiiine. If J-Lo and Eva Mendes had a baby, it would look like Elena."

Casey ignored the scientific implausibility of Cummings's statement. "Where'd you see them?"

"J-Lo and Eva?"

"Elena and Narziss."

"He snuck her into the assistant coaches' locker room once."

Narziss was Mr. Entitlement. "Bet he knew the coaches looked the other way," Casey said.

"Hey," Cummings said, "they have different rules for Todd 'The Prez' Narziss."

"Have you seen him with Elena anywhere else?"

"At Club Addiction. A couple of us went out the other night with the girls."

"Not Friday, the night Elena disappeared?"

"No," Cummings said. "Monday? Yeah-yeah, the Monday before that. I had a bad feeling about it."

Casey didn't respond.

"CT?" Cummings said. "You there?"

Casey couldn't respond. He had fallen into partial cataplexy and sleep paralysis, hunched over. His momentum took him to the floor. As he rolled, he snapped out of it. He recovered his phone. "Marshon? You still there?"

"I'm in the hospital with broken legs. Where would I go? What's up *witchyou*?"

"I fall asleep sometimes. It's how I roll." He reached into his jeans pocket, extracted a caffeine pill, and swallowed it. He marched out of Leila's bedroom, into the kitchen, opened the refrigerator, grabbed a Red Bull and drank it to wash down the pill.

Silence.

"Anyway," Casey continued, "you were saying—about a bad feeling..."

More silence.

"Marshon?" He looked at his phone, and the call was still connected.

Pause.

"You there?" Casey said.

Cummings burst into laughter. "That's how I roll, dawg." He cackled with glee. "A-ight, CT, A-ight."

Casey rolled his eyes.

"I got this vibe from The Prez like he had something to hide," Marshon said. "He was acting all nervous. I asked him about it, but he denied there was anything wrong."

19

Hailangelo lay back on his king-size bed, staring at the print on the ceiling directly above him. Gustav Klimt's *The Kiss* portrayed a man smooching his lover on the cheek, both of them cloaked in golden robes with turquoise and blue flowers in their hair. She knelt before him, eyes closed, enraptured by his presence, as if their passion and soul connection had drained her energy to the point of exhaustion. She clung to the man, who was the only force keeping her upright, her right arm draped over his and his hands embracing her porcelain skin. Hailangelo envisioned a sculpture that would bring *The Kiss* to life. He had already found the proper fabric for the cloaks—one for the statue and another for himself. Now he simply needed the muse.

Earlier in the day, he had poured himself a Black Russian and watched people outside his window. One of his neighbors, Rihanna

Morris, played with her daughter, Shantell, who sat in a red sled. He had seen Elena Ortega walking little Shantell to school each weekday morning.

Rihanna pulled a rope attached to the sled carrying her daughter. The sled left a wake behind in the snowy grass. A truck had plowed several days' worth of snow into the back corner of the parking lot outside their apartment, and Shantell jumped out of the sled so she could use the embankment as a sledding hill. The ride was brief, but so was the climb up for more. Without fail, the girl squealed with glee each time down.

Hailangelo had thought Shantell would be perfect for a statue based on the Norman Rockwell painting, *The Problem We All Live With*. It featured a little African-American girl, just like Shantell, walking to school while escorted by deputy U.S. marshals, amidst racist protestors hurling tomatoes. Hailangelo viewed every race as equal—equally vile—and delighted in different tones and hues to use as material. He didn't care if his statue's race matched that of the original painting; only that they matched the beauty and spirit of the inspiration. Still, the resemblance was obvious.

Hailangelo knew he had a problem: he created unique, rare works of art that couldn't possibly be fully accepted or appreciated by his contemporaries. Perhaps long after his death he'd be heralded as a visionary master. But for now, he would have to contend with the law. To him, blending into society, mimicking "appropriate" behavior and avoiding detection were realities, necessary skills he could develop and hone. He was certainly not the first persecuted artist to have his creations destroyed by religious zealots, morality police, or dictators—and he wouldn't be the last. Like the statues themselves, he sculpted his life according to his own preferences, but also took into account the reaction of his adoring public.

For these reasons, he had to let the giggling girl glide down the snow bank forevermore. He couldn't take her. Society would rise up and not allow it. He drained the last of the vodka and set the glass in the sink.

Society couldn't control his compulsions. The hunger remained. Just because he couldn't bring Rockwell's *The Problem We All Live With* to life didn't mean Rihanna couldn't ripen for his kiss. Yes, she would look gorgeous in a golden cloak. He closed his eyes, content with the vision for his next statue.

§

Casey dreamed they were dead, and he couldn't believe it. In the dream, he looked around Cresh Funeral Home. His mother wore black and yammered on to her friends and relatives. Those around her searched for an escape route from her dissertation.

Mother's long gray hair hung down under a black-brimmed hat as she stood near the caskets, peach drapery adorning the walls behind her.

Weird, Casey thought, *that the two caskets are empty but the lids are open.*

The one on the left moved a few inches periodically, even though nobody touched it. He suddenly needed air. "Excuse me," he said, leaving a circle of people listening to Aunt Dorice, who was about five-foot-three and two hundred pounds. She was ten minutes into a story about her Plum French Toast Bake, which she insisted was low in fat.

Casey opened a golden door handle, walked through oak doors and a vacant room. He continued through a second empty room and arrived at a third door. Instinct told him not to open it. He couldn't tell why.

He opened it. In the backyard, people lay on the snowbanks, convulsing. Maggots covered their faces.

Robert Cresh, the funeral-home owner, stood right in front of Casey in a black suit but wearing no winter coat, watching the victims as a shepherd would survey his flock. Cresh's nametag was pinned to his lapel. Despite the fact that Casey had never formally met him, Cresh's face lit up as if Casey were the prodigal son.

"Casey!" Cresh said, his face covered in corpse makeup. "Glad you could make it." He held up a wine glass. "Care for some vintage formaldehyde?" He drank the entire glass and said, "Ahh."

Casey smiled uncomfortably and scanned the backyard. "What's going on?"

"What do you mean?" Cresh smiled. He had a bushy unibrow.

"Oh, I don't know—the convulsing, maggot-infested zombies, maybe?"

Cresh chuckled and shrugged. "They're just lawn gnomes."

Casey stared blankly.

Cresh frowned. "Fine. This is where the dead come when their hearts stop beating. And they remain here unless revived."

"How comforting." Casey started to wake up, but still felt tired and wanted to explore this dream. Something beckoned him...

Annoyed, Cresh pointed to the corner of the backyard. "If you must know, Leila and Elena are right over there." Sure enough, their bodies were contorted on the ground, gesticulating and making distorted snow angels.

Casey blinked rapidly. "Who else knows about this place?"

The Cresh-ire cat smiled. "You mean does anyone else know you let that rapist ravish your sister?"

"How do you—"

"I see the trees rot," Cresh said. "The maggots feed, the birds circle, the rabbits turn away."

Casey looked at his feet, ashamed. "I didn't think she'd get raped."

Cresh raised his brow. "Or commit suicide."

"What? Who? Leila?"

No answer.

"Leila committed suicide?" Casey grabbed Cresh by the lapels. Or did he mean Elena?

"Release me at once!" Cresh said, and Casey complied. "Even a dog knows when a friend needs him, Casey. Instead, you chased squirrels. No matter." Cresh smoothed his lapels and turned his back to Casey. He faced the convulsing bodies. "I'll have you here soon enough."

Behind him, Casey heard someone approach, giggling.

"He's right, Casey."

Casey turned.

His mother stood there, holding a kabob of two meatballs with a carrot in the middle. She smiled at him. "Delicious!"

Casey awoke in a cold sweat, sitting up in his hotel bed. "Whoa." The clock read 3:13 a.m. He paused as images of Leila, Elena, Cresh, and his mother spun in his head like clothes in a dryer. He waited for them to settle at the bottom. Just a dream, he thought. Dream, dream, dream. Not real. He rolled over and tried to go back to sleep. He knew he'd need a lot of energy for the trip to the taxi driver's cottage.

§

Later that morning, Casey did his best to forget the nightmare, but the image of his mother holding the kabob persisted until about an hour into the Hail's practice, during which Narziss caught three passes and barreled over defenders after each catch. He seemed to have no fear.

"That's more like it, Narzy," Coach Druthers said. Teammates pounded their fists on Narziss's shoulder pads and Oakley swatted his star tight end on the butt to show approval. If the pressure from his rough first playoff game was getting to Narziss, he sure didn't show it on the practice field. Coaches said, "You play like you practice." Casey bought into that to a certain extent. However, players knew that maintaining focus in practice to execute techniques and strategy correctly was one thing. Doing so in an actual game—especially in the playoffs—was quite another.

"Todd Narziss is ready to play," Narziss told reporters in the locker room after practice. "Nothing affects his mentality, especially his own dropped passes. That's in the past. Last time I checked, this next game against New York will start out tied at zero, so it's a fresh start. We plan to win fifty-two to nothing."

The room buzzed about the upcoming conference championship game on Sunday with a bid to play for the world title at stake. The media throng had expanded to include a famous writer from the *New York Times* and a hotshot reporter from ESPN. One might have expected the players to be excited by all the national media attention, but by this point in the season, it just annoyed most of them.

"Narziss is tired of waiting around, answering all these questions," Narziss said, clenching his jaw as he sat on the bench in his varnished locker. "I just want to play football and forget about everything else."

The reporters did not know the half of it.

The questions that seemed to rankle the players the most concerned the weather forecast predicting zero degrees and a wind chill of minus-twenty at kickoff. Narziss had the advantage of large hands to catch the frozen football—oversized even for a pro athlete's. Casey wondered if Narziss had used those paws to call Skeeto and ask him to kill Elena and her unborn child. Narziss played American football for a living, which was by definition a violent sport. But he also did charity work and had two little kids. Could he really have ordered a murder?

It would not be without precedent. In 2001, Carolina Panthers player Rae Carruth was convicted of conspiracy to commit first degree murder of his pregnant girlfriend, as well as of shooting into an occupied vehicle and using an instrument to destroy an unborn child. Doctors saved the child but his girlfriend died. Carruth was convicted and sentenced to prison.

Narziss stood behind the herd of reporters and their recorders, cameras, mics, and lighting equipment. Casey wondered, if Elena had been a blue-eyed Swedish American, would there have been a huddle of reporters this size around the police chief all day? Maybe they would be onto Narziss as a suspect by now. As it was, news coverage of Elena's disappearance waned. The *Times* reporter asked players about the missing Pro Shop employee, and whether the circumstances affected their focus on the championship game. Narziss claimed that, as far as he knew, none of the players admitted to even thinking about the missing Pro Shop employee, much less knowing anything. The only person truly questioning the Philanderer-in-Chief on the circumstances surrounding the crime itself was a narcoleptic freelance magazine reporter who was supposed to be writing about the team's epic championship drive, feeding fans what they craved — all Narziss, all the time.

20

After the locker room session, Nell picked up Casey and they drove three hours northeast from Green Bay to Minocqua. By the time they arrived, the Tuesday sun had set. The rural tourist town in northern Wisconsin had a population of fewer than 5,000 people. Log cabins were the norm and they spotted almost as many bait shops as street lights. A lighted sign outside a pub proclaimed, "14th Annual Wife-Carrying Contest, March 14."

Nell said, "Did you see that sign?"

"You mean I didn't hallucinate it?"

"Is it a race?"

"Or a dead lift?"

"Who does that? 'Let's join the gym, honey.' 'No, I have a better idea—*Wife-Carrying Contest!*'"

When Nell turned off Highway 51 onto Blue Lake Road, the Z4's headlights provided the only illumination on the single-lane road. Like most of Wisconsin's Northwoods, the area was largely virgin forest, dominated by pine and birch trees. Neither Nell nor Casey said a word from the moment they left the highway. They were both tired and talked out. An occasional cottage dotted the roadside; Casey absorbed the space between them—the isolation, the connection to nature, the stillness. It was so different from a big city, where most homeowners could barely fit a garbage can between their houses and sounds rang out every second of every day. Yet somehow Casey could relate to this stillness, to the isolation he'd felt since his sleep attack with Elena. Before Skeeto died, he and Casey had found less and less in common and less reason to fight for the friendship. His profession required hours to write. The introvert in him loved it. But after a while, even Casey yearned for human interaction. He hadn't understood that until now, riding in a car in the dark somewhere in the Wisconsin Northwoods, so near Nell yet so close to nowhere. He felt a strong attraction to Nell, to her intelligence, spunk, and verve, but he couldn't be sure how to sort it out or act on it until they found Elena.

"You okay, sleepyhead?" Nell said.

"Yeah. I've enjoyed spending time with you."

She smiled. "Aw, me too."

Casey paused. "Thank you."

"For what?"

"For, I dunno, driving me to the ends of the earth."

"Don't thank me." She winked. "You're going to pay for gas and dinner. What's wrong?"

"Ah, I just don't know how to feel about Skeeto. We used to be best friends."

"Did something happen, or did you just drift apart?"

"We drifted."

Nell sipped her cappuccino and set it back in the cup holder. "Friends can be so circumstantial, especially if you lose a common activity. You think you're such great pals and, in a way, you are. Then you quit the softball team, change jobs, move, or—Heaven forbid—have kids, and boom! It's over."

Casey felt melancholy for times gone by. "Skeeto and I used to play in a band together called the Filing Cabinets." He felt a twinge of guilt for breaking up the band after college to focus on his job. He loved reporting, but he would never know how things would have been different with Skeeto had he stayed in the band.

Nell tucked her hair behind her ear. "Love the band name; so square it's cool. Were you guys any good?"

Casey scoffed. "Of course not. But we had fun."

She giggled and curled a strand of her hair with two fingers. "I wish I could have heard you guys play."

"I wanted to play a reunion gig…" Now it was no longer possible. He felt hollow.

"I know you won't have Skeeto," Nell said, "but you could still play your songs for me."

Casey thought a moment about that, and pondered whether he could play those songs without his friend. Physically he could. But emotionally? It would be tough, but he knew Skeeto wouldn't want the songs to die. Casey smiled. "Maybe when this is all over."

They drove another mile to the end of the street and the GPS prompted Nell to turn right onto a gravel road.

The driveway ended at a patch of woods. Casey spotted a cottage tucked back about thirty yards. The female GPS voice—Nell called her "Joan" because it sounded like a robotic Joan Cusack—said, "Arriving at destination." The headlights illuminated an address marker, a wooden sign nailed to a tree. It had an 8 carved into it, painted blue.

Nell parked the Z4 and turned off the lights, leaving the area pitch-black. "Sure this is it?"

Casey opened the car door, and sensed the same fear he had felt during childhood when he descended alone into the basement for the first time. "Guess we'll find out." He grabbed a large yellow flashlight and got out. A grassy path led to the cottage. As they walked, pine needles and snow crunched underfoot.

Nell took out her standard-issue Glock 22 pistol.

"Is that really necessary?" Casey said.

Nell popped in a clip and readied the chamber.

"All righty, then," he said.

She said nothing.

"It's not like Elena's dad followed us here," he said, looking over his shoulder to make sure.

"We don't know this cabbie," Nell said. "He could have shot Elena and buried her out here. He could be working for Narziss. Or Elena's father. Or—"

"Next, you'll say he could have night goggles," Casey said.

"If he's a diehard hunter, sure."

Casey frowned.

"But if it makes you feel better, I'll holster it." She had no holster, so she tucked it into the back of her jeans and pulled her green cosmo jacket over it.

Casey rolled his eyes. "Yeah, much better."

The flashlight revealed old birch trees along each side of the trail. Halfway to the cottage, they came upon an abandoned wooden cart overflowing with rusted chairs, poles, and grills. The cart looked ready to buckle under the weight. He shone the flashlight around it, checking for signs of life, wondering what the heck the cabbie planned to do with all that junk. They passed the cart, nobody there. Casey exhaled.

They heard a rustling behind them and quickly turned. A pair of yellow eyes reflected the light about fifty yards away, then disappeared. "Wolf," Casey said, and exhaled hard. For a moment, his feet felt encased in cement.

They trudged toward the cottage and spotted the taxi's back fender and yellow trunk peeking out from behind the cabin. The cab had reflective red-and-silver stickers on the side.

Faded green paint flaked from the cottage, illuminated by a single bare light bulb. The wooden door featured three horizontal windows stacked vertically, draped by old cream-colored cloth. The place looked like it had been abandoned for years; did Ed Plasky want it that way? Casey stood outside the door, peering at Nell. "I think we should go," Casey whispered. "Nobody's here." He started back toward the car.

She placed her hand on his chest to stop him. "Then why are we whispering?"

Casey cleared his throat and said in a normal but quiet voice, "Really, we should go."

She frowned at him as she pulled her curly blonde locks back into a ponytail, and knocked.

"Okay," Casey moaned, "I guess we're not going."

The flashlight faded, then extinguished. Dead batteries. Casey tossed the flashlight to the ground and illuminated his smartphone, creating a yellow glow on the door. Nell and Casey stood outside the cottage with that glow for twenty seconds. He wanted to run. But he kept remembering his mother holding that kabob outside the funeral home in his nightmare, chastising him for never finishing anything. He breathed deeply, quietly, concentrating on not having a sleep attack. *Your most important breath—*

Something human flashed past the window in the cabin door.

Nell pulled out her FBI identification.

A man pulled back the curtain and peered at them through the window, his sclera appearing like lights in the darkness. But they weren't the only things starring back at them. So did the pitch-black eyes of a double-barreled shotgun.

21

Casey had a sleep attack.

"Don't shoot!" Nell yelled. She held up her badge to the shotgun muzzle. "FBI."

The man in the door had a comb-over, just as Sandy from the gas station had described the taxi driver. They had found Ed Plasky, driver of Cab Twelve.

He didn't open the door. "*D'respassing* at night is a good way *da* get shot, don'tcha know," he said through the glass. Casey recognized his Upper-Michigan accent—he was a Yooper. "Put yer hands up."

Nell shook Casey out of the attack. They both raised their hands.

The man opened the door, aiming the gun at them. He looked Nell up and down, smiled, then pointed his shotgun at Casey. "What do *yas* want?"

"Mr. Plasky, I'm Agent Jenner, FBI. Can we come in and talk?"

He aimed the shotgun at her. "About?"

"The last customer you picked up by Hail Stadium," Nell said.

He glared at her. "Oh, I don't dake notes on my customers, sweetheart. I just drive 'em."

Nell and Casey shared a glance.

Ed backed into his cabin, closed the door, and disappeared from view.

"He's running," Nell said, sprinting around the cabin, gun in hand.

"Wait!" Casey said, following her around the corner, slipping on the snow, falling, and catching himself with his hand on the ground.

Nell halted, hunched a bit, pointed the gun in front of her with her flashlight right under the pistol barrel, her elbows slightly bent. They heard a car door slam and the taxi engine turn. Headlights illuminated. "Stop!" Nell said, standing next to the vehicle, gun aimed at the front windshield. "We just want to talk."

Ed pointed the shotgun at them. Casey froze in partial cataplexy and sleep paralysis, his head and shoulders slouching. He wished it could have been complete cataplexy so he'd be out of the line of fire, and envisioned a headline:

NARCOLEPTIC MAN NEARLY FILLS HIS PANTS

"Get out of the car!" Nell shouted. "Throw the weapon out the window. Now!"

To Casey's surprise, Ed electronically lowered the passenger-side window, chucked the gun out and to the ground, then raised his hands.

Nell ran to him, opening the car door, pulling him out of the cab and cuffing his wrists behind his back.

"Ow. I ain't done a ding."

"Then why run?"

"I dought yas were da ones dat kidnapped Elena."

Nell winced. "I showed you my badge."

"Dey got dem badges at Halloween stores and dat. Can't trust nobody dese days."

"Who kidnapped Elena?" Nell said.

"I don't know," Eddie said. "But I read in da papers she's missing."

"How do we know *you're* not the kidnapper?" Nell said.

"Can I explain inside? It's freezing out here and I ain't got no shirt on."

Nell scoffed. "You were the one that ran out here half-naked."

Ed walked toward the house, wearing blaze-orange hunting pants and matching suspenders. He had graying chest hair. "Am I under arrest or something?"

"No, we just have a few questions," Nell said. "First, let's see the trunk."

Casey knew why she demanded that. After Jeffrey Dahmer had committed his first murder and shoved the victim in the trunk of his car, police had pulled Dahmer over but failed to check the trunk thoroughly.

Ed bit his lower lip, then said, "It's empty."

Nell calmly held her Glock in her right hand and held out her left hand. "I would really like it if you gave me the keys now."

Ed turned from the house and waddled to the trunk of his taxi. "Can I get dese cuffs off?"

"No."

"De keys for the trunk are in my pants pocket."

She released the cuffs.

He reached into his pocket, extracted the keys and opened the trunk. "See?"

Nell nodded, aiming the gun at him with two hands.

Ed slammed it shut and they walked toward the cabin, out of Casey's view.

Casey hoped she'd return to shake him out of his sleep attack.

He heard Nell ask, "But you *did* give Elena a ride?"

"Yep," Ed said. One of them opened the back screen door to the cottage. "What's with your friend?"

"Oh, he'll be back in a few minutes."

Casey heard the door close and imagined the headline:

Jilted Narcoleptic Literally Left Out in Cold

Even during an attack, Casey could feel the bitter cold turn his skin numb. All he could do was wait it out.

Eventually, he snapped out of it and returned inside. He flexed his fingers and toes, which had nearly frozen. On the wall above the mantel hung a stuffed deer head; below it, a fire popped occasionally in the fireplace.

"Where's Elena?" Casey said.

Ed grinned, buttoning a red flannel shirt. "Look what da woodchuck drug in."

"Where is she?" Casey demanded.

"Dat I'm not at liberty da dell yas."

Nell held the Glock and pointed it at Ed's feet. "Why is that?"

"Elena gave me a pretty penny not da dell."

"She paid you to disappear?" Nell asked.

"Yah der hey," Ed said. It meant yes.

"Where did she get that kind of money?" she said.

"I don't know." Ed worked a finger in his ear, apparently cleaning out the wax.

Casey smirked; they all knew she sold drugs.

"We're not the only ones looking for Elena," she said.

"Todd Narziss of the Hail was dating her," Casey said.

"I'm not dalking, don'tcha know."

Casey walked toward the door. "It sure would be a shame if Narziss were to find out that you picked up his mistress and unborn child and they never showed up again. If he knew you were hiding up here, in the woods all alone, there's no telling what a six-foot-five steroid maniac would do to you."

Ed snapped his fingers and pointed into the air as if to say, Eureka. "Oh yeah, I just remembered I dropped Elena off on South Madison Street in Green Bay."

"Do you *just remember* the address?" Nell said.

Ed stared at her for a moment and then said, "No."

"Bull," Casey said.

The cabbie massaged his forehead with both palms. "I don't remember."

Nell relaxed her hands to her side, gun pointed at the floor. "Don't you keep a log?"

"Not for Elena. Mr. Oleysniak wants her deliveries off da books. She pays cash only, directly da him."

"Then Mr. O. gives you a monthly fee under the table," she said.
Ed shrugged.

She activated the safety on the Glock, placed it back in her waistband and folded her arms. "Can you describe the place where you dropped her off?"

"No."

"No you *can't?*" Casey said. "Or no you *won't?*"

"Both," he said.

"In that case," she said, taking her gun back out, "we'll just charge you with felony drug trafficking."

"What? Why? You have no evidence."

"We talked to Tyrese," Casey said. "He's willing to testify." Casey hadn't asked him, but it seemed like the way to leverage information out of the cabbie.

Ed's face drooped.

Nell picked up where Casey left off. "And if you were an accessory to a felony while a murder happens in the process, we'll charge you with first-degree murder under the Felony Rule."

Ed sat back in an old chair, rested his elbows on his knees and rubbed his temples.

"How did you find her?" Casey asked.

"I was waiting in my cab for an assignment because I had a scheduled pickup for Elena outside da stadium."

Casey fell into sleep paralysis, fading in and out of hallucinations and reality. The stress had taken its toll on him. He watched Ed talk about Elena, then swore he saw him in a safari hat and khaki outfit, with a rifle, shooting at a black bear that lumbered through the door. Couldn't be, he thought, and started to pull out of it, tried to move, couldn't. Heard the bear's roar, drifted again…trapped. Terrified. It sounded so real. Others had asked him if his hallucinations were entertaining. His answer: not for the one trapped in the condition, unable to affect his own destiny. Nothing was scarier than losing control.

"Elena had me on speed dial," Ed said. "She called my cell and asked me da pick her up, said it was an emergency."

"What kind of emergency?" Nell said.

"She said da DEA was closing in. An informant dold her dey were going da raid her apartment any day now."

"So she wanted to disappear," Nell said.

Eddie nodded. "Just for a couple days, until it blew over. She wasn't planning da disappear for good."

"Did the feds raid her place?" asked Casey.

Eddie shrugged. "Heck if I know. She paid me da disappear, remember? So I came here."

Nell exhaled frustration. "Where did you drop her off?"

"Oh fer cry-yi-yi and a half-a-wheel of cheese. Yer high n' mighty, ain't-cha? I'm gonna do what da little lady asked."

Casey shook his head, tried to regain bearings.

Nell readied her gun, and pointed it at Eddie's knee. "Let's try this again. You said South Madison Street. Sure you don't remember the exact address?"

22

Hailangelo sat in his car, parked in the lot outside Elena's apartment complex. He knew Rihanna Morris and her daughter would return home any minute. They had gone out to eat at McDonald's like they did every Wednesday, probably so that Shantell could burn off energy in the play structure. The Morris family always left around five-thirty and returned an hour later.

The Morrises' old economy car pulled into the parking lot on schedule. Shantell, four years old, hopped out of the car and ran through the parking lot without looking for cars.

"Shantell, wait!" her mother called, getting out of the vehicle.

Shantell skipped toward the building obliviously, gripping her bedraggled stuffed-animal kitty, its tail dragging in the snow and marking a thin line up the steps.

Hailangelo pulled off the plastic cover on his hypodermic needle with his teeth, and slunk out of his car. As Rihanna power-walked toward the steps, perturbed, Hailangelo closed in behind her, covered her mouth with one hand, and injected hydrocyanic acid into her neck with the other. Rihanna—frozen in surprise and fear—struggled less than the others.

Shantell made it to the top of the stairs and skipped out of sight. Hailangelo figured the girl would stand outside the apartment door.

"Momma?" Shantell called. "Did you know my nose has two holes for digging? Momma? Momma?"

For a moment, Hailangelo feared she would come back down the steps and see him. He couldn't allow there to be a witness. Nobody ever spotted him in the act; he was far too meticulous.

Shantell kept calling for ten more seconds. By the time he had dragged Rihanna back to the car, she had become limp; he placed her in the passenger seat of the car. He closed the passenger door, hurried to the driver's side and got in. He extracted the keys from her purse and turned the ignition. It needed a new muffler and the floor was so thin it sounded like it was made of cardboard lined with balsa wood.

What a beater. He glanced at her. She was older than the others, poorer and more worn, but had a pride and grittiness they didn't. She would endure. He liked that, and would take great care to preserve that in her statue. He cocked an eyebrow at her and bowed his head like a butler. "Ma'am, allow me to give you the tour of my studio."

§

Nell stepped close to the cabbie. She considered threatening to arrest him and bring him back to Green Bay. Instead, she chose a tactic that psychologists called motivational interviewing. "You don't want her baby's blood on your hands, do you?"

"Oh jeez," Ed said, running a hand through his thin hair. "No."

"And you don't want to go to prison?"

"Heck no."

"You want to save the baby, and yourself."

"Yeah."

"Then what should you do?"

He stared at his shoes like a little boy sitting in the principal's office. "Dell you where I dropped her off."

"Very good," Nell said, winking at Casey.

Ed looked up at Nell. "I dropped her in front of da church. But she didn't go inside where I dropped her off anyway." He tugged on the skin under his chin. "She ran up da sidewalk. Could be anywhere by now."

Nell stared at him silently for a moment. "Do you really want to go to prison?"

"What?" he said.

"You dropped her off in front of the church. Then you started lying. Where did she go, Eddie?"

He looked her in the eyes this time, hands on his thighs. "Okay, okay, she went into da church. Said she didn't want da be deported."

Nell grinned and nodded at him. "Thank you, Mr. Plasky. That will do." She headed for the cabin entrance.

He reached out toward her. "Wait. How did you guys find me?"

"Friend of a friend," Casey said, following Nell out the door.

They walked toward the Z4 with purpose, got in, and exhaled in unison. Nell started the car and drove down the gravel driveway.

Casey said, "How did you know he was lying?"

"He looked up and to the left and tugged on his double chin. It's his tell for when he's getting nervous and creative."

"Do you think Ed was involved in her disappearance?"

"No."

"How can you be so sure?"

"Believe me," Nell said. "I've interviewed countless criminals, and I know when they're bullshitting. It's not always implausibility that gives it away; some perps are terrific liars, especially serial killers. It's their posture, delivery. When they're telling the truth, there's frankness to it. Ed had that."

"What do you make of his story about Elena seeking refuge in the church?"

"I believe him."

§

Hailangelo parked his car, turned off the lights, and carried Rihanna into the studio under the cover of darkness. He laid her on the couch, bending her knees, tilting her head to the side and kissing her cheek. Something was missing. He'd done this several times before, and had become inured. Like any other addict, he needed to kindle more stimulation to experience the same titillation. But how?

He could double his pleasure. Yes, and make the kiss between two of his muses. Twice the danger, power, control. He had been tracking one other lovely. He went to his laptop, woke it, logged in, and opened the tracking software he'd installed on her mobile phone. Now blood rushed to his nether regions. His amygdalae lit up.

To his surprise, his muse had left Green Bay. She'd traveled by car south on Highway 151. Could she be headed to Madison?

§

Nell and Casey rode in the Z4, headed home from the cabin, still about thirty miles from Green Bay. Nell said, "Think we could convince Leila to sell Baciare cosmetics?"

"Ha. Good luck to us." He yawned into his fist and thought: *Elena, on the other hand, could probably sell make-up to a dictator.*

"My mother always said, 'Never count someone out.'" Nell pursed her lips.

"Mine always said, 'Never count Casey in.'"

"Moms come around."

"You met my mother."

"She could change. For example, mine never let me wear makeup until my sophomore year. By my senior year, I entered the Pulaski Dairy Princess contest."

"No way!" Casey said.

"Yes, I really did."

"No, I mean, *no way* there can really be a dairy-princess contest."

"Don't laugh. I won." She playfully stuck out her tongue. "I didn't have bodacious curves, but I have talent."

"Curves shmurves. You have gazelle legs and wit." His eyelids felt like they were made of iron.

"Thanks."

Casey swallowed the last fourth of his cappuccino. "What was your talent?"

"Kickboxing."

Casey raised his eyebrows.

"What?" Nell said. "I'm very good at it."

"I noticed. Do I want to know your prize?"

"Two hundred bucks and a day off of school, thank you very much. It was so embarrassing, though."

"What?"

"The runner-up and I had to sit on the stage at the city fair, inside this glass dome, like a giant snow globe, refrigerated inside. We sat in chairs while artists carved our heads out of cheese."

Only in the Midwest. Casey glanced at her. "With people watching?"

"Yes."

"You're kidding." This story was like a car wreck and he couldn't look away. It might even become an article—*reporter Casey Thread looks at the unseemly underbelly of Midwestern dairy-princess contests.* "That does sound embarrassing."

"Get this: a few dirty old men stood off on the side, drooling. Many were my girlfriends' dads."

"Ew."

"One of the dads waved to me every time we rotated."

"Rotated?" Casey thought she had been making it all up, but this was so bizarre it had to be true.

"Yes, we rotated like those wax dessert displays at the cashier's desk in family restaurants. The worst part was the artist who carved my face didn't use just any cheese," she said with disdain. "He used Colby."

They drove past farmland, and Casey could make out dark outlines of barns and livestock. "What's wrong with Colby?"

"It's part orange, part white. It made my complexion look heinous."

Casey grinned. "What I'd give to see that carving."

"Check my mom's freezer."

Casey stared at her and blinked slowly.

"You think I'm crazy," Nell said.

"Nooo…"

"You do."

"I'll tell you who's crazy—our mothers."

Nell laughed.

"You know what I like most about you?" he said.

"Aside from my Milan-runway height and voluptuous bosom?" Nell said facetiously.

"Well, that's obvious. But I also like that you roll with it whenever I pass out."

"My college boyfriends passed out a lot, so I've had practice."

"And with me, you don't have the puking."

"True. Your narcolepsy is like my grandma's compulsion to clip coupons. You can't control it."

"Most people snicker when I pass out. They make assumptions. You don't."

"Right, I only tease you to your face."

"I appreciate that."

"It's a part of you, Casey, and I love everything about you."

He looked at her, trying to decide if she were real or a narcoleptic mirage. It wasn't a straight-out "I love you," but the reporter in him debated the ethics of trimming the extraneous words.

23

When Hailangelo caught up to Leila, she was walking along State Street in Madison, Wisconsin, about two hours southwest of Green Bay. Another woman accompanied her. State Street featured eclectic shops and family-owned local businesses, although more recently a few chains had moved in. The law only allowed pedestrians, bicycles, and city buses on State Street. The air smelled clean and parents didn't hesitate to bring their kids there for ice cream. Hailangelo made sure to stay half a block away, and pretended to window-shop.

From the middle of the street, Hailangelo could see the university at one end and the Wisconsin state capitol dome at the other. A homeless man, evidently mentally ill, roamed the sidewalk, but his friendly nature added character. He would make nonsensical jokes and belly laugh. Middle-aged trees lined the sidewalks on each side, and vintage twenty-foot-tall store signs beckoned customers. Leila and her companion ducked into a boutique.

Hailangelo hastened his way and peered in on them through the storefront window. Leila wore her typical black wool coat. She had a knack for appearing presentable without seeming like she put forth a great deal of effort. She held up a bright pink dress off the rack with a yellow feather boa.

Her companion laughed. They posed like over-the-top socialites, returned the apparel to the rack, left the store without buying anything, and passed Hailangelo, who had turned away. The women moseyed along the sidewalk and ducked into a coffee shop. Inside, a skinny bearded musician in his late thirties sat on a stool in the corner, playing a folk song.

Later, Leila and her companion walked to the University of Wisconsin Union at the end of State Street, entered, and sat in a dim room called the Rathskellar. All the entrances were doorless arches seven feet high. Hailangelo sat at the table next to Leila, the backs of their chairs nearly touching. He drank a dark ale and eavesdropped as best he could. Small shaded wall lamps illuminated the medieval German décor. They ordered dark beer in wax-paper cups.

Leila's companion was telling a story. "So I'm at my sister's for Halloween, right? The doorbell rings. My sister says, 'Amelia, can you grab the door?' So I do, and there's a little boy dressed in a superhero costume. I give him a Snickers, and I'm thinking I'll get a hearty thank you, right?"

"Right," Leila said.

"But he just stands there, eyes and mouth agape like he'd seen a ghost. I turn around and my sis is breastfeeding Baby Jake in the kitchen."

"Not sure if that was a trick or a treat," Leila said.

Hailangelo drank his ale and briefly contemplated taking them both. Then he thought better of it. He had to remain focused on his true muse, and not allow distraction. Patience, patience, patience.

Leila said, "I've missed you."

"You just like free beer." Amelia smiled, then sipped.

Leila raised her soggy cup and nodded. "Cheers." When they finished, she said, "Shall we?" They exited the Union and walked down the steps toward the street.

Hailangelo followed.

As they entered the crosswalk, Leila saw something that stopped her movement. A man walked toward her and brushed her shoulder in the crosswalk. She turned toward him and stopped in the street just beyond the yellow dotted line—frozen there like Lot's wife.

Amelia laughed. "Come on, Lei, I was kidding—I can't stomach another waxy beer. Leila. Lei, come on, there's a bus coming."

The bus drove right for Leila. Buses in Madison didn't stop for pedestrians unless they were over the age of 90—and only then if they had a cane.

Hailangelo had tunnel vision for Leila; the world around him blurred in kaleidoscopic fashion.

Amelia lunged for Leila.

At the last moment, the driver hit the brakes and stopped.

Hailangelo exhaled relief.

"Lei!" Amelia grabbed her friend's arms.

Leila didn't flinch. She just stared at the man from the crosswalk as he walked away.

Amelia guided Leila to the curb. As the bus passed by, the driver opened the door and shouted something indistinct at Leila, but she didn't react.

Amelia looked into Leila's eyes like an emergency responder. "Leila? What is it?"

Leila was pale. She glanced back at the man from the crosswalk.

"It's him."

24

Nell and Casey turned onto South Madison Street in downtown Green Bay and pulled into the parking lot. The temperature was an unseasonably warm forty degrees. The snow had melted to half its normal height. Casey approached the ornate cathedral, looking up at the steeple and a round carving above the door which resembled a doily like the ones his mother used to make. Two statues stood above the door. He recognized one as Saint Francis, whose serenity and kindness attracted wild animals. The world could use more people like that. They entered the narrow narthex.

Inside, the pews were empty. Nell said, "Let's start downstairs." They found the staircase that led down into the community center underneath the cathedral. At the foot of the stairs, an old male parishioner held the glass door for them. "You folks here for the soup kitchen?"

"Yes, we're serving dinner," Nell said.

"That's very kind. Where's the food?"

Casey glanced at Nell.

She shrugged. "The other volunteers are bringing it."

"We all do our part," the parishioner said. "Here's the key. Please give it to Paul, the coordinator, after lunch. God bless you." The man left.

They searched the basement but found no sign of Elena. Nell left the key on the counter with a note for Paul. Casey stuck twenty dollars under the note. As they walked upstairs, he kept hearing his mother say, *You never finish anything.*

They searched the balcony, including the large organ and pews for the choir, but didn't find Elena. They checked the altar: nothing. The last place to search in the entire complex was the sacristy. It was locked, of course. Something lay under the door. It was small, black, and plastic. Casey stuck his fingers under the door and tried to grab the object but only succeeded in pushing it further inside the sacristy. He stared at it then exhaled. "We can't break into a sacristy."

Nell smirked. "I never said we should." She pulled out a tool from her purse that resembled a tiny flattened screwdriver.

"That doesn't look like eye liner," Casey said.

"It's not. It's an offset diamond pick." She extracted a second object from her pocket—a small black tension tool with a twisted tip, as if someone had cornered the end of a screw driver.

She inserted the tension tool at the bottom of the deadbolt lock and manipulated the diamond pick in the upper part of the keyhole to move pins inside the lock, feeling her way. She twisted the tension tool to open the lock with a *pop*. She returned the tools to her pocket and quickly opened the door.

Casey shook his head. "Holy—"

Nell turned toward Casey with the universal sign for shush. He had never been more attracted to anyone in his life, and that included Elena the night of his, ahem, unfortunate sleep attack. She flipped on the lights, drew her gun, unlocked the safety and systematically searched the area. Nell approached the closet door and swung it open: there was nothing inside but black frocks and white robes. Nell rifled fearlessly through them with one hand, holding the gun with the other.

On the floor in the sacristy lay a black plastic object, the one he had inadvertently pushed under the door. He grabbed it. In silver letters it read, Baciare Cosmetics. Casey held it out. "Drop a compact?"

"No," Nell said, extending her hand. "Let me see." She took and examined it. "Oh my."

"What?"

She showed him the back. A white sticker with printed black letters said, "Nell Jenner, Independent Sales Consultant, Baciare Cosmetics," with her contact information.

"You sold makeup to a nun?"

"Not yet." She squinted.

"A priest?"

"No. But this is odd."

"What?"

"This compact is out of production."

"So?"

"They stopped making it right after I started selling."

"And?"

"And the only person I sold one to was Elena."

"Come on, there had to have been others."

"No, I remember everyone wanted the new compact with more compartments because it came with free cleanser. Elena bought the old one to help me clear inventory."

Tightness formed in Casey's stomach, round and hard like an avocado pit. He sighed.

"No sighing, yawning, or doubting," Nell said and walked out the door.

"Where are you going?"

"The cabbie said she was only hiding here while the DEA raided her apartment," Nell said. "She may be back in her apartment."

Or she's hiding out in Florida, Casey thought. Or Quito. Or Uzbekistan. As they strode to the car, he wondered if Elena knew Nell was a federal agent. He guessed not.

Even if Elena is safe, he wondered, what would happen to her baby? After all, the fetus's mother sold drugs and its father was a famous married man prone to steroidal rage. If that scenario didn't set the baby up to be a future student-body president, what did? Even if Elena avoided prison and deportation, what life would she and the baby have?

To whom would Elena turn if the infant had colic and screamed and screamed—*and screamed*—until Elena wanted to rip off her own ears? She couldn't turn to her mother, who lived thousands of miles away. Would Narziss be there if Elena had post-partum depression? Would he care about her hemorrhoids? Yeah, right. Elena probably didn't have health insurance. Would she pay the hospital in cash with drug money?

They exited the church and walked toward the car. Casey turned to Nell. "So, are you investigating Elena for drugs or something?"

"Me?" Nell said. "No, that's the DEA's bailiwick."

"Don't you partner on cases?"

"From time to time, sure. But I'm on a different case."

"What case?"

"I'm tracking a serial killer."

A *what*?

Nell continued. "But I do happen to know a guy at the DEA who would love to know all about this. He's tall, dark, and handsome; Elena would love him."

They got into the Beemer. Nell turned the ignition and said, "Elena was here illegally."

"You didn't report her?"

"She's my best friend."

"And you're a federal agent."

Nell pulled away. "Look, reporting her to Immigration would get her sent back to Ecuador. I'd lose a friend, she'd be back with her drug-dealing father, and what would we gain?"

"One less drug dealer in town."

Nell glanced at him as if he were trying to sell her on the Easter Bunny. "Like someone else wouldn't take her place? All her customers would quit cold turkey?"

"I guess you're right."

"You know I am. And it wouldn't help Elena one bit. I was trying to get her some help, connect her with people who could show her how to change her behaviors, get out of drugs and into a better life."

"What happened?" Casey said.

"She disappeared."

25

As houses whipped past the Z4 windows, Casey tried to remember anything Elena might have said or done that could offer a clue to her whereabouts. Nothing fresh came to mind. As they wove through town, nearly everyone had navy-and-white Hail license plates or mini-flags sticking out of their car windows. A few houses had gigantic inflatable balloons adorning their front yards, made to resemble cartoon Hail football players. The team was a perennial focus but now, with the championship in sight, Hail hysteria had never been higher. Most Green Bay residents were not out to impress each other with fancy cars or tailored clothes; they were out to pull together and bond through civic pride.

As they approached the stadium on Chippewa Street, Casey looked ahead at Elena's apartment. He yearned to see her at her door, perhaps returning from a trip. That would have been a surprise, but nothing compared to who he actually saw. "What the—"

"What?" Nell said, following his eyes to the apartment. On the second floor outside the apartment stood Shantell, with her spindly appendages, hugging her stuffed animal, crying, her mouth in an open frown. Nell pulled into the lot, parked hastily and got out. She sprinted up the stairs.

Casey followed. He stopped a few steps short from the top—close enough to listen but not so close as to scare the girl.

Nell leaned down to Shantell's level and placed her hands on her own knees. "Hi, Shantell, remember me?"

Shantell nodded, sniffling.

"I'm Elena's friend, remember?"

Shantell nodded again, tears streaking down her cheeks.

Nell hugged the child. "Sssh, it's okay, sweetie. It's okay. Where is your momma?"

Shantell sniffled and spoke in serrated breaths. "I. Don't. Know."

"How long have you been out here, sweetie?"

Shantell wiped tears on her kitty's head. "Since dinner."

Nell looked at Casey then turned back to Shantell. "You mean since breakfast?"

Shantell shook her head emphatically. "Last night, Momma took me out for dinner. I got a Happy Meal!"

"A Happy Meal?" Nell responded with inflated grandeur and a slight smile.

Shantell nodded, pulled out a plastic toy from her pocket, and grinned for the first time, flashing dimples.

"Wow!" Nell said. "That's the coolest pink pony I've ever seen."

"Thank you," Shantell said, chewing on one of her braided pigtails. At least the poor girl wore a winter hat, a hood, and fleece mittens. Without them, she might have gotten frostbite or pneumonia.

"Didn't any of the neighbors invite you in?" Casey said.

"Momma says not to talk to strangers, and never to go with them."

"You have a smart momma," Nell said gently. "Where did she go?"

Shantell shrugged. "I ran up here, but Momma never came up."

"Did you go back down to look for her?"

Shantell nodded. "Mm-hmm, but our car was gone."

"Did you see her leave with anyone?" Nell said.

Shantell worked out knots in her pony's hair with a small plastic brush. She nodded. "I'm hungry."

"We'll get you some food soon, sweetheart. But first, it's really important to talk about who was with your mom last night before she went away, okay?"

Shantell glanced at Nell. "Our neighbor."

"Do you know the neighbor?"

Shantell nodded.

"What is the neighbor's name?" Nell said it ever so gently, as if the answer were an eagle's egg she had to delicately return to its nest.

Casey's heart fluttered with the thought that perhaps Rihanna had left with Elena. Could this be the key tip to find her? From a four-year-old?

Shantell stroked the toy pony's mane.

"Can you describe your neighbor?" Nell tried.

No response.

"Was it a boy or a girl?" Nell said.

Shantell looked up from the toy. "A man."

Nell glanced at Casey. "*A man*. Okay, very good, Shantell. It's safe to tell me what he looks like. Remember, I'm not a stranger. I'm here to help your momma. You know that, right?"

Shantell nodded, tending to her pony. Casey wondered if Happy Meals were her only source of toys.

"Who was with your momma?" Nell said.

Shantell looked at her and said, "I came down the steps and saw Momma drive away in our car with the statue man."

26

WEDNESDAY, JANUARY 26

Hailangelo wanted to hold Leila, place her in a bubble to protect her from harm. But he knew he couldn't and kept his distance, in order not to risk her recognizing him as her customer from Fixate Factory.

Leila and Amelia sat on a bench along the sidewalk across the street from the Union. Hailangelo looped around them to eavesdrop.

"I knew the city was small enough that I could bump into him," Leila said, "but it was like preparing for a tornado—I bought the insurance but never actually thought a twister would rip through." A single tear trickled down her cheek.

Amelia wiped it away. "Are you sure it was him?" Victims of violent acts often thought they saw their attackers.

They watched the rapist walk to his car in the adjacent uncovered parking lot across the street next to the Union. "Yes," Leila said, as if in a trance. "It's definitely him."

"Let's go write down his license plate number." Amelia stood up.

"I can't believe he hasn't learned a thing about fashion all these years," Leila said in a hollow drone, staring blankly after the man. "I mean, black shoes and a brown belt? Where are the fashion police when you need them, right?"

"Lei, are you okay? If you don't want to check his license, I under—"

"I wish he would have just killed me," Leila said angrily.

Hailangelo raised a brow. He could fix that.

Tears trickled down both women's cheeks.

"No, no," Amelia said, moving so they were face to face. "I know you're upset—you have every right to be. But please, don't say that."

"At least if he had killed me, I wouldn't have had to live with the rape. He takes a girl's virginity, innocence, and mental health."

Amelia glanced at passersby. "Do you want to find someplace private?"

Leila ignored her, already in her solitary world. "Then he doesn't even recognize me. He steals my dignity and now the theft is complete. He has gone free while I'm behind mental bars. If self-respect was like housing, I'd be homeless."

Amelia squeezed her upper arms. "You have people who love you."

Hailangelo rolled his eyes, half-expecting Amelia to break into a maudlin pop song encouraging listeners not to commit suicide.

Arms at her sides, Leila's tears flowed. Then, Hailangelo noticed her countenance harden, as if magma boiled below. She said, "I gotta go."

"Where are you going?" Amelia asked.

Leila kept walking without answering.

Amelia followed her. "Wait, Lei. Stop."

Leila stopped and pivoted, fists at her sides. "I'll text you later. Let me go."

"But—" Amelia tried.

"This is something I need to do on my own, okay?" Without giving Amelia a chance to answer, Leila turned and left.

§

Casey and Nell escorted Shantell to the Z4 and drove her to Leila's apartment. They had no carseat for the child, but saw no alternative that wouldn't delay their search for Elena—and now Rihanna. A few moments could save Shantell from becoming an orphan.

Casey called ahead to make sure his mother was there. She was, and agreed to watch the girl so Casey and Nell could follow up on Shantell's tip about the "statue man," whom she later identified as their neighbor and said his yard had a lifelike statue of Todd Narziss in it.

"Hailangelo," Casey said. He suffered a sleep attack, his head and shoulders slouched over. Nell shook him out of it.

"Why do you do that?" Shantell said.

"It happens when I'm surprised," Casey said.

"Like scared?" the girl said.

"Yeah, like that. Or it could be a happy surprise. Any sudden change of emotion."

Adrenaline surged, and Casey struggled to maintain his composure. He explained to Shantell that his mother would take care of her until hers came back. He hoped it would be soon. Shantell seemed fairly unfazed, content with playing with her new pony in the back seat. "Is Momma at work?" Shantell asked the grown-ups.

Casey turned to face the girl. "We're not sure, big girl. But we're going to find her for you."

Shantell's lower lip swelled into a pout. "Why does Momma have to go to work all the time?"

"Well…" Casey glanced at Nell for help but got none. "I guess so she can pay for your food and apartment."

Shantell exhaled. "I'm sick of that answer."

Nell grinned.

"Me too, kid," Casey said, turning back to face forward. "Me too."

Nell typed Hailangelo's street address into her phone and conducted a reverse search. "The property owner is Thomas Meintz."

"That's him," Shantell said. "The statue man is Mr. Meintz, my neighbor."

Nell looked gravely at Casey. "I have the address for his shop. Leila's apartment is on the way."

27

Hailangelo drove his car, following Leila's rusty Buick LeSabre, who in turn followed her rapist in his sparkling blue Shelby Cobra. They wound down the road, passing colonial after Victorian after Frank Lloyd Wright house. The sculptor wondered what Leila would do when her rapist arrived at his destination. His instincts told him to abduct her before the rapist could. But he couldn't bear to interrupt—the volatile situation titillated him.

Finally, the rapist drove into a driveway. Leila parked diagonally across the street, and Hailangelo a block behind her. Could her rapist really live in Maple Bluff, this upscale suburb of Madison just blocks away from Governor Moeller's mansion?

Hailangelo squinted and his lips curled up slightly. Status didn't prevent people from committing felonies.

Hailangelo used his smartphone to run a Web search for the street address of the man in the Cobra, and it came back as owned by a Brian and Rachel Twig. Hailangelo giggled. His name was Twig? How brittle, anemic, infertile. He searched for that name in Google. A Tennessee newspaper article appeared. Brian Twig had been previously charged with sexual harassment in Nashville, but the charges were dropped. There were thirteen more articles, all about dropped rape or harassment charges. Tsk, tsk, tsk. Brian had been a very naughty boy. This had to be her rapist, and this had to be his house.

Hailangelo and Leila watched Twig walk into his abode. He embraced someone, probably his wife Rachel, inside the door. Hailangelo had brought binoculars, and noticed Rachel wasn't classically beautiful by any stretch but was still out of Twig's league.

A minute later, Twig returned to his car. He retrieved something out of the back seat—a briefcase—and then closed the door and walked toward the mailbox near the end of the driveway.

Leila ducked down in her car to be out of his sight. But when she peeked through the window, Twig wasn't paying attention. He pulled letters and magazines from the mailbox and walked toward the house, his back now to Leila and Hailangelo.

She quietly opened the car door and approached Twig's house, jazz-running as one would learn to do in dance classes. By the time Twig heard her, she had halted five feet behind him.

Twig startled and turned.

Hailangelo held his breath. Leila pulled a pistol out of her coat pocket. She muttered something to Twig, but Hailangelo couldn't hear it. He rolled down his car window.

Twig started, "I—"

Leila shot him in the groin. The blast echoed throughout the neighborhood. A dog barked from a neighbor's yard.

Brian grabbed his crotch and fell. He managed to turn his face to the side before impact, but skinned his temple on the icy ground and began to seep blood. "Ah, God, aaah!"

Leila shoved her shoe under his stomach and rolled him over. "Recognize me now, Brian? Maybe it's the blue hair."

"Ah, God!" He writhed on the ground.

Hailangelo grinned. God's not going to help you, Brian. He didn't help all the women you raped.

As if on cue, Leila pointed to her scar from the burn. Hailangelo wondered if it was her permanent scarlet letter.

Blood coated the snow around Twig. "You shot me!"

"Astute observation, Twiggy."

"You crazy b—"

"Brian? Jesus!" Rachel came out the front door, back straight, palms out, fingers flared. She tucked her long brunette hair behind her ears and bent down by her husband. She glared at Leila and screamed. "You *shot* him?"

Leila just stood there, amused, gun held casually at her side.

Hailangelo slunk in his seat and gazed out the window. *This woman is insidious. Someone after my own heart.*

Brian vomited on Rachel's designer shoes. She recoiled and exclaimed. Leila put a fist to her mouth and looked away, giggling. Hailangelo laughed with her.

Rachel yelled, "Get away from my husband!" She reached inside her pocket, retrieved a cell phone, and dialed 911. She spoke into the phone but Hailangelo couldn't hear her.

Leila held up the gun and wagged it back and forth admonishingly. She leaned over Brian and said something Hailangelo couldn't hear.

Rachel appeared to age a decade in two seconds. She suddenly snapped the cell phone shut.

Brian Twig writhed in the red snow. Hailangelo read his lips as he said, "Help me, Rachel."

Leila clenched fists at her sides and screamed vitriol at Twig.

Rachel stood over him on the other side, slowly shaking her head. Hailangelo guessed her husband had promised to change his ways, to start anew in Wisconsin and leave all those "false, audacious" accusations in Tennessee. His wife had given him extra chances and he had betrayed her.

Rachel nearly choked on her tears. "How could you…"

He writhed.

Leila trotted to her car and drove off. Hailangelo followed, delighted his muse had gotten her wish and escaped unscathed. He would allow her to enjoy it for awhile, until the timing to immortalize her was just right. It delighted him to get to know her better. Leila got two blocks away from the Twig residence when an ambulance and two police cars passed her en route to the scene. Hailangelo simpered.

§

As they drove, Casey's cell phone rang; it was Leila. "Oh, hey sis. How are you?"

"Never been better. I feel…amazing."

"What's gotten into you?" Casey said.

"Nothing much. I only found my rapist."

Found him? "I didn't know you were looking for him."

"That's because I wasn't looking for him. But I found him. Who would've thought, right?"

Casey frowned. "You saw him and you feel better?"

"Yep. I shot him in the balls."

"With a snowball?"

Leila scoffed. "No. A gun."

"A squirt gun."

"No, a real purse pistol. I bought it online."

"Cut it out, Lei, this isn't funny."

"Last time I checked, the Second Amendment stands. Plus, now Wisconsin has a concealed carry law."

Casey glanced back at Shantell, who stared out the window in the back seat. He lowered his voice and covered his mouth with his other hand. "You're saying you actually did that?" He extracted his trusty credit card and dug it into his palm to avoid an attack.

Nell glanced at Casey with a look of curiosity.

"At first, I was traumatized just to see him," Leila said. "For a moment, I could barely move—it was like I was in a clear glass tank and water had rushed in, compressing my lungs. But then I envisioned him prowling the lakeshore for another unsuspecting university student."

"What were you thinking?"

"I've read in psychology journals that rape is about power. I doubt he's self-aware enough to realize it. He's like a spider that crawls inside a house to catch flies. It would be better off outside where food is available. But it's not about making sense. It's about instinct and compulsion."

"Did you call the cops?" Casey glanced at Nell, who squinted back at him.

She ignored the question. "I've been thinking about all the rape victims in history: slaves, refugees, women in newly occupied nations, victims of ethnic cleansing. How many rape victims have there been? If someone bottled all their tears and stacked the bottles, would they reach Jupiter? And back? So many of those women never uttered a word about it. How could they hold it in? I'd combust. Anyway, he won't be raping again."

"That's a bit...extreme," Casey said. He purposely spoke in vague terms, so as not to arouse Nell's suspicion any more than he already had.

"Not really. He'll survive."

"No, that's definitely extreme," he muttered through his teeth. "Aren't you worried you'll get arrested?"

"I told him the statute of limitations on the rape hadn't lapsed, and that's true. I looked it up. I told him that I'd go to the media. He knows his other rape victims would come forward. He has victims in Tennessee, too, not just Wisconsin."

"Damn," Casey said.

"You're such a buzz-kill. You can't just let me bask in something positive happening. I have closure here, after all these years. I can finally move on with my life. But no, you always have to pull me down. I'm damaged goods, right, Case? Always will be. Do you feel better now?"

"That's not what I—"

"What would you have done?" Leila said, agitated. "Sent your rapist to timeout with a scolding?"

"There are laws, Lei."

"The lab lost the only physical evidence from the rape. According to the news, he has gotten away with this five, six, seven times."

Casey said nothing. He had a headache from hell and felt both exhausted and nauseous—either due to hunger, anxiety, narcolepsy, or all of the above. He needed to stay focused and alert. He slapped his cheeks a few times.

Leila sighed. "Look, I'm sorry, okay? I'm on my way home."

"Good. We're bringing a little girl over to your place."

"A girl?"

"Her mother's a friend of Nell's. I asked our ma to watch her at your apartment. She agreed."

"Okay...you asked Mom to babysit for a friend? That's kind of random."

"I'll explain later. How far away are you?"

"Ninety minutes."

"We're dropping the girl off and have somewhere to go. Thanks in advance for watching her. She's sweet. Her name is Shantell."

"Yeah, sure. Thanks for listening, Casey."

"What are brothers for?"

28

Casey and Nell dropped Shantell off at Leila's apartment. Elzbieta tried her best to smile and welcome Shantell, but it was like a cactus attempting to be a pillow. Elzbieta turned on cartoons and it entranced the little girl. It reminded Casey of Saturday mornings from his youth. At least now Shantell was safe. He and Nell thanked Elzbieta and left.

As Nell drove toward Hailangelo's studio, she asked Casey about the conversation with Leila.

"It's nothing," Casey said.

"You said something about calling the cops," Nell said.

"I did?"

"Yeah. And you mentioned laws, as if she'd broken some."

Casey chuckled nervously. "Ah, just some irate customer at Fixate Factory giving her a hard time."

He wanted to vent to Nell, to tell her about Leila shooting Twig. But he couldn't be sure Nell wouldn't feel obligated to report his sister to authorities. He had no reason to believe Leila would harm anyone again, and he tried to put himself in her shoes. What if he had identified the rapist? Would he have flashed back to that night, to the helpless feeling he'd had while trapped in a narcoleptic attack and a stranger attacked his sister? Would he have kicked this man, punched him? Yes. Would he have shot him? Probably not. Casey didn't own a gun, for one thing. Then again, he wasn't the one who got raped. He tried to block out the conversation with Leila and focus on the future. Casey searched for the exact address in the GPS and set it so "Joan" would announce the driving directions. After Joan's initial instruction, Casey said: "So what's this about investigating a serial killer?"

Nell glanced at him as if to say, *who, me?*

"Please, we've come this far. I think I deserve to know."

Nell nodded. "You didn't hear this from me. Six women have gone missing—four in western Illinois, one in Iowa and one in Colorado, all during the last two years. We have reason to believe they were taken by the same person. Our intel suggests the unsub operated for a while in Galesburg and migrated to Green Bay."

"Unsub?"

"Unknown subject. The killer we are chasing but have not yet identified."

"Why would the killer move to Green Bay?"

"I can't tell you." Nell looked straight ahead as she drove, never glancing at him.

"You mean it's classified?"

"I don't even tell my mother classified information." Nell slowed the BMW and hung a left.

"Your mother saved your head carved out of cheese. I'd hope you wouldn't tell her."

That got her to smile. "Suffice to say there was a clear pattern from Galesburg."

"What kind of a pattern?"

She gave him a knowing look.

"How did you track him from Galesburg to Green Bay?"

Nell hung another left at a stoplight. "That I can tell you—it was in the news. In late July, Green Bay PD found a car in a wooded area along a county road on the outskirts of town."

"What kind?"

"A Dodge Caravan."

"A minivan? That sounds innocuous."

"Right, and that's exactly why the killer drove it. Well, that and it gave him room to store and transport his victims."

"What tipped you off that it belonged to the Galesburg Killer?"

"It matched the description of the vehicle he drove out of town. We had a BOLO out for the vehicle in neighboring states."

Casey jotted details in a reporter's notebook.

She continued, "Police in Green Bay impounded the vehicle and inspected the interior. We found a hair follicle and traces of blood from one of the missing women."

"Nothing that ID'd the killer?"

"*Nada*. We had crime techs tear apart the minivan piece by piece until there was nothing left but the frame. He had bleached most of the vehicle."

"So he knew what he was doing."

"If he made prints, he'd washed them clean. None of his blood was detectable, no finger prints, no license plates. He even melted the vehicle identification number, probably with a blowtorch. I've been chasing whispers in the wind. A psychotic wouldn't be organized enough to destroy evidence. Our unsub is narcissistic, intelligent, and has an ego the size of Hail Stadium. But even the most conniving criminals make mistakes. This guy's no different—a hair had stuck in a nook of the minivan's frame."

"Great, so you have DNA?"

"Unfortunately, the hair had no root, so we could only conduct subjective analysis. That carries a twelve-percent error rate. But the blood on the hair yielded white cells, and the DNA sample matched one of the missing victims. That error rate is about one in a billion."

Casey stopped writing and stared out the front windshield. "That's why you wanted to help me find Elena, isn't it? You thought maybe your suspect abducted her, that he had finally made his big mistake."

"I didn't rule it out."

"I don't believe this. You've been using me this whole time."

"Hey, I was undercover."

"But if Narziss ordered the abduction of Elena, that would be a dead end for you."

"Well, sure, that would be a police case. I'm following a killer who crossed state lines. I'm keeping an open mind." She turned onto the street leading to Hailangelo's art and taxidermy shop.

"Why the cosmetics cover-up?" Casey had wanted to ask her that earlier, but opportunity had eluded him.

"Agents pose as prostitutes to catch killers. It gives them access to johns. By selling cosmetics, I have an excuse to meet any young woman I see. Now I know almost every chick in Green Bay who fits the profile for the killer's preferred victim."

"If you can't go to the unsub, you let the unsub come to you."

Nell nodded. "Something like that." She parked the car in the lot behind Hailangelo's store and pulled the emergency brake. She turned off the safety on the Glock, put it into her purse, and zipped it shut. Casey and Nell got out of the car and walked along the sidewalk around to the front of the store.

Glass windows formed Hailangelo's storefront. A bell chimed when they entered. Casey nervously checked his phone: no new messages.

Inside, Hailangelo had displayed a plethora of African drums, wooden animals and ivory Buddhas on shelves. Incense and Middle Eastern music—set to a techno dance beat—filled the air. Fine scarves, hand-carved African masks and heads of dead deer, elk, moose, panthers, lions and cheetahs adorned the walls. A stuffed Siamese cat perched on a shelf, fangs flaring. Casey shook off chills.

As Casey scanned Hailangelo's shop, he noticed a teenage girl sitting on a stool behind the checkout counter in the center of the one-room shop. Casey said hello.

She looked down from his eye contact and didn't respond. So much for customer service. Women did this to him all the time defensively and, while he understood that they didn't want to convey the wrong signals, he wished it didn't have to be that way. Couldn't people greet each other with a respectful hello and a smile? She rested her chin on her palm.

"Hi," Nell approached the teenager. "What's your name?"

"Olivia."

"Hi, Olivia," Nell said. "We're looking for the owner."

"Mr. Meintz was supposed to be back an hour ago," Olivia said.

"Did he say anything about where he went?" Nell said.

"No."

"Have you been back there?" Casey pointed.

"His office? Hell no. Reeks back there, probably another dead mouse. Oh my god, is there *anything* more disgusting?"

"Hence the incense?" Nell said.

"Exactly," Olivia said. "I mean, I'm supposed to sit here with that smell and nothing to do? Screw that. Meanwhile, I've got a freaking Chemistry exam tomorrow. This is total B.S."

Casey looked at Nell. "What now?"

She shrugged. "I guess we wait." She walked past him; her hair smelled like mangoes. The fragrance faded fast, overcome by the incense. She grabbed a rain stick on a shelf.

He bashfully looked away from Nell and stared at an African mask on the wall, painted in a checkered black-and-white pattern. It had blue beads for eyebrows and tiny white seashells on its forehead. Curved lines in red, yellow and orange began under the oval eye slots, ending at the cheeks like Technicolor tears. It unnerved him in a way that held his gaze. He tore away and glanced at Nell. "So is there anything else you want to tell me?"

"About?" Nell said.

"Was anything you've said to me in the last week true?"

"I told you, I really do sell cosmetics."

Casey said nothing.

She motioned with her head toward the front door and then went back outside. "Let's see…I'm concerned for Elena, I'm really FBI and I'm tracking a serial killer. That's all true."

"Where are you really from?"

"Galesburg, originally. Although I've lived up here the last two years."

"They assigned the local girl?"

Nell paused as someone walked by the front of the store. When the man was out of earshot, she continued. "Technically, I work out of the Chicago FBI field office. But yeah, I knew the territory, had connections."

"Did it help?"

"I knew a Galesburg resident who reported suspicious activity. He said that, on a number of occasions, he saw a neighbor in his twenties or thirties moving large objects from his minivan late at night. Said it happened about once a month, sometimes twice. We had it narrowed to the owner of the local art shop. His name was James Meickle. Mr. Meickle used the same social security number as a Jack Meilenti of Des Moines."

"Another art-shop owner?" Casey said.

"Nope, coffee shop."

"Hailangelo's real name is Thomas Meintz," Casey said. "So he's our guy?"

"Can't say for sure," Nell said. "But if it's not, it's one hell of a coincidence."

"I don't believe this. I interviewed him years ago for the paper."

"What did he say?"

Casey shrugged. "We just talked about his work."

198

Nell nodded. "Let's go back inside." She opened the door and they went in.

The cashier glanced up, then went back to checking her phone.

The middle-eastern techno song ended. Led Zeppelin's "The Battle of Evermore" began, an ethereal tune featuring ukulele and acoustic guitar. Nell held up the large rain stick, about five feet long, made from dark brown wood with colored squiggles painted on each end. "Heavy," she said, weighing it with both hands and knocking on the thick wood. She turned it over and the sound of rain flowed perfectly with Jimmy Page's plucked strings. "Is it true Led Zep were into the devil?"

"I dunno," Casey said. "But God *wishes* he played like Jimmy Page."

"My favorite band is The Beatles," Nell said. "They sang like angels."

"Can't beat the Fab Four," Casey agreed. "Nearly three-hundred songs in a decade and countless hits. Are you kidding me?"

Olivia made a disgusted noise and said, "Are you two going to get a room? Or actually buy something?"

"Can we take a look in back?" Nell said.

Olivia made a "pfft" sound. "Even if it were allowed, and it's not, it's locked. I don't have the key."

Strange.

Nell walked to the back of the room and tried the door handle. Indeed, it wouldn't open.

Casey whispered to Nell: "Flash your badge."

Nell whispered back. "I don't want to tip him off. He'll run."

"Jimmie the door."

"Not with her here."

"So we wait?"

"No. Go see what you can get out of Miss Employee of the Month."

Casey approached Olivia, and noticed her sweatshirt promoted her school. "How do you like East High?"

Olivia scrunched her face. "Ew, I have a boyfriend."

He raised his hands and eyebrows, pivoting back toward the scarves and masks to take his place among the dead animals. "Just making conversation."

"If you aren't going to buy anything, I'm leaving," Olivia said. "My shift is over."

"Don't you have to lock up?" Casey said.

Olivia lazily moved one shoulder.

Casey said, "You'll get fired."

"I was planning to quit after final exams, anyway."

"Well, don't stay on our account," he said, smiling and clasping his hands behind his back.

Olivia gave him a poisonous look, grabbed her purse and left. The door chimed.

Casey jogged to the cash register, looked through drawers and cabinets for keys to Hailangelo's office. He didn't find any. Nell extracted her lock-picking kit from her purse. This lock fought her more than the one at the church, but after a few minutes it popped open.

The back room couldn't have been more than fifteen feet long by ten feet wide. To the left of the door was Hailangelo's desk. Nell stood in front of his computer, staring at something. The foul odor grew stronger.

"This is interesting," Nell said, snapping a photo of the desk using her cell phone.

"Isn't that evidence inadmissible?" Casey said.

"Right now, I'm more concerned about finding Elena and Rihanna. We'll worry about evidence later."

"Mamma mia," Casey said, stepping back. "Are those real?" There were two rats perched on the desk—one on each side of the computer—standing on hind legs, with black fur and long, pink tails.

Nell turned back toward him. "Well, yeah, but they're stuffed."

Casey shuddered. "I loathe rats." Stacked on the shelves were small texts on taxidermy, as well as larger, glossy books displaying works by hyperrealist sculptors George Segal, John De Andrea, and Duane Hanson. A thick book on Hanson, an American sculptor, lay on Hailangelo's desk. Casey opened it and flipped pages. It depicted Hanson taking plaster molds of people's entire bodies—including faces—to use for his statues. Hanson took realism to an extreme with his art. Not only did the statues measure life size, but Hanson had added hair, clothing, and other props to make them look alive. One of Hanson's statues from 1981 depicted a dejected Miami Dolphins football player sitting exhausted on his helmet, the clear ancestor of Hailangelo's Todd Narziss statue. Both were impeccable.

Another book showed a picture of Hanson's apartment, where officials found more than 1,000 Polaroid photographs hung on his wall, pictures of people he had snapped as inspiration for his art. Hailangelo had placed a white paper in the back of the book. Casey thought it was a bookmark, but it turned out to be a folded cover letter or term paper Hailangelo had written. Casey unfolded it. It read:

Hanson's work is a commentary on human nature, depicting the monotony and emotion of everyday life. They have a living presence that inspires conversation. I tried to create these same traits in my statues.

The front door of the store chimed. Casey and Nell scrambled through the office door and pretended to examine scarves in the back of the show room.

Nell set her purse down on the floor. "What do you think of this one?" she said to Casey, wrapping a hazel scarf around her.

"Beautiful, dear," he responded, playing along.

Thom "Hailangelo" Meintz approached, stroking his chin. "Have you been helped?" he said to Nell.

Casey felt a cold, damp chill flow into the shop, and it reminded him of the nastiness that pushed up the shores of Green Bay on misty, foggy days when storms approached.

29

Hailangelo walked to the back of the shop and stood next to Nell. "That hazel color in the scarf really makes your eyes pop, doesn't it?" The artist removed his navy pea coat and red scarf and hung them on a wooden coat rack. He approached them in a gray tailored blazer with a red silk handkerchief and dark jeans. Casey had to admire Hailangelo's sartorial prowess.

Nell turned toward the mirror and sized up the scarf. "Yeah, it does."

"Mixed with the gold highlights...perfect colors on you," Hailangelo said.

Nell turned toward Casey and thumbed in Hailangelo's direction with confidence and flair. "Now here's a man who knows what to say to a woman."

Casey shrugged, hands in pockets. "I think every color looks great on you. And it doesn't make you look fat."

"Casey, right?" Hailangelo said. "How…interesting to see you again. When I saw you at Fixate Factory, I meant to tell you how much I appreciated the article you wrote about me in the *Green Bay Times*."

"No problem. How's business?"

"I have a new exhibit in Manhattan," he said. "Just opened to rave reviews."

"Congratulations," Nell said.

"But the real news is this Hail Pro Shop girl who disappeared." Hailangelo said it in a tone that implied he shouldn't have had to verbalize it. He stepped toward Nell and nearly tripped over her purse. He looked down. "Oh, pardon me."

"You're fine," she said.

Casey wished Nell had taken her gun out of the handbag when she had the chance.

Hailangelo checked the clock on the wall. "Can I wrap this scarf up for you?"

Nell turned in front of the mirror. "Hmm, I don't know…"

Hailangelo gazed at her. "You're his…girlfriend?"

She nodded without hesitation. "Yes."

Casey swallowed. Clearly, this was part of their act, right? Or was it?

"How did you hear about Elena's disappearance?" Nell said, still sizing up the scarf and turning her shoulders to different angles in the mirror.

Hailangelo smirked. "It's all over the news, quite the tragedy; Elena Ortega is such a beautiful creature."

Nell and Casey shared an uncomfortable glance. "So you know her?" Casey said.

"Sure. She's my neighbor."

"Do you know her well?" Nell said, no longer looking in the mirror but at Hailangelo.

"People move in and out of that apartment complex like it's a hotel," Hailangelo shrugged. He glanced at Casey. "Aren't you supposed to be working on a story?"

"I'm writing about Todd Narziss of the Green Bay Hail."

"That's right. Are you going to mention my statue?"

"How could I not?"

"How about a photograph?"

"That's up to the editor. But I've actually turned my attention to Elena's disappearance."

"I thought you stuck to sports?" Hailangelo said.

"She's a friend. And I'm multi-talented."

Hailangelo scoffed. "What does Elena's game of hide-and-seek have to do with the team?"

Casey shrugged and pursed his lips. "Nothing in and of itself. But she happened to be having an affair with Narziss."

Hailangelo grinned at Nell. "Men with statues are hard to resist." He stepped closer and sniffed her as if she were pie fresh from the oven. "Your makeup looks beautiful."

Nell forced an awkward smile, removed the scarf and placed it back on the rack. "Thanks, I sell Baciare cosmetics. Always have my 'face' on." Casey marveled at how nonchalantly she played it.

"No scarf?" Hailangelo said. He stepped between her and the purse, and Casey couldn't tell if that was intentional.

"Maybe next time," she answered, trying to move around him.

Casey really wanted a cigarette. He hadn't taken his quit-smoking pill in a couple of days, and the packaging specifically warned not to miss a dose. But the events that occurred during the course of the last week had made a joke out of everyday routine.

Hailangelo grabbed a steel dagger from a small redwood display rack. He grinned and examined the ornate wooden handle, carved to look like a dragon.

Casey really, really wanted a cigarette.

Nell looked at Hailangelo and swallowed. "Where's Rihanna?"

The sculptor raised a brow. "Who?"

Nell said, "You know who I mean."

Hailangelo smiled. "What do you do for a living, hmm?"

"I sell cosmetics."

"So inquisitive for a cosmetics shill."

"You feel close to her, don't you?" Nell said.

Hailangelo held the dagger at his side, as if there was nothing to see. "Can I interest you in any of our other merchandise?" With his other hand, he gestured like Vanna White toward his inventory.

"You want to keep Rihanna close," Nell said.

"I already do," Hailangelo said, stepping toward her. "Remember: 'The two will become one flesh. So they are no longer two, but one.'"

Casey wasn't sure what he meant by reciting that biblical passage, but he knew he didn't like it. He glanced down at Nell's purse, not sure he could get to it before Hailangelo made use of his dagger.

"You can't keep her close forever," Nell said. "Eventually, the authorities will find her and take her away."

"Quiet!" he waved at her. "You may leave my store."

Nell took a step toward him, easily within his striking range. She softened her voice. "You have the power to change that, Hailangelo. You are in charge here. She does what *you* want, and you want to let her go."

"No, no I don't."

Casey cleared his throat. "So you do know where Rihanna is?"

The artist squinted at Casey. "What do you care?"

"We're her friends," Nell said. "And you left a little girl in the cold, alone, overnight…"

Hailangelo held the dagger up to the light, as if examining it for smudges. He appeared completely calm.

Casey's chest felt as if Hailangelo were standing on it. Out of breath, he could only whisper. "Where is she?"

Hailangelo placed his hands over his heart in mock-romantic fashion, as if he were a melodramatic actor in a 1950s musical. "We had such a great time. Don't worry, she's golden." He approached Casey with a sedate look, sliding his thumb up and down the dull edge of the blade, rolling his eyes back as if it were erotic to him.

Nell stepped toward them. "Wait."

Hailangelo stopped in front of Casey, his brows crooked. He leaned in, held the tip of the dagger inches from Casey's chin and said, "Boo!"

Casey flinched into a narcoleptic fit—instant partial cataplexy and sleep paralysis.

Hailangelo waved his hand in front of Casey's face and turned toward Nell. "What the hell's the matter with him?"

"He has narcolepsy," Nell said.

Hailangelo cackled. "*Voila!* Just like a statue. It's brilliant. He belongs in the Louvre."

Nell stepped next to them. "Casey?"

Hailangelo slapped his palm on Casey's shoulder blade. "I'm just playing with you, Thread." Hailangelo's breath smelled like alcohol. A Nirvana song, "Heart-Shaped Box," played through the stereo system.

Nell said, "Rihanna is attractive, slender, full of life, just like Elena."

Hailangelo turned his head toward her. "You see more in people than simply what blend of makeup will accentuate their cheekbones, don't you?"

"It's my job."

"Maybe you can give me some tips," Hailangelo said, slowly walking around her.

"You wear makeup?" Nell said. She tried to act nonchalant.

He stood behind her with the knife. "Tips on how to see more in people." He gently brushed Nell's locks off her shoulders and inhaled deeply. "You forgot that I like long hair. *Definitely* long hair…"

"Jenny Bachowski," Nell said. "Remember her?"

Casey could hear the anger in her voice. This was as personal for Nell as it was for anyone. He wondered why she didn't just kick him, tackle him, or dive for her purse.

"Can't put that name to a face," Hailangelo said in a monotone voice that suggested ambivalence. "Sorry."

"That's funny," Nell said. "You knew her face meticulously when you stalked her in Galesburg. You knew her name when you abducted her."

Hailangelo blinked slowly. "I only deal in fine art." He gestured around the shop. "Well, that and things that sell to the bourgeois."

Nell didn't look at the art and taxidermy on the walls. Her eyes remained focused on Hailangelo. "You can't perform sexually. You feel inadequate."

The artist frowned. "What?"

Casey realized she had been baiting him this whole time. She needed more evidence for an arrest.

Nell took leisurely steps until she stood next to her purse. "Did you hear about those statues left out in public on college campuses?"

Hailangelo held his breath for a moment then chortled. "Yes, it has created quite a buzz in the artistic community."

"I saw them on the news," Nell said. "They bear a striking similarity to your techniques."

"Do they?" He pivoted, grabbed her wrist and held the dagger to her neck. "You're not a cosmetics shill."

Nell shrugged a shoulder, seemingly nonchalant. "You're wrong. I do sell makeup."

"Drop your gun," he demanded.

"I don't have a gun." She held out her hands, as if inviting him to search her.

He touched the tip of the knife to her chin, not enough to cut her but enough to make an indentation.

She glanced down at the floor.

He followed her gaze, spotted the purse, and kicked it across the room—the gun still in it. Hailangelo stepped back, extended his arms and formed a square with his thumbs and forefingers, as if framing her. "I'd love to see you under perfect lighting."

"Where's Jenny?" Nell whispered with intensity. "Where is she?"

No answer.

"Where's Rihanna?" she said. "I would really like it if you told me."

Hailangelo paused, then spoke as if they were recapping a boring day at the office. "They're just innocent girls who ran away from home." He gestured in the air like a magician who had just made something disappear and was acting as if it were easy.

"What's your real name, Hailangelo?" Nell said. "Tommy Meickle? Thomas Meintz?"

Hailangelo said nothing, just looked down and half-grinned, as if to show that he knew what she'd say before she did.

Nell continued. "Galesburg is my home town. My first school was there. I used to play freely with neighborhood kids: Tag, Four Square, Ring Around the Rosie. We never locked our doors. Things have changed. *You've* changed things, Hailangelo. I want to turn back the clock."

Casey hoped Nell would disarm him.

"You can't reverse time," Hailangelo said. "What's your little game? Are you a detective?"

"Think I'd give a crap about a petty killer from Galesburg if I were stationed in Green Bay?"

Hailangelo said nothing. He backed away, pointing the dagger at her. "You're a fed."

"Where's Rihanna?" Nell demanded.

Casey would have given his right arm to be able to slug Hailangelo, but still couldn't move.

"Tell me, Agent, what field office are you from? Milwaukee?"

"Now I'm afraid I don't know what you mean," she lied. "You're gentle with your girls, aren't you?"

"Yes," Hailangelo said. "I put my date on a pedestal and treat her with the reverence she deserves. Doesn't every gentleman?"

"I understand," Nell shrugged. "It's not your fault."

"Is this the part where you use your motivational interviewing to make me feel empowered, Agent? Hmm? Next you'll mix in a bit of the Reid interrogation tactics, standard FBI procedure. You'll develop a theory to see if I respond to it, yes?"

Nell said, "The chemicals in your brain are imbalanced. There's a disconnect between your ventromedial prefrontal cortex and your amygdala. Just come clean and we'll get you help."

He laughed. "Excellent, Agent. Well played. But I know your game."

Nell remained cool as an orange from the refrigerator. "Where's Rihanna?"

"She ran away from home," he said.

Nell tilted her head slightly. "Where do you hide the bodies?"

That triggered something for him. He paced, impersonating her in a condescending, singsong voice: "Where is she? Where are the bodies? Where do girls go to shower?" He stood before Nell, invading her personal space. "Where do bada-bada-dee-dee-gobba-gobba-goo?" He cackled as his brows flared.

Casey expected Hailangelo's eyes to burst into flames, but it never happened. They simply looked bottomless. The sculptor spoke cryptically but had admitted to nothing criminal. Nell practically hyperventilated. "Where...is Rihanna?" He had gotten to her, and they all knew it.

Hailangelo grinned, leaned in, and again held the dagger up to her chin. "Maybe you should look in the woods."

Casey thought, *Was that a joke? Or his way of coming clean?*

Hailangelo backed away and sized her up. "You inspire me, Agent. You are dignified, well-dressed, composed, educated. In short, you remind me of the woman with the umbrella in *A Sunday Afternoon on the Island of La Grande Jatte.*"

30

Hailangelo licked his lips and tapped the side of the blade in his palm. "I happen to have an umbrella in the corner of the shop."

"Really?" Nell said flatly. "Feel free to grab it."

Hailangelo grinned, then wiped it away. "Now, that would make me an impolite host to you, Agent. There are...accommodations you deserve. Services I can provide. After all, not many walking this earth have the expertise I possess."

Nell stared blankly for a moment, swallowed, tried to laugh it off. "Tommy. Don't do this." Her voice sounded like her throat had gone dry.

The sculptor high-stepped toward Casey like the drum major of a college marching band, using the dagger as a baton, mocking her. "*Tommy, don't do this.*" He cackled, palmed his chest again as he caught his breath and turned toward Nell. Hailangelo's voice suddenly turned angry. "I can do whatever I want. My father showed me that when I was six years old; he killed my mother, had sex with her corpse then buried her in our back yard." He waited for Casey and Nell to react, but Nell didn't and Casey couldn't. "When Pops finished burying Mom, he handed me her panties and said, 'Something to remember your mother by.'"

"That's...awful," Nell said, shaking her head, short of breath.

"A real gentleman, my father," Hailangelo said.

Now Casey could see why Nell hadn't disarmed him. As long as he had the upper hand, as long as he thought Nell would die, he would tell her what she needed to know.

"Dad re-sodded the yard," Hailangelo chuckled. "The poor bastards who bought that house never knew their kids were playing football and building sand castles on top of Mom's grave." His grin evaporated as he rubbed his temple.

"No one reported her missing?" Nell said.

"Just my aunt, but she was the crazy one in our family."

"Did you bury Rihanna in your backyard?" Nell said.

"You think I'm some ogre?" Hailangelo growled. "Like my father?"

"Are you?"

He composed himself, straightened his posture. "I'm an artist. Just an artist. I haven't buried anyone in my entire life."

Casey swore the African mask with the Technicolor tears leapt off the wall right at him. More middle-eastern music set to techno played over the stereo system: riffs from violins and woodwind instruments danced atop a combination of hand drumming and electronica beats.

Nell relaxed her stance, smiled at Hailangelo, and said, "You are a terrific artist, Hailangelo. You do beautiful work."

He grabbed the stuffed Siamese cat off the shelf. "Thank you, Agent. This is my favorite piece."

"Nice taste in music, too," she tried.

He strode to Casey, held the stuffed cat in front of the reporter's face with one hand and brandished the dagger with the other. "Cat got your tongue?"

Casey's heart pinged around in his chest like a ball in a racquetball court. This was it. He would die right here, right now. It would end, just after finally finding someone who could see past his narcolepsy, someone beautiful and intelligent and cultured. Just his luck.

Hailangelo laughed, expecting a reaction, but Casey still couldn't give him one. Hailangelo looked at Nell for an explanation.

She shrugged. "Still narcoleptic."

Hailangelo sneered at Casey. "Freak." Disappointed, he set the cat down next to Casey with a thump. For once, Casey thought, narcolepsy actually helped—it took the fun right out of it for Hailangelo. The sculptor kicked over a wooden rack of scarves.

Nell broke for her purse, dove to the ground, and unzipped it.

Hailangelo turned.

She rolled to her back, pulled her gun, and aimed.

He lunged, swung the dagger, knocking her Glock off target—*BLAM!* A bullet went into the wall. The blade slashed her blouse diagonally across her chest. She shrieked, pressed forearms against her wound, and moaned.

Casey finally snapped out of sleep paralysis and shook his

head. Hailangelo kicked Nell's gun into the corner of the room and fled toward his office.

Casey reached for Hailangelo's bicep as he raced past, but the sculptor shook off the reporter's arm tackle. Casey grabbed the rain stick and pursued.

They entered the office in the back of the store and Hailangelo sprinted across to the left and reached for the door, above which was a sign reading, "Emergency Exit Only."

"Stop!" Casey shouted, catching up across the room, knocking the book on Duane Hanson to the floor. He raised the rain stick above his head and Hailangelo opened the door. No alarm sounded.

Casey whacked him square on the shoulder. The rain stick cracked. Splinters flew; beads scattered on the floor like sleet on a tin roof. Hailangelo staggered through the door, dazed, swinging the dagger back behind him but missing his pursuer.

Casey had expected the alarm to sound and cold air to rush in, but instead of an exit, the door simply led to steep stairs en route to the basement.

Hailangelo tried to slam the door behind him, but the reporter stuck his hand in the way. As Hailangelo ran down the stairs, Casey threw the remains of the rain stick down the staircase at his feet, tripping him. Hailangelo fell down the last two steps but bounced off the basement wall and rolled to the ground out of view.

Casey looked back for Nell, but didn't see her. He descended the stairs cautiously, peeked around the wall, and scanned the room. A brushed-chrome post-modern lamp illuminated the room from a black coffee table. No sign of Hailangelo.

Casey had expected a dungeon, but this place looked immaculate, inviting. The décor was swanky, including a black leather sofa. Hanging along the wall at the base of the steps was a framed print replicating Edgar Degas's masterpiece "Stage Rehearsal." It depicted a man in a top hat and tuxedo fixatedly watching young ballerinas stretch and dance. Casey had seen the original painting at the Metropolitan Museum of Art in New York. On a shelf along another wall rested a diamond necklace on a black mannequin bust.

A thin hallway about ten feet long led out of the room into the larger portion of the basement. Since the hallway was dark, Casey couldn't see into the room from the end of the hallway. He could definitely smell a stench emanating from somewhere in the basement.

Casey had neither a weapon nor any idea how to defend himself. Hell, he'd have broken his beloved guitar over Hailangelo's head. Instead, he retreated up the stairs, the smooth soles of his black loafers slipping on the linoleum surfaces. "Nell?" he called, darting through Hailangelo's office like a kid playing tag.

Back inside the store, he spotted her. She had wrapped a scarf around her chest as a makeshift bandage. She tied a second scarf diagonally in the other direction, forming an "X" on her chest. "Nell! You okay?"

"Never been better." She winced.

"Is it deep?"

"Deeper than a paper cut. Where'd he go?"

"You've lost a lot of blood."

"*Where'd he go?*"

"Downstairs."

"There's a downstairs?"

"I whacked his shoulder, but the rain stick shattered and he made it down there."

"You hit him with a rain stick?"

"That thing was heavy."

"Where is he now?"

"I didn't follow him without a weapon."

"Good call, sleepyhead." Still sitting, she opened her cell, winced in pain, and dialed. "Meyer? Listen, I need your help. I found him, I found the bastard I've been hunting for three years. Name is Thom Meintz, at least that's his most recent alias. Goes by Hailangelo. Yes, *the* Hailangelo. No, I'm serious. I'm at his store."

Meyer said something, but Casey couldn't hear it.

She answered, "Well, for starters, the bastard slashed me and ran. We lost him. He could be in the basement, or he might have fled the building. No, I'm fine. What I need is for you to set up a ten-block perimeter around his store. Great. We'll make sure he's not hiding in the back lot." She hung up.

Casey went around behind her, laced his arms under her armpits and helped her to her feet. "Now what?"

"Would you grab my gun?" she said, adjusting her makeshift bandage and wincing. Blood had saturated the scarves.

Casey retrieved her gun and handed it to her. "You should rest."

"I'm fine," she said. "Lead the way."

31

Casey hesitated, stared at Nell and, when he could tell arguing would be futile, led her back into Hailangelo's office, past the stuffed rats guarding the computer. She extracted a small black flashlight from her coat, turned it on, held it out backhanded, and braced it under her gun.

"Wow, that thing is bright," Casey said.

"It's a CombatLight. Standard flashlights don't cut it at La Casa de Psychopath."

Casey headed for the door to the basement.

"Wait," she said, motioning with the gun to let her go first down the stairs.

He let her pass.

She descended. Downstairs, she cleared the initial room.

"This guy's a piece of work," Nell said.

"It's strange that his place is so swanky," Casey said.

"There's a reason. This was part of his ruse. He'd woo them with his dark looks, his vocabulary, and his artistic achievements—then close the deal in this tempting environment."

"Creepy, if you ask me," Casey said. He headed toward the hallway to the right, the last place he had seen Hailangelo.

"Wait." Nell spotted a door Casey had missed to the left. The scarves around her chest had turned reddish-black. Nell paused for a second, gathered her strength, then kicked open the door.

It released a rotting odor. Nell pointed her flashlight and gun around the room to make sure they were alone. She took a tiny jar out of her pocket and rubbed something that looked like VapoRub under her nose, then did the same for Casey. It blocked most of the stench.

Inside this room, Nell flipped a light switch with the barrel of the gun. Blood had stained the cement floor, especially around the drain in the center. The wall paint had chipped. Industrial sinks and butcher tables lined the exterior. Knives and cleavers of various shapes and sizes hung on one wall. A desk was covered in tubes of paint and brushes. In the center of the room lay a wooden stool and crate. On one wall hung a replica print of *Madame X*, on the other *Pygmalion and Galatea*.

Five large green rubber garbage cans stood in the far right corner. Casey peered into the largest sink: Empty.

Nell grabbed a pair of latex gloves out of her pocket and pulled them on, releasing them with a snap.

She opened the lid on one of the five garbage bins. The smell bombarded them.

Casey turned away as if punched in the jaw.

Nell slammed the lid back down on the bin. "Mercy!"

"What's in there?"

"Nothing."

"*Nothing?*"

"Well, it's empty now. Obviously, it contained something nasty very recently."

"Maybe it's dinner scraps," Casey squinted, "like pork or chicken."

"I wish," Nell said as she walked a few feet to an old, rusty, white refrigerator with a slot-machine handle.

She opened it. Inside, there were no shelves, and nothing except for the body of Rihanna in the fetal position, an elaborate golden cloak wrapped around her from the chest down, turquoise flowers in her hair.

Casey had a sleep attack. He could have sworn he saw Rihanna come to life, step out of the refrigerator, and giggle.

"It's okay, it's okay," Nell said, pointing her weapon at the floor with one hand and gently placing her other on Casey's shoulder. Nothing about it was okay. She shook him out of the narcoleptic episode and the life-like Rihanna evaporated, leaving only the corpse in the fridge.

Nell bent over, holding her wound in pain. After a moment, she examined the body. "No signs of struggle, no blunt-force trauma to the head, just a needle mark."

Casey turned away from Rihanna's body, took two steps and placed his forearm across his face, trying to collect his thoughts. He thought about Shantell, and what might become of her. Foster

221

care? Adoption? He didn't cry. Somehow, to his surprise, his brain compartmentalized everything without any conscious effort. Everything in this basement seemed surreal. He struggled to believe that the very woman whose daughter he'd found outside their apartment hours ago had been murdered.

"Which poison caused her death is undetermined," Nell said. "But at least now we know who's behind it all."

"What do we do now?"

"We need to leave her here for authorities so they can photograph the place and collect evidence."

"We can't just *leave* her here."

"Backup is coming."

Casey stared at the refrigerator.

She grabbed his wrist. "Come on, she's already gone."

He slowly turned and exited the room. They walked through the door past the couch. Nell handed Casey the flashlight and motioned to him to switch it off.

Pitch-black darkness encased them. They slid down the narrow hallway with their backs against the wall—the only way to be sure Hailangelo wouldn't sneak up behind them. With every step, Casey wondered if Hailangelo would grab him, or worse. They continued down the hallway wall until they reached the end of the corridor. It opened to a large room. Where was Hailangelo?

Nell paused a moment. Silence.

Casey flipped on her flashlight. On the far wall was a bulletin board displaying at least two hundred photographs printed on regular computer paper. Casey's stomach tightened as taut as the threads inside a baseball.

"Oh my God, there's Elena," Nell whispered.

"Which photo?" Casey whispered back. "How can you see that far?"

Nell shook her head and pointed instead at a mannequin. "Over there. The statue."

Casey moved the flashlight, flinched, and stepped back, afraid it was the killer.

Nell slowly walked along the wall, feeling for the switch, and flipped on the overhead light. "Don't move," she instructed, aiming her gun with two hands in front of her as she checked the room for Hailangelo.

Casey squinted, fighting the brightness as his pupils constricted. After a few seconds, he could see a statue that looked just like Elena, in her bra and panties, posed bent at the waist with one arm reaching out for an embrace. Her hair was down and her skin flawless. Airbrushed? Had Hailangelo built this statue to taunt Casey for not finding the real thing? This was personal.

There were five other statues of beautiful young women. "They're more realistic than even the Narziss statue."

"No kidding." Nell checked behind each, and behind a bar with a marble countertop. "We're clear. He's not in here."

"Where the hell is he?" Casey's eyes darted around the room. He spun in place, and his heart pounded so fast he could practically hear it.

Nell pointed at a staircase in the far corner of the room. She slowly approached it, ready to fire her Glock.

Casey approached the Galatea statue. Elena's eyes were glassed over, or were they fake? She stood still as a boulder. Yet, she was breathtakingly beautiful. He couldn't make sense of it.

Nell joined him, reluctantly touched Elena's bare arm—only to recoil. "Oh my God!"

"What?" Casey said, stepping back, afraid of it but not sure why. His head and tailbone bumped into the wall, but his adrenaline peaked, masking any pain.

She touched the statue again. "It's…warm."

"Warm?" Casey guffawed. "Come on."

"It feels so real. It's like…"

"Like what?" Casey said. "Nell?"

"Like she's…*alive.*"

That didn't make sense. "It's just a statue," he insisted.

Nell nodded an invitation for him to join her.

"It's not breathing," he said. "Not real."

"You're right on both counts," she said. "Come here."

Casey pressed up against the wall. "No, thanks. I'm good."

Nell looked at him. "I've touched statues, mannequins, and corpses. They all feel cool to the touch."

Casey stubbornly remained in place and pulled at the collar of his shirt. "It *is* sort of warm in here."

"It's not the ambient temperature. Not the humidity, either. Come here."

He knew he had to move sometime if he wanted to get out of there and away from these…things. He sighed, pushed away from the wall, and joined Nell.

Nell felt Elena's wrist. "No pulse. Touch her."

"Are you crazy?"

"Touch her."

He touched her arm and squirmed. "Ah!"

"See?"

"It feels so…real."

"It should," Nell said. "That's really her."

32

Casey stared at Elena, transfixed, confused. Even in death, she looked radiant. "No...no-no-no-no." He shook his head, chuckled maniacally, and suffered a sleep attack.

"Casey." Nell shook his shoulders and he snapped out of it.

He crouched to the ground and whispered, "First Skeeto, now Elena." Tears welled. He sniffed, wiped his eyes with his sleeve. He gagged then breathed through his nose to get past the initial nauseating shock. *Your most important breath is your next one.*

Nell placed her hand on his shoulder, but this time it was for comfort. Tears streaked her cheeks, too. They hugged and cried.

"We failed," Casey said. "Weren't fast enough."

"He killed Rihanna within hours. We didn't stand a chance with Elena." Nell pulled away from him and paced, wiping tears.

She recovered quickly, no doubt due to her training at Quantico, like flipping a switch. She thought out loud. "He's no sadist, though. Doesn't torture, because he views these as art. He's punctual, efficient, clean. I see no signs of a struggle. He probably killed her before the abduction."

"How does he *do* that?" Casey said, looking up at Elena's face.

"Hard to say until the autopsy."

"No, I mean: how does Hailangelo get his statues to look so alive?"

"He's an exquisite craftsman."

"It's not just that. There's a spark there. It's gorgeous…and terrifying." He removed his blazer and held it out to drape it over Elena's body, but Nell intervened.

"Crime scene," she held out her hand. "Don't contaminate it."

"Oh. Right. Sorry." Never mind that they had already touched her. He put the coat back on and bashfully looked down at his feet, like a teenager at his first dance. He had admired Elena for so long, first as a friend with whom he'd never thought he stood a chance. With nothing to lose, it made it easier to ask her out. To his surprise, she had responded, "I would love to spend time with someone genuine." *Genuinely drowsy*, he remembered thinking, having no clue at the time she was comparing him to someone else. Narziss? Oleysniak? Her father? All of them?

He cleared his throat and forced himself to look away. Another victim sat on a chrome stool before the chic bar. A thin, blue, fluorescent string of lights traced the underside of the marble.

"That's Jenny, from Galesburg," Nell said. "I think she was his first victim. I interviewed her parents about Thomas Meickle right before he left town."

227

Casey shook his head. "We have to stop him."

Jenny had blue eyes, long-brown hair, and exquisite cheekbones. She had been clothed in a skimpy black dress and matching heels. One elbow rested on the bar and her hand was nestled under her chin, bored for all eternity.

He pulled himself away from Jenny's eyes and glanced around the room at the other women. They looked alive, unnervingly erotic. He hated himself for thinking it, but his instincts and hormones took over. Aside from what this said about Hailangelo, what did it say about the onlooker? "How does he do it?"

"He used taxidermy techniques," Nell said, prodding Jenny's arm with a gloved hand, "and airbrushed them."

One woman had been posed like an expressionist painting, resting her right elbow on a table and her right knee on a stool. She wore an orange sweater and an olive skirt.

Another victim was seated, dressed in an immaculate white French dress and a black bonnet with a striped ribbon tied below her chin. As with Jenny, her elbow rested on her thigh, her chin on her palm.

Perhaps the most beautiful of all, however, was the one that depicted a woman wielding a sword aloft.

Nell frowned. "I've seen that before!" She grabbed her phone and did a quick internet search. "I knew it!" she exclaimed. "It's based on the image of *Motherland Calls*, the world's tallest statue, in Volgograd, Russia. Says here that the statue commemorated the Battle of Stalingrad—a victory over the Nazis."

Casey wondered if Hailangelo viewed his gallery as a similar triumph—but in this case, over law enforcement. His statue also wore the scarf around her head and the large pearl earring, with an innocent countenance that defied the setting.

"Wait a second," Nell said. "The statues left on campuses were all based on famous paintings. I wonder if each one is in homage to a famous work of art."

Casey quickly ran a search for famous paintings of women. "The one in the bonnet appears to be this painting," he said, handing his phone to Nell.

"Yes. And this other statue seems to be modeled after the Johannes Vermeer painting, *Girl With the Pearl Earring*."

"They all match a masterpiece. Except for Jenny."

"Most first victims are experiments for serial killers," Nell said. "The serial killer adapts as he goes, just like anyone else learning a trade." She paused in disbelief. "He thought he could bring the classics to life."

"How do you explain the warmth?" Casey said.

"Heating coils, maybe?"

Casey glanced down and saw extension cords leading from the ankles of each statue—each *victim*, he reminded himself—the cords adhered to the ground with clear packaging tape.

"His permanent harem," Nell said. "No need for souvenirs to remember the crimes. He can literally relive his ritual with ultimate control, forever."

Casey approached the bulletin board that displayed all the photos. There were at least a dozen showing Rihanna.

Nell stood among the statues. "Well. That explains why Rihanna was in the refrigerator."

Casey turned from the bulletin board to look at her. "Why?"

"At room temperature, rigor mortis sets in on facial tissue as quickly as an hour after time of death," Nell said. "And the limbs are usually stiff in four to six hours under normal conditions."

Casey turned back to the images on the wall. "This ain't normal."

"Exactly. He'd want to maximize elasticity in Rihanna's skin, and keeping her in the fridge would buy some extra time by delaying decay." Nell joined him by the bulletin board and pointed to a collage of photos. "Here's Elena." Indeed, the pictures showed Elena Ortega leaving and entering her apartment, with a date and time written below each image in black ink.

"He was stalking her too," Casey said, with an urge to look over his shoulder to ensure none of the statues crept toward them.

Nell opened her cell, dialed, and paced. "I found him, sir. I'm in a basement at the Art East Gallery & Taxidermy Shop in Green Bay. He's preserving them like animals."

While she spoke to her boss, Casey examined a photo of one of the victims. Hailangelo had labeled it *Aqualibrium by Mark Cross*. Casey had never heard of the painting. When Nell was off the phone, he showed it to her.

"This mean anything to you?" Casey said.

Nell typed it into Google. "Looks like a realist painting of a woman in a blue dress wading in clear ocean water."

"Another work of art to 'bring to life.'"

"Elena and Rihanna were murdered for art. But why kill Skeeto? What's the common thread?"

Casey swallowed. "I'm afraid to ask."

"I think I know. They all knew *Elena*."

Casey dug the shard of credit card into his palm to remain alert.

Nell took a deep breath. "Let's go back to the last contact with Elena. I talked to her on her cell phone while she was at the gas station."

"Then she gets in the cab."

"Right, and the cabbie drops her off at the church. Maybe Hailangelo grabbed her there."

Casey stole glances at the statues to make sure none of them moved. "But what does that have to do with Skeeto?"

"These kinds of crimes are about fantasies. The more intelligent the criminal, the more complex the fantasies and the more meticulous the execution of the crimes. If he lusted after Elena, and it's pretty clear he did, I could see him clearing a path to both get her and take out anyone he thought might stand in his way."

Casey scanned the bulletin board. There were fifteen different women with multiple images. "How many do you think he's killed?"

"Obviously the six women in here, plus Rihanna makes seven, and possibly the four statues left in Colorado Springs, Iowa City, Galesburg and Columbia."

"Wow," Casey said, shaking his head. "Eleven victims?"

"Maybe more. Hailangelo feels no remorse. They're just clay in his hands. He'll do it again and again until someone stops him."

A door opened and Nell pointed her gun up toward it. They heard multiple pairs of feet coming down the steps into the room. "Police," said a uniformed officer.

Nell lowered her gun and flashed her badge. She nodded toward Casey and said, "He's with me. Special agents from the Milwaukee office are already on their way."

"The exterior is secure," one police officer said. "The perimeter is set."

Casey saw two tall wooden dressers against a wall. "Nell, look."

She pulled another pair of rubber gloves out of her pocket. "Here, put these on."

Casey opened a drawer. Inside were panties in plastic bags, each with computer-generated labels, including details on each woman's name, measurements, birthdate, and address. "Think he obsessed much?"

"His childhood trigger was his mother's demise. He has always connected panties to sexuality."

Casey nodded. "Doesn't every guy?"

Nell placed her hands on her hips. "But you don't keep a bag of women's panties in the same room as your statue harem, do you?"

"That would be a no."

The bottom drawer contained a stack of unlabeled photos. Casey grabbed them to see if he could recognize the woman in the photos. "Aaah!" He threw them in the air as if they were tarantulas.

"What?" Nell said, grabbing one of the photos and flipping it over.

Casey could say nothing and when she looked, Nell knew why.

"It's your sister."

33

Hailangelo drove toward Hail Stadium, wondering if the reporter had discovered his treasured statues. Yes, he had to have. He couldn't believe he had led Thread down there. But what choice did he have? He knew better than to battle a federal agent to the death; he was a sculptor, not a pugilist. He could have run out the front of the shop instead of exiting from the basement. But he had the fed's blood on his shirt. Besides, how was he supposed to know the reporter would come out of his little trance right then? He cursed, knowing he should have stabbed Thread when he'd had the chance. But, at that moment, he'd wanted only to get out. He was sure that the fed had called for backup.

Even if Thread hadn't discovered the statues yet, it was only a matter of time until he would. Hailangelo cared deeply about his statue *Young Lady in a Boat* because the original artist, James Jacques Joseph Tissot, was his ancestor. Or so his mother had told him. He had no reason not to believe her, but also had no evidence. Thomas "Hailangelo" Meintz chose to envision Tissot's blood pulsing in his own veins, to channel the painter's genius. Tissot—who fought in the Franco-Prussian war to defend Paris, who later studied there, whose 15 large-scale masterworks *La Femme à Paris* exhibited to high regard, whose ability to portray dramatic lighting had taken art connoisseurs' breath away—inspired Thomas Meintz.

In this regard, Casey and his FBI girlfriend had taken his family from him — his supposed great-great-great-great-uncle — not to mention his beloved Galatea. Hailangelo would never, ever forgive Casey Thread for this. He would make him pay. He wished he had killed the fed but, alas, could tell that her wounds had been little more than superficial. She would survive; the FBI would comb his shop and basement for evidence, confiscate his sculptures, and hunt him.

The thought of *them* in his studio was like pond scum in Perrier. *The indignity of it all.* He reached over to the passenger seat, grabbed the bottle of vodka, and drank from it as he drove. He knew he would be healthier if he abstained from these passions. Was he addicted to the alcohol, pornography, and sculptures? Was addiction even a vice? Could anyone blame him for desiring something, anything, to numb the pain of his mother's demise? To get him through the day with a little less pain?

He figured other people would judge and chastise him, but they did the same thing—except they used nicotine, caffeine, sugar, chocolate, alcohol, or the stimulation of exercise. It was all dopamine flooding their brains, just a matter of what triggered it. He had created gorgeous statues that brought masterworks to life and immortalized beautiful women. They'd never wrinkle, fade, or return to dust. *You're welcome*, he thought. He considered himself enriched and better educated than those who had no idea what he felt. And yet, he knew full well that what he did was illegal. Man-made laws were pathetic attempts to nanny others. Like a drug addict, Hailangelo rationalized that he would prefer a shorter life with titillation than a longer one without the euphoria he garnered from his dark thoughts and statues. Screw the feds, he thought, they can have my old works. I'll sculpt a new collection.

But first, he had unfinished business with one of his former muses. He parked along the curb near the Hail practice field, among other vehicles left behind by fans who had come to observe the team preparing for the big game. Passing those who stood along a chain-link fence risking frostbite just to get a glimpse of their heroes, Hailangelo walked to the parking lot where players parked their luxury vehicles.

He had met Narziss a year before during the creation of the statue bearing the athlete's likeness. At the request of the team, he had gone to the star's mansion and created a mold of Narziss out of plaster. It had been a painstaking process to coat the bare tight end with the soft plaster and, at times, he had had to remind Narziss that this would immortalize him in the atrium of the most popular football team in the world. That equated to endorsements and a political future. Once he had sold Narziss on that, he could have dipped the man in bronze if that's what it took.

Now he recognized Narziss's red Dodge Ram pickup truck. *Compensating much?* Hailangelo climbed into the back of the truck and lay down. Fortunately for the artist, the temperature hovered around thirty-six degrees. He kept his gloved hands warm in his coat pockets. Like a surgeon's, his hands were his most valuable asset— for procuring his materials, sculpting, and painting his materials. He had to protect his hands and pamper them.

Some people liked to be spontaneous. Not Todd Narziss. The team's co-captain made no secret of the fact that he took pride in arriving first at the Hail facility and leaving last. He spoke about it in the media as if he deserved a purple heart, how he'd catch hundreds of passes from the "jugs" machine, a device that used two spinning rubber wheels to shoot footballs harder and farther than most humans could throw or kick them. Hailangelo loathed the tedium of waiting for Narziss to return, but the excitement that came with his plan outweighed it. When it came to his craft, his patience knew no bounds. Better to take longer and do it right.

The team practiced outdoors despite the wind chill because they knew they'd be playing in the same conditions on Sunday. Hail fans viewed it as home-field advantage. Players viewed it as a price to pay for fame, fortune, and glory.

Thirty minutes after practice ended, Hailangelo heard the truck beep twice to signal that the locks had been opened. If adrenaline rushed through Hailangelo's system, he didn't feel it. His heart rate remained the same. Narziss's defenses would be down—he'd be exhausted from the workout at the practice facility and ready to drive leisurely to the locker room to shower and change.

When Narziss opened the truck's door, Hailangelo stood up from the deck and stabbed the syringe into the player's neck. Before he could deliver the full dose of poison, Narziss reached back, grabbed

Hailangelo's hand and bent the needle into the shape of an *L*. The needle broke away from the plunger, came out of his neck, and fell to the ground. Narziss turned toward his assailant, his eyes bugging.

Hailangelo could tell Narziss wanted to sculpt him into an ashtray. As the superstar reared back to strike, the partial dose of hydrocyanic acid stunned his system. He dropped to his knees on the parking lot, then went down in a heap. Hailangelo, who'd spotted pedestrians coming down the sidewalk, leapt out of the truck and risked being seen by standing over Narziss. "You tried to steal Elena from me," he said. "You defiled her, you hack. You led them to my studio. You're about to die, but don't worry. Your statue will live on."

With that, he calmly walked back toward his car.

A man in his fifties followed about thirty yards behind. "Hey! Stop."

Hailangelo kept walking. He had never made such an egregious mistake. Then again, he'd never killed in such a rash fashion.

"Hailangelo, stop!" A man in a Hail sweatsuit hustled behind the sculptor. Hailangelo froze, pivoted, and came face to face with one of the assistant coaches.

The old-timer huffed and puffed. "Can I get your autograph?"

Hailangelo raised his brows, smiled, and peered over his shoulder at Narziss's truck. The athlete's body lay out of sight on the other side of the Ram. Hailangelo took the coach's pen and signed his clipboard.

"Thank you so much," the coach said, "I walk past your statues every day. Sometimes I still have to tell myself they're not real."

Hailangelo forced a chuckle. "Thank you, very kind of you to say." He turned to leave.

The coach didn't want him to go. "Are you going to do another statue soon?"

"Oh, I'm always working."

"Thank you so much, it's an honor," the coach said.

Hailangelo strode to his car and drove away. That had been too close. None of this would have happened if that damn reporter hadn't stuck his nose into it. Hailangelo knew just how to repay him.

Ten minutes later, he parked outside Leila Thread's apartment. He walked to the front door of the complex and buzzed her room. After a moment, someone answered via intercom.

"Who is it?" An older woman's voice.

"Thomas, a friend of Leila's from Fixate Factory."

"Leiiiii-la…" the woman called. "It's for you."

Hailangelo could hear her through the intercom. A girl giggled. "Oooh, Thom-as and Lei-la sitting in a tree, K-I-S-S-I-N-G." That's odd, he thought. He knew Leila didn't have kids from his thorough surveillance.

Leila scoffed. "Hardly. Thomas? Is that you?"

"Yes, it is."

"First comes love, then comes marriage," the kid sang.

The intercom cut out. The door buzzed and unlocked. Hailangelo opened it, scaled a flight of steps, went to her door, and knocked.

The door opened.

§

Casey and Nell vaulted the steps leading from Hailangelo's basement, and the door they reached indeed opened to the outside. They sprinted to the Z4, got in, and sped toward Leila's apartment.

Snow had begun to fall. Casey examined his hands and slapped his own face to ensure this whole ordeal wasn't a narcoleptic hallucination. His brain felt like it would boil over while his fingertips tingled from the cold. *Breathe.* He mentally cursed the snow for impeding their progress as he picked up his cell phone and called his sister.

Voicemail. He hung up and tried again. No answer. He gripped the armrest tighter. "Think he's inside her apartment?"

"He probably went to his own place to collect his things before leaving the country. But if he did go to your sister's, I think he would hover around and wait for Leila to come out. That would be the easier way to surprise her and take her to a vehicle without anyone noticing."

"What about my mother? He threatened her life."

Nell pressed down on the accelerator.

§

Hailangelo stood in Leila's doorway, grinning. "Hello, Leila." His pea coat covered the blood from Nell on his shirt.

Leila smiled. "Hi. Come in."

Hailangelo stepped in and nodded at Elzbieta. "Hello, Mrs. Thread?"

"Yes," Elzbieta said.

"I'm Thomas, a friend of your daughter. It's a pleasure." He took her hand, bowed, and kissed it.

Elzbieta chuckled and said, "Charmed, I'm sure."

Leila looked impressed. "He's taking me out to dinner."

"That's nice," Elzbieta said.

Hailangelo smiled. "We met by chance at Fixate Factory, and I must say you've raised a wonderful young woman." He noticed animal fur on Elzbieta's sleeve.

"Oh, well, thank you."

Hailangelo grinned at Leila. Their date was off to a stellar start. And now, having watched her in Madison, her interaction with Amelia, and the shooting of Brian Twig, Hailangelo knew just what to say to Leila. He would relate to her in ways nobody had ever done before. Tell her what she thought before she said it. He might not even have to use blackmail or poison.

Shantell marked an *o* on the Tic Tac Toe grid, looked up at Elzbieta and said, "Your turn, Mrs. Thread."

Hailangelo looked at Shantell. His grin evaporated, replaced by wide eyes. Rihanna's daughter! How could it be? *Crap crap crap.* Had Leila known Rihanna and picked her up? Was this the reporter's doing? The FBI's? He had to get out of there before the kid recognized him and squealed.

Shantell dropped her pencil on the floor and leaned down to pick it up.

Hailangelo waved to Elzbieta and said, "Thanks for letting me borrow her. I'll be sure to bring her back in one piece."

Elzbieta scoffed. "You better."

Hailangelo turned his back to the table, away from Shantell, and held his arm out to Leila. "Shall we?"

"My pleasure," Leila said. With that, they left. En route to his car, her cell phone rang.

"Need to answer that?" he asked.

Leila checked the caller I.D. "It's just my brother. I'll call him later."

§

Nell and Casey arrived at Leila's complex. Casey jumped out of the car before it had completely stopped and sprinted to the entrance. He pressed the buzzer. Nobody answered. He pressed the button frantically like a telegraph operator on uppers. "Come on…come on. Where are they?"

"There," Nell said, pointing at a car across the lot, about fifty yards away.

Elzbieta's voice came through the speaker. "Who is it?"

Nell and Casey had no interest, already running toward Leila, who spoke to someone Casey couldn't see. Casey's heart pumped liked pistons. "Lei!"

Her companion opened the passenger-side door to his 1970 black Chevelle. She got in the muscle car.

Casey closed in, sprinting, forty yards away from the car. Thirty.

The man walked around the Chevelle, got in, and started it.

"Lei!" Casey shouted, twenty yards away. "Wait!"

As the car pulled away, Casey felt himself lose control.

34

This time, the sleep paralysis was accompanied by mental numbness. As Hailangelo drove away with Leila, Casey felt... nothing.

Certainly, the déjà vu wasn't lost on him. But the first time his little sister had been attacked, he'd been caught off guard. This time, he had seen it coming, tried his best, yet still hadn't been able to stop it.

Nell caught up to him and shook him out of it.

He made fists. "Dammit, dammit, dammit!"

The Chevelle took a hard turn around a corner—tires squealing—and vanished. Again, Leila was going to be attacked by a predator and, again, his mother would be right—he couldn't finish when it mattered most.

"Casey, look at me. Are you all right?"

He clutched his hair with both hands and fell to his knees. "No—he *has* her!"

Nell grabbed his shoulder and tugged him toward her car.

He resisted, yearning to punish himself.

She tugged harder. "Let's go."

"I can't."

She got in his face. "Get a grip. You already broke open an interstate-murder case. It's downhill from here."

"Look, some of us didn't go to Quantico," Casey snapped, pushing her away. "I'm not cut out for this—I can't even stay awake!"

"Casey?" A familiar voice. "Casey!"

He turned.

"Where on earth did you go?" his mother yelled, standing at the doorway of the apartment complex. Shantell peeked out around his mother's legs. "I thought you were coming back for Shantell."

Casey was relieved to see she wasn't holding a kabob. He couldn't begin to formulate the words. He ran to the car and Nell followed his lead.

"Wait," his mother called. "What's going on?"

They sped after Leila and Hailangelo. Casey waited a few minutes then called the phone in Leila's apartment. "Hi, Ma. Listen, Leila just took off with a murderer."

Elzbieta chuckled. "Oh, Casey, you and your imagination. You just had another hallucination."

"No, Ma. I saw this. Nell did, too. Right?"

"I saw it, too," Nell said.

"That's impossible," Elzbieta said. "She left with the nicest man. He makes the statues around town and in Manhattan."

"That's how he gets away with it, Ma. It's all in the ruse."

For the first time ever, Casey's mother didn't have a comeback. "Oh dear." The words sounded like they fell out of her mouth solely due to gravity. Casey hoped she wasn't having a stroke.

"You let this happen," Elzbieta said in monotone. "Again."

"Ma, I tried. It's not over. We'll get her back."

Elzbieta let out a cry like a wounded animal. "My baby. You were supposed to be watching out for my baby."

"Ma. We're going to find her. Nell has the entire Bureau on this. The cops, too."

"They haven't done squat."

"We found evidence at his store. We've got him. We just have to catch him."

"Casey Jerome Thread. How could you let this happen again? How?"

"Ma, I gotta go. I'll keep you posted."

Elzbieta bawled.

Casey ended the call and slammed a fist on the dashboard.

"Sorry, sleepyhead."

Casey said nothing.

"You can talk to me." She said it in a caring tone Casey had rarely heard from others.

He didn't know what to say. He envisioned Hailangelo stabbing his sister in the car, before they could find her.

"You know I can't promise we'll find her," Nell said. She took a right turn at an intersection.

"I know." Snow fell gently on the road, serene and peaceful like a scene in a snow globe. Under any other circumstances, Casey might have considered it gorgeous.

Nell said, "I can send an agent to watch your mother and Shantell."

"Thanks, but I'd be more worried about your agent with my mother there."

She smiled and called it in anyway. "They'll watch the place, make sure he doesn't circle back there on us."

Casey's phone played the song "Message in a Bottle" by the Police, the ring tone to signal a text message had arrived. He grabbed his phone. It was from his editor at *Sports Scene*.

"Holy crap," he said. "Todd Narziss is in the hospital." Casey's article had just careened in another direction.

"Hospital? Why?"

Casey scrolled down. "Apparently some sort of violent altercation."

"Is he okay?" Nell said.

Casey wasn't sure which type of answer he wanted to see. He scrolled down further. "He's in stable condition at Green Bay Hospital."

"Well that's a relief."

"Yeah, tough break for the team. *And* him." Casey stared out the passenger window. For now, he had nothing else to do.

Nell placed her hand on his thigh. "I really do care about you. You know that, right?"

His heart fluttered. Did she mean that in an "In Your Eyes" kind of way, or in a "We Are the World" kind of way?

She put both hands on the wheel and focused on the road. "I didn't lie about anything."

Casey looked out the window, at a dog rubbing its back into the cool, white ground; how he longed to be so whimsical and free. "At first, I didn't know what to believe."

She turned a corner. "But now you do."

Their eyes met. "Now I do."

She smiled.

He returned it. "Where are we going?"

"To get your sister back."

"But we don't know where he went."

"We're not following him."

"What the hell are we doing then?"

"Ye of little faith. If you're hunting an animal and lose the trail, how do you track it?"

Casey shook his head. He had never hunted anything in his life, besides a job.

Nell answered, "You go back to where you know the animal has been."

35

Casey and Nell pulled into the back parking lot of Hailangelo's shop, got out of the Z4, and hurried to the art studio. Casey racked his brain thinking about Leila and how to stop her from becoming the next statue. He saw her as a survivor, and knew she'd give the killer a fight.

They stopped at the door and Nell handed Casey another pair of latex gloves. "Any chance he could have brought Leila back here?" Casey said.

"Even if he did, he would have bailed after seeing the police presence."

Casey looked around and didn't see Hailangelo's car. "I don't think I can go in there again."

"You can," she said, and opened the door. They entered and hustled down the steps. Nell placed a call. "Cindy? Listen, can you access some computer records for me? His latest alias is Thom Meintz. Thom with a T-H."

"They're not here," Casey said. "Where did he take her?"

Nell covered the phone and pleaded with him to trust the FBI process.

He nodded.

As they passed between the statues, Casey got goosebumps and the hair on his neck stood on end. Talk about awkward. Hailangelo's studio was now well lit, thanks to the addition of large lamps to illuminate the crime scene for investigators. The harsh light did nothing to dampen the statues' beauty. If anything, it brought their radiance to full relief. He had to remind himself that these had been people, real living women. Hailangelo had lived his fantasies, just as Nell predicted.

Casey closed his eyes yet still saw the statues behind his eyelids. He didn't dare keep his eyes closed for too long, either, lest he risk another sleep attack and imagine the statues coming to life. He had forced himself to compartmentalize Elena's murder. But he had no idea how he would handle a hallucination about her. He wondered if he'd wake from that at all.

He wasn't a violent man, but the thought that Leila could end up as one of Hailangelo's eternal love slaves made him want to rain hellfire on the sculptor.

Nell flashed her FBI identification to two police officers, who were discussing the crime scene while their partners snapped photos. One of the officers nodded at Nell as she walked by. Casey and Nell passed through the narrow hallway. Nell placed her cell on her collarbone, turned to Casey and whispered, "The Bureau is checking Hailangelo's computer records." Nell spoke back into the phone. "Wait, did you say Narziss? Okay. Thanks." She snapped the phone shut and nodded toward Hailangelo's office. "Let's go."

He followed her through the swanky room and up the staircase.

"Our Bureau computer specialist accessed Hailangelo's e-mail and says he recently exchanged several messages with none other than Todd Narziss."

"Damn," Casey said. They stood before Hailangelo's computer. The two stuffed rats stared back at their unwanted guests.

"Hailangelo sent about twenty text messages from his cell phone to Narziss." They now had evidence linking the two on the night of Elena's disappearance.

"What did they say?"

"Hailangelo wanted to know if Narziss would consummate a deal they had previously discussed."

Something told Casey it wasn't about the Narziss statue.

Nell pulled open the heavy metal desk drawers and rummaged through the contents. "Help me look."

"For what?"

"Receipts, checks, financial records…"

Casey joined her search. They didn't find any financials in his desk or in the filing cabinets.

"For the record," Nell said, "it's legal to do a search without a warrant under the emergency exception that someone's life is in imminent danger."

Casey raised his hands in innocence. "I didn't say anything." The rats each stood on metal boxes. He hated the thought of touching the rodents, even while wearing gloves, but moved them to the floor, repeating to himself, *they're dead and stuffed, they're dead and stuffed*...and opened the boxes. Inside they found cash, checks and IOU's. Casey examined a check, and it sent him into a sleep attack.

"Casey?" Nell said, shaking his shoulders. "Wake up, sleepyhead." Casey snapped out of it.

"What is it?" Nell said.

He shook his head and pointed in horror at the floor. "It's made out to Thom Meintz—signed by none other than Todd Narziss and dated a week before Elena disappeared."

"How much?" She reached to the floor and picked up the check.

Casey looked from the check to Nell. "Ten-thousand dollars."

Ten minutes later, they pulled into the ER entrance at Green Bay Hospital and raced to the front desk. Nell showed her badge, and after asking for Narziss's room number, burst through double doors and ran down a hallway.

Casey followed close behind. Something about the near-empty halls chilled him. There was no telling what might pop out at him—hallucinated or real. They raced past the ER and into the post-op recovery room. Monitors beeped and bleeped. Curtains separated each patient, and they checked seven beds before they found the famous athlete, his head wrapped in a wide white bandage.

Casey went to his side, shook Narziss, and called his name. "Wake up. Wake up."

Narziss started, struggling against the wires and straps and Nell and Casey as if they were football foes trying to tackle him before he could score the winning touchdown in overtime. Wires popped off his chest and stomach. He groaned.

Two nurses tried pushing with all their weight on Narziss's chest. "Settle down," a male nurse said, "Mr. Narziss. Please!" Two more doctors and two nurses pressed their hands on his chest. Narziss finally surrendered and let the medical staff tackle him in his own private end zone. Sweat beaded on his forehead.

"You look like you could use some spinach," Casey said.

A female nurse said, "It's a miracle he's alive."

Nell showed her identification to the nurse. "What happened to him?"

"He was attacked. Someone poisoned him with hydrocyanic acid. That caused him to fall to the cement. He hit his head on the parking lot and fractured his skull."

Nell nodded. "What's his prognosis?"

"He's in a great deal of pain, but the morphine should keep him comfortable until he recovers enough to go home."

"No long-term effects from the cyanide?" Casey said.

"It was a small dose. He's a big guy, and we were able to promptly treat it with hydroxocobalamin," the nurse said.

"Right. Hydroxocobalamin," Casey joked. "That's what *I* would have done, too!"

Nell grinned.

The nurse folded her arms and frowned. "He's fortunate."

Casey glanced at Nell and shivered. Narziss was practically the next Grigori Rasputin.

"The point of the needle was still in his neck, broken off with poison still in the syringe," the nurse continued.

"What if he had gotten the full dose?" Nell said.

The nurse raised her brows and shook her head.

"Can we speak with him for a few minutes?" Nell said.

"Don't keep him too long," the nurse said, "I'll be back in a bit."

Casey faced Narziss with urgency. "Hailangelo has my sister."

Narziss slowly moved his head and met the reporter's eyes. He slowly blinked and said nothing.

"Where is she?" demanded Casey.

Narziss blinked again and gave a faint shrug.

Nell leaned down to Narziss and softly said, "You wrote a check for ten grand to Hailangelo."

"*Din't.*" Narziss slurred, closing his eyes.

"We have the check," Casey said.

Nell showed her badge. "Agent Nell Jenner, FBI. It's going to be logged as evidence. What's it for?"

Narziss said, "*Stashoes.*"

Nell winced. "Statues?"

"Bull," Casey said. "I didn't see any statues at your house."

No response. Narziss closed his eyes.

"What was the check for?" Nell repeated sternly.

"I want my lawyer," Narziss said.

"You've got a little girl," Nell said. "What would you do if Hailangelo had her?"

"Kill," Narziss managed.

"You don't trust him," Nell said.

Narziss closed his eyes and firmed his lips.

"How did you end up in here?" Nell said.

Narziss said, "Attacked."

"By Hailangelo?" Casey said.

Narziss said nothing.

Nell pressed. "Where *is* he?"

Narziss fought back a smile and shrugged again. Casey pressed his palm on the bandage on his head and the superstar screamed.

"Where is he?" said Casey with clenched teeth.

"Prick!" Narziss said. He struggled to retaliate and, failing, clicked the morphine button beside him several times.

"Does he own any other property?" Nell said. "Maybe his father's old place?"

Narziss closed his eyes and shook his head ever so slightly.

"Are there any abandoned or foreclosed homes where he might hang out?" Nell said.

Narziss pulled on a string that signaled for the nurse to come immediately.

Casey said, "It's going to be fun testifying that you hired Skeeto to kill Elena."

Narziss opened his eyes. "What?"

"You had an affair with Elena, knocked her up, and you wanted to be governor," Casey said.

Nell tilted her head, twisted her lips, and nodded. "Three strong motives."

"Screw you," Narziss said.

"You realize that I will tell Samantha everything," Casey said.

Narziss said nothing.

"Mr. Narziss, Hailangelo is a serial killer," Nell said.

Narziss's eyes sprang open even wider. "Huh?"

"We found his victims in the basement of his shop," Nell said. "One of them is Elena."

Narziss's eyes bugged. "What?"

"And we've got your check to him, written a week before she disappeared, for $10,000."

"No," Narziss said. "Wrong...idea."

"Talk to us and maybe I can put in a word for you with the DA," Nell said.

"I asked Skeeto...to follow Elena. A baby...would be bad press."

"And during a championship run," Casey said.

"Skeeto followed her. She admitted...baby is mine."

The baby *was* his. Narziss paused a moment and, perhaps not coincidentally, pressed the morphine button several times.

Casey tried a different tack. "You know I'm writing about this for *Sports Scene* magazine. That's a given. But what I include is still up for debate."

The athlete looked the reporter in the eyes. "I never...paid Skeeto...to hurt Elena."

"Did you ask him to do it as part of his employment duties?" Casey said.

"No."

"Did you drop hints to that effect?" Nell said.

"No, damn it. I cared about her. Skeeto was only going to talk sense into her. He followed her to the church. But he never got the chance—Hailangelo took her!"

Nell said, "You can make him pay."

Casey said, "Where did he take my sister?"

The female nurse returned. "Can I help you?"

Narziss said, "I want them to leave."

The nurse echoed, "I'm afraid I'll have to ask you two to leave now."

"You know him," Nell said to Narziss, composed. "Think. Where might he take her?"

The nurse grew impatient. "I'll call security."

"Todd, please," Casey said.

The nurse left.

Narziss blinked. "Studio."

"You mean the store?" Casey said.

Narziss nodded.

Nell shook her head. "We already checked there. Where else?"

Narziss cleared his throat, blinked, and winced. "Deer stand."

Casey paced. "That narrows it down to all of wooded Wisconsin."

"Permanent...stand in oak tree," Narziss said. "He has a blind."

Casey squinted and frowned. "A what?"

Narziss pressed the button for more morphine.

"A blind," Nell explained, "is camouflage so the deer can't see your pasty tuckus." She glanced at Narziss. "Where is it?"

"Highway 32...County Road B...railroad tracks...fifty yards north."

Casey wrote it down on his hand, his mind racing. Did Hailangelo have Leila up in some tree like an owl with its field mouse? He sprinted out the door with Nell on his heels. As they ran down the hallway, she took out her phone and dialed.

"Who are you calling?"

"My boss," Nell said.

Somebody answered and Nell began reporting to the man on the other end that they were headed for the deer stand. "Can you send a team there?"

A hospital security guard approached. Nell showed her badge and he backed away.

"Everything okay?" Casey said.

"Yes," Nell said, "the Chicago bureau chief is communicating with his counterpart in Milwaukee, who has agents in the area. They're sending a chopper from Milwaukee and trying to trace Leila's cell phone."

"Nice. She's going to be okay, right?"

Nell glanced at him but said nothing.

They arrived at the Z4 and climbed in. Nausea clung to his stomach like gum to the bottom of a shoe—he tried pulling it free, but the tension stretched and stuck and he couldn't scrape it off. He searched for something useful to occupy his mind. "So, if Narziss didn't pay Hailangelo to *kill* Elena, what was it for?"

"Hailangelo did the statue of Narziss and they both knew Elena, who sold drugs."

The truth dawned on him. "They *partied* together."

Nell slowed the car down at a red light, then sped through the intersection.

Casey's mind was racing too. "Nell, are you a criminal profiler?"

"I'm an FBI field agent."

"You'd like to be working in Quantico?"

"Yes, my dream has been to make the Behavioral Sciences Unit. But there aren't a lot of openings."

Casey suddenly wanted her to succeed more than anything he could think of, to feel the euphoria that comes with it. He hoped that, when this was all over, he could be a part of that, and that his future would involve spending more time with his sister too.

36

Hailangelo drove his Chevelle down Highway 33. He whisked the car past farmland, enjoying the symmetry of the agricultural rows and the perspective of them. Cows and horses grazed near faded red barns ready to topple at a moment's notice. Phallic silos and cylindrical hay bales challenged him to maintain his focus—his admiration for Leila's long blue hair, the black eyeliner around her eyes.

He glanced at her in the passenger seat and smiled. "Can you feel the horsepower?" he said.

"Yeah, it has giddy-up. It's nice to get away from the everyday monotony, you know? My mother is always so concerned about success, money, safety, blah-blah-blah."

"I'm so excited you're posing for my next statue."

"Me too! And for an exhibit in Manhattan." Leila twirled a strand of hair with her finger and giggled.

He had never heard her laugh. "Well, I'd have asked you long ago had I seen you earlier."

Leila blushed.

"You weren't working the first few times I patronized Fixate Factory. The place seemed so…empty without you."

Leila surveyed the country landscape. "Where exactly is your studio?"

He ignored the question, continuing his stream of thought. "Your blue hair is like a stage curtain, your personality and uniqueness bursting out from behind it like rays of light, transcending the stage, unable to be contained."

"Nobody has ever said something like that to me before."

That was the idea. "What do you think of your mother?"

"My *mother*?"

"Yes. Do you try to be like her—or the opposite of her?"

She said nothing. As they drove farther and farther out of town, Leila grabbed the back of her neck. "Are we close yet?"

"Yes, another five minutes or so. It's out here so I can have peace and quiet while I work. Even a slight jerk of the hand can ruin a statue. I require complete serenity." He smiled at her, and seemed genuine. It seemed to calm her anxiety.

"I know we met a few months ago," Hailangelo said. "But I feel like I've known you all my life."

"Me too," she said. "I've admired your sculptures since I was a girl. Anyway, I find it apropos we met at Fixate Factory, the most laid-back scene I know."

He didn't go to Fixate to relax. He went there to become energized, pent up. "I do enjoy the ambiance."

"It is peaceful out here," she said, somewhat grudgingly.

"Exactly. And when I have such exquisite material with which to work, I get lost in the process. I can't allow it to go to waste because of some intrusion. Your statue will be a Greek goddess."

She demurred. "I've never seen a blue-haired goddess before."

"True art is about taking risks. Pushing boundaries. But more than anything, of course, it's about undeniable beauty." He slowed the Chevelle and turned right off the highway onto a gravel road about twenty yards long. It ended at a patch of snow-covered grass leading up to a frozen cornfield. He parked the Chevelle. Outside, dusk set. There were no streetlights. He smiled at Leila. "We're here."

She gripped the armrests, scanned the endless fields, and snickered. "We're…where?"

He pointed across the field. "There. See that oak tree?"

"Uh, yeah." The thick, mature trunk protruded about eight feet out of the ground before sprouting its first branch. The limbs were bare, but she could tell that, when fully leaved, the branches formed a half-circle. "Is that a tree house?"

He frowned. "It's my studio."

"Oh. Right." She winced. "Sorry."

His mind raced, as if flipping through TV channels with no time to spare. He tapped his temple as if it were the remote. "It's where I like to do the preliminary work. I have another studio in my office back at the art shop."

"You don't park next to this…studio?"

"I don't want to deal with cars driving up and disturbing me, especially when they occur right as inspiration strikes. We'll walk." He opened his door and stepped out of the car. "And inspiration is most definitely striking now. Come."

Leila hesitated. She rummaged a hand in her purse. Hailangelo saw her through the car window, prepared for her to pull the gun she had used on her rapist. Instead, she extracted her cell phone, glanced at it, and realized it had no reception.

"Coming?" He smiled, his teeth so white they nearly glowed in the dusk.

She got out of the car, closed the door, and stood there. "How do you get your statues down?"

"By rope." His face froze like his statues.

She didn't budge, didn't utter a word, like a squirrel when a twig snaps behind it. Hailangelo's heart rate didn't change a bit. But he figured hers did. He laughed. "I'm kidding. I have a hydraulic lift I use to lower them. It runs on a gas cylinder." He pointed at it in the distance. "See? It's right there, partially obscured by the tree trunk."

"Oh, yes, I see."

He waved for her to follow. She did, and they walked together, side by side. "It's okay, I know why you're nervous."

"Why?"

"I know about what happened to you when you were fifteen."

She half-laughed, then frowned. "I'm sorry…"

"The rape. Don't worry—I don't judge."

"You…you *know* about that?"

He raised his palms as they walked. "Yes, but I don't look at you *any* differently."

"How? How do you know that?"

"Well, to be honest, I saw you crossing Langdon Street in Madison."

She recoiled and halted. "You did?"

"I was having a beer in the Rathskeller, saw you leave with your friend, and was going to catch up with you and say hello. It's a small world, seeing you there."

Leila squinted. "But, I didn't see you."

"Yes, I know. As I drew nearer, I saw you in the crosswalk, and you broke down, and the bus nearly ran you over. I was horrified. You cried, but your friend helped you."

Leila looked down. "I...I'm sorry you had to see that."

"Tut-tut. Don't be silly."

"I was sort of in shock."

"I overheard you telling your friend about that man. I'm sorry, I shouldn't have eavesdropped on you — it's just that I was concerned."

Leila reached up and massaged her neck. "This is so embarrassing."

"There's nothing to be ashamed about. It seemed like you were in great hands with your friend."

"Amelia. Yeah, she's fabulous."

"Is she...just a friend?"

Leila's already fair complexion went completely pale. "What do you mean?"

"Do you feel a butterfly fluttering off the walls of your heart when you're with her?"

Leila shuddered. "She's my best friend. She helped me through the rape. I owe her my life."

Now they were getting somewhere. "You would…give yourself to her?"

Leila hugged herself and began walking toward the tree. "It's cold out here."

Hailangelo chuckled and followed. "My apologies. I've been a horrid host. Your pedestal in Manhattan awaits."

"I doubt that."

"What's to doubt? I have the gallery, the skills, the brand, the contacts."

She said nothing.

"What did Amelia teach you?"

"She taught me to conjure thirty seconds of courage, get through the anxiety, and settle in a comfort zone."

How he adored Amelia at that moment, as a spider might appreciate a human who swatted at a fly, succeeding only at hastening the insect's capture in the webbed quagmire. "I know it looks like a treehouse or deer stand from here. But inside it's carpeted, furnished, and the generator feeds a space heater, so it'll warm up quickly. I'll pour us some spirits."

"Great, I could use some liquid courage."

Hailangelo felt more and more confident in her compliance with every step. It's not like she had anywhere else to be. They neared the tree, now about twenty yards away. "Have you always loved to paint?"

She glanced at him in surprise.

He winked. "I saw the paintings on your wall. It just seemed so… you."

She folded her lower lip into her mouth and bit down on it, flattered.

"You're talented," he said.

She smiled and looked down. "Thank you. You're too kind."

"No, I mean it. Ever consider moving to NYC?"

"New York? Me?"

"I could introduce you to friends there, in the art scene."

"I don't think my mother would approve of a profession without built-in health insurance."

"You can't let your mother run your life. Besides, after your statue, you may become an in-demand model." They arrived at the base of the tree. His flashlight extinguished.

"Whoops," Leila laughed nervously. "Paul Revere, your torch is out."

The light flicked back on as Hailangelo pounced, striking her with the flashlight, first on the neck—temporarily shorting her air supply. He kicked her in the stomach and she doubled over.

If only he hadn't run out of hydrocyanic acid. But fortunately, he had more in the deer stand.

Hailangelo slammed the flashlight against the back of her head. She fell into a heap, dazed but not yet unconscious. Grabbing her, he knelt down and lifted her onto his right shoulder. "Come now, Millie," he said, grinning, "we have a lot of work to do to get you ready for the grand unveiling."

37

As they drove toward the deer stand, Nell's cell phone rang. She answered and listened for a few moments, then ended the call.

Casey said, "What is it?"

"They've tracked Hailangelo's car."

"The deer stand?"

"Yep. Right where Narziss said it was. Once you leaned on him a little."

§

Hailangelo stepped onto the hydraulic lift, his muse draped over his shoulder like a burp cloth, and flipped the lever to turn it on. He moved a joystick to raise the machine into the air. It buzzed as they ascended. The snowy cornfield grew smaller as they reached the top of the tree.

She made fists and pounded on his kidneys.

The buzzing stopped and he hoisted her onto the deer stand.

She rolled onto her back while he entered the stand from the hydraulic lift. She tried to run away from him, but he jumped up and kicked her in the side. She froze in pain.

He surmised that panic had set in, that Leila would harken back to some pithy statement Amelia had made about felons who lusted for power over women.

She slid back along the floor to the corner and sat there.

"This is cause for a celebration." Hailangelo smiled. "I've got a bottle of 1977 Cognac worth two hundred dollars." He started the generator in the stand and turned on the space heater. He walked to an old trunk straight out of a pirate tale, opened the lid and extracted the bottle and two champagne glasses.

Leila tried not to blink so she could watch him closely to make sure he put nothing in her drink.

He poured the amber liquid into a glass and held it out to her. "A glass of spirits, Millie?"

She didn't move—instead, she glanced around the interior of the deer stand. He had painted the walls with a hyperrealist mural depicting six Supreme Court judges in black robes gazing at them through binoculars.

"You like the décor?" He grinned at her, wide-eyed. It heightened his sense of being scrutinized, assessed. He adored the audience.

She raised her chin defiantly. "I'm not Millie."

He chortled. "Oh yes, you are."

"Why do you call me that?"

"Millie was the cousin of artist Edvard Munch, creator of the painting *The Voice*, which was inspired by his affair with her. You are special. You remind me of her."

Leila folded her legs to her chest and hugged them. "How am I special if I remind you of someone else?"

"Because you're the only one who ever has. Come now, drink up."

Leila didn't.

"Drink!" he demanded angrily.

She hustled to her feet, took the glass, and drank, expecting bitterness. It was sweet.

Hailangelo beamed. "You like it, right? Tell me you do."

"It's fine," she mumbled.

"You're worthy of the bottle *and* the wait." He went to a stainless steel cooler and extracted an ice pack. "Here, I know it's frigid, but let's put this on your neck." He applied it to her bruise. She winced and scanned the room.

"If you're looking for your phone," Hailangelo said, "I've crushed the SIM card so we won't be interrupted by any calls from telemarketers. 'Press one if you're a serial killer. Press two if you're a victim.'" He winked at her. "Stick with me, kid, and you'll go far. Just think—all your friends will be able to visit you in Manhattan."

He expected Leila to break for the lift, but she didn't. She simply stared at her shoes, dejected.

He continued in the earnest tone of Andy Griffith. "I'm sorry I was so forward about it. I shouldn't have struck you. It's just—"

He chuckled innocently. "I didn't want you to get scared, is all…and run off screaming, only to miss the opportunity of a lifetime."

She held the ice pack out to him. "It's too cold."

He applied it again with a sympathetic expression. "Ssh-ssh…we don't want your contusion to leave a permanent mark. They're really difficult to cover up.'"

She broke down. "I…can't go through it again. Please."

"Go through what, Millie? We're only making a statue that looks like you."

"Please, please don't rape me."

Hailangelo looked hurt.

"My dear cousin, I'd only dream of it."

38

Nell and Casey raced in the Z4 through the last suburb, past an endless string of McMansions. "You think he poisoned the women, like he did Skeeto and Narziss?" Casey asked.

"It fits the evidence," Nell said. "He could poison them a number of ways, but I'd guess from the mark on Elena's neck that he injected them all."

Casey imagined Hailangelo attacking his sister in that way. He wished Nell's car had jet propulsion, anything to get there faster. He felt so damn helpless. He wanted to say something, anything, but there was nothing left to say.

An awkward silence ensued.

"Nice part of town," Casey tried.

"Urban sprawl," Nell said. "Not so beautiful, if you ask me."

"At least there's a sense of community," he said. "I grew up on a farmhouse—not many kids around to play tag or football."

"Back in the '50s, relatives lived near each other," Nell said. "Everyone knew the barber, the butcher, the baker. Big cities and scattered families allow killers to be anonymous. More important, they can stalk victims who are strangers, who they can disassociate from being human. That allows serial killers to harm a human in the same way someone else might step on an ant."

"In the twenty-first century, there are more people and yet more isolation than ever," Casey said. "Then again, we have text messages, webcams, smartphones, so many ways to stay in contact."

"Texting Uncle Ralph a few times a year isn't the same as living a mile away."

There were days Casey wished he lived far away from his relatives. "Sometimes that's not all bad."

"Unless you're a kid from a broken home and there's nobody else to serve as a role model," Nell said. "Used to be that neighbors could help raise a child."

"Now, too often, there's no sense of belonging within the typical village."

"Exactly. People don't trust each other. Think it's a coincidence that the prevalence of serial killers has ascended over the last half-century?"

"Come on," he said. "Is that really true? Or is it that we're better at detecting and tracking them?"

They left a residential area and turned onto Highway 33, a single-lane roadway that had been plowed and salted, leaving the pavement clear of snow. Two sheriffs' cars blocked the highway, with chains of spikes across the lanes and shoulders designed to puncture tires. Nell slowed, pulled up to a halt, and showed her ID. The deputies moved the chains and allowed them to pass.

Nell pressed the accelerator to the floor.

Casey sighed. "Well, at least they set the perimeter."

"Yeah, but Hailangelo might have beaten us to it. Anyway, we are better equipped to fight crime than at any point in history. Authorities can now access joint databases like the National Combined DNA Index System. There's ViCAP to share details about violent crimes, and even a growing facial-recognition system."

"Then again, we can't forget that guys like Jack the Ripper pre-dated all of that," Casey said.

"True," Nell said. "There was Gilles de Rais, the French sadist from the 15th century, or the 'Blood Countess' Elizabeth Báthory of the 16th century."

Casey sighed. "Or pick your average warrior. Serial killers are as old as the human race." He glanced at the speedometer. They were going a hundred miles an hour and it barely fazed her or the car. He was glad she was driving. "Are we there yet?"

"Not far yet, sleepyhead."

"If divorces created serial killers," he said, "there'd be a lot more serial killers—half the couples in America get divorced."

"Certainly not all kids from broken homes become murderers," Nell said. "But researchers have partnered with the FBI to study a part of the brain called the hypothalamus. It regulates emotion and motivation. It's part of the lower part of the brain, called the limbic brain." She decelerated as they approached a stop sign, looked for oncoming traffic, and sped through the intersection. Fortunately, the highway remained in favorable driving condition. "If it's damaged by genetics, poor diet, or injury, the person can lose control of emotions, temper, and the ability to relate to other people. He becomes more withdrawn, creates vivid, violent, sexual fantasies, and is not equipped to put them into perspective. It's a breeding ground for deviant behavior. So if the parents are irresponsible, deranged, or violent, the child is at greater risk for developing into a killer."

Casey smirked. "So you don't blame the media for the destruction of society?"

She guffawed. "Certainly not. Most journalists simply report what they see. Although, giving serial killers catchy nicknames like The Green River Killer sensationalizes crime and gifts the perpetrator an emotional spike from fame…"

Casey emitted a spitting sound. "Nice to know you've got my back."

Nell continued. "To be fair, those same monikers also help investigators track murderers and learn from past cases. It sparks the public to take precautions, and to pressure authorities to catch the offender before he kills again." She tilted her head. "The positives might outweigh the negatives."

"And you don't blame the porn industry?"

"Past killers have blamed their actions on it."

"Come on, serial killers pre-date the printing press. Plus, how many people see porn and don't commit murder?"

Snow drifted across the road. Only slightly daunted, Nell slowed the car to a virtual crawl—eighty miles an hour. "Millions, obviously," Nell said. "But mainstream pornography is the gateway to violent porn, which becomes the trampoline to violent fantasies."

"And acting them out," Casey said.

Nell shrugged. "Most don't. But again, if you're someone prone to such behavior—"

Hailangelo certainly was. Now he had Leila, and Casey clutched the armrest so tightly he practically crushed it. "Is the behavior the cart or the horse?"

"Who knows. But the subject then substitutes control for intimacy. Hailangelo thinks these women are objects he can collect. And as much as he loves his mother, he probably feels slighted she wasn't there for him."

"But that's not her fault," Casey said. "You heard him—his dad killed her."

"I didn't say it should make sense."

"He's crazy."

Nell glanced at Casey. "But not legally."

Casey shifted restlessly, tugging on the seatbelt. "How far are we from Leila?"

Nell glanced at the odometer. "A couple miles. He's not crazy. Irrational, maybe. He led a double life. He duped Narziss and others into posing for his statues. Probably lured them with drugs. Might have used that to bait Leila too."

"I don't see Leila doing the hard stuff."

"No offense intended."

"None taken."

"Regardless, if Hailangelo is rational enough to stalk his victims and hide their remains, he is not legally insane."

"So is Hailangelo just a monster who gets off on anarchy?"

"That's a cop-out," Nell said. "There's always more to it, even if the killer doesn't realize it. He probably is sexually dysfunctional, but with his statues, there is no one to laugh at him if he can't perform. He's not psychotic, he's psychopathic."

"Tomato-tomahto," Casey said. "If we don't stop him, he'll kill my sister."

39

Hailangelo laid a golden tablecloth over the fold-out table. On it, he set champagne glasses. "Come, Millie, have a seat."

He could tell Leila had no desire to sit but she realized she had no choice. She appeared still to be dazed from his initial assault. She half-fell into the wooden chair next to him at the table. Hailangelo opened a textbook on realist sculpture. It offered pictures of the casting process for creating the molds for each statue.

"This is how it's done," Hailangelo said. "It's the same process I used with Todd Narziss."

She choked back tears.

"I'll mix the plaster and cover you in it. It's like being covered with wet sand at the beach. Did your friends ever do that to you when you were a child?"

She nodded.

"You see? This will be like that."

"That was sort of fun." She sniffed.

"Precisely. And it leaves your complexion brilliant, like a mud-and-cucumber treatment. Then we'll take off sections piece by piece and I'll build the mold for your statue from there." He watched her closely to see how she would react.

"I'm sorry I've been so silly. It's just…with the rape when I was younger…"

"Of course," Hailangelo handed her a glass of champagne, toasted her, and smiled. "It's only natural to assume other men are monsters. But I assure you, I'm just an artist who is quite fond of you."

She pulled her hair to one side.

"It's an honor to work with you," he said. "In return, you'll be immortalized."

She acted pleased as she tipped back half her drink. He guessed she felt resigned, and that the last thing she desired was to keep living her imperfect life forever. Maybe death would release her from the memories of her rape.

"Think of how pleased Amelia will be to see your statue."

Leila scoffed. "I think she'd be creeped out by it. One of me is more than enough for anyone."

"Oh, it's pretty clear she adores you."

She yawned, stretched, and swayed, trying to focus on Hailangelo's face.

He beamed back at her. "It's nappy time, Millie."

For a moment, she defiantly held her head up with her hands. The wine was uncontaminated, but he had spiked her glass before they arrived. Hailangelo snickered, calmly stood, stretched his arms, and walked away. The last thing she saw before losing consciousness was her captor striding toward her, holding a rope. Suddenly her head slipped through her hands and planted on the folding table with a thud.

§

Casey and Nell sped down Highway 33 past the sign for Junction B. The sun had melted into the horizon. Casey's eyelids drooped and he wished he had a latte with a double shot of espresso. He pointed ahead. "There are the train tracks." The headlights illuminated them.

Nell passed through the intersection, then pulled to the side of the highway. Farmland, snowy fields, telephone poles, and patches of trees extended into apparent infinity. They got out of the car.

Nell turned on her flashlight. Walking together, they headed toward the train tracks. The frigid air nipped at their ears. On the other side of the tracks, Nell flashed the light on two cars: an old black Chevelle and a black Chevy Suburban, the latter of which had several antennae.

"I recognize the SUV from the Milwaukee bureau," Nell said.

"How'd they get here so fast?"

"We had a unit in the area."

"The Chevelle is Hailangelo's." Casey yawned and squinted. "Is that it? In the tree back there?" He used his hand to shield his eyes from the swirling wind and snow. In the distance, though it was dark, they could just barely make out the gargantuan oak with what looked like a deer blind at the top. He sprinted toward it.

"Wait up," she called after him, pursuing.

Casey slowed as he got about thirty yards from the tree. He could barely see his feet.

Nell walked behind him. She took out her gun and held it under her flashlight. They marched through a cornfield. Stalks, snow, and frozen dirt crunched underfoot with each step. Wind gusted across the fields, sucking moisture from Casey's cheeks and leaving his skin raw. He could barely see, but Mother Nature would not keep him from his sister.

Nell flashed her light along the base of a tree and, as she panned the beam upwards, she found the deer stand. "Has to be ten feet in the air."

A hydraulic lift stood next to the tree, elevated. The wind picked up, lowering the chill factor and blowing even more snow, forcing Casey to shut his eyes. He focused on not falling into a narcoleptic attack. *Your most important breath is your next one.*

When the wind died down a bit, he could see that the wooden structure was as big as an apartment and completely encased in the deer blind's camouflage. Nell turned off her flashlight. They walked ahead in the dark, eyes still adjusting to the night.

Casey tripped over a stump and fell to the ground, giving himself a face wash in the snow. He couldn't decide what stung worse—the fall, the snow, or the embarrassment of it all.

"You okay?" she said, crouching down to him.

Casey rolled to a sitting position, wiped his face, and turned to look behind him. "What the hell was that?"

Nell turned the light on the stump. It wasn't a stump at all.

It was a corpse.

40

Casey scrambled away from the corpse, kicking snow, some of it bunching under his pants and biting his ankles. "Aaah! Holy crap! Is that real? Can you hear me?"

"Shhh!" Nell whispered. "Yes, it's real, you're not hallucinating."

Casey patted his legs. "I'm awake. I'm freezing. This is happening." Who was it? Please don't be Leila, he thought. Please please please.

Nell flashed her light on the body—it was a male. She reached in the dead man's pocket and pulled out a wallet. She flipped it open and shined the light on the identification. "No."

"What?" Casey scrambled to his feet and looked over Nell's shoulder. The badge belonged to FBI Agent Nmandi Agu. He was bald, fit, and chiseled. His face had been scarred. "Did you know him?"

Nell exhaled, holding the light on Agu's body. She whispered, "When I turn off this light, crouch down."

"Why?"

"Just do it." She turned it off.

Casey did as he was told. "What's going on?"

Nell whispered, "The bullet wound in Agent Agu's chest suggests a forty-five degree angle. The shooter is in the tree."

"How could he shoot in the dark?" Casey whispered.

"He could have used a night scope, a standard tool for hunters. Or, maybe it was just a lucky shot."

"Well, if he's got a night scope—" ...*crack! Pop-pop! Crack!*

They dropped flat to the ground. Death—cold and impersonal—stared Casey in the face. Would they lay here for a short time? Or indefinitely, objects to be stumbled over in the dark? Would crows pick at them in the morning, before authorities arrived? He expected the rifle shots to ring out, the bullets to pierce his body, at any moment. But they didn't.

"He's not shooting at us," Nell whispered. "It's coming from the other side."

"The other agents?" Casey said.

"Probably."

Pop, crack, pop-pop-crack! Most of the shots sounded like they came from the ground level, but a few definitely originated from above. "Come on," Nell whispered.

As his eyes adjusted to the dark, he could still barely see Nell or the tree. They trudged through snow another ten yards and fell at the base of the huge oak. Two-by-fours had been nailed to the trunk, forming a ladder. But the hydraulic lift blocked part of it. The deer

279

blind reminded Casey of a tree house he and Leila had had as kids, where they'd sit and eat s'mores, read comic books, and suck on long blades of grass.

Nell handed him the flashlight and whispered in his ear, "Shine this for me." He did.

Pop-crack-crack-crack-pop! The gunfire sounded closer. Not near enough to buzz in his ear, but close enough to make him sweat despite the wintry temperatures.

Nell climbed, first on the hydraulic lift, then on the wooden ladder on the trunk. She held her pistol in her chapped, pink hand, her other hand covered by a thin, leather glove. Nell ascended half-way up the tree. Then two-thirds.

The gunfire stopped. Had one of the shooters died? Had all of them? Silence never sounded so wonderful.

Nell reached the top without a peep or even a shadow from Hailangelo. It hadn't been this quiet since they'd arrived; it was as if even the tree held its breath. Disconcerted, Casey aimed the flashlight with care, such that she could see but not so that it would be visible from inside the stand. Nell slowly moved the gun over the top of the ladder, pointing it into the deer stand, above her head and out of view.

Four heavy footsteps emanated from inside the stand. Hailangelo kicked Nell's gun from her hand like a soccer striker; the weapon fell in an arc into the darkness, landing with a staccato crunch on the field about ten yards away.

Nell lost her balance, fell backward, groped for the ladder, but only succeeded in catching a handful of air. She fell ten feet and landed on her side with a thud and a crack.

Casey extinguished the CombatLight so he couldn't be seen, then lunged to her. "Nell...Nell! Wake up." He felt weird saying that to her; usually it was the other way around. "Don't leave me now, please." His eyes adjusted to the darkness enough that he could see her chest rise and fall with each breath. But her arm appeared broken and her eyes rolled back; it looked like she had hard-boiled eggs in the sockets. He glanced up at the deer stand and, when he saw no shadowy figures, used the flashlight to scan the field for her pistol. He couldn't find it. Had he hallucinated the gun falling? No, not unless he had imagined Nell plummeting, and clearly that wasn't the case. He turned to confirm she was still there. He crouched down and touched her. He wasn't having a sleep attack. He really was standing at the base of Hailangelo's lair in the middle of nowhere, without a weapon. Meanwhile, the psychopath had the rifle, the higher ground, and Leila. Casey began to panic, frantically searching the snow for the gun. Had it sunk deep in the snow, out of sight? In the shadows, the black metal of the pistol couldn't be more camouflaged. Casey closed his eyes, recalled the trajectory of the gun, and scanned the light—back and forth, back and forth, back and forth, walking toward the location where he'd heard the sound of the gun landing. He saw nothing but snow and footprints.

Eventually, he realized he'd gone beyond where it could possibly have landed, and backtracked toward Nell. He knew it meant risking Hailangelo seeing him, possibly shooting him, but without her weapon he'd stand little-to-no chance. He walked back to Nell, but found no gun.

Should he wait until more help arrived? Would his sister be dead by then? Would she be half-human, half-statue? He had no choice but to crawl around in search of the gun. It had to be there. He held the light under his chin, got down on his knees and groped the ground. The snow quickly coated his jeans, and soon his body heat melted the snow and saturated his pants around the knees. And still he had no pistol to show for it.

His stomach ached from the realization that he wouldn't find the weapon, that his nightmare about losing Elena and Leila would come true, and possibly Nell to boot. He flinched at a sharp pain in his knee.

Had he knelt on a rock? It was too hard for a stick. He reached down into the snow, and couldn't quite get the object dislodged. He used both hands to dig around it, then extracted it. Nell's gun!

He held it in his right hand, the CombatLight in his left, and aimed them both up toward the top of the tree. Still no sign of Hailangelo. He turned off the light, tossed it at the base of the tree, tucked the gun in the back of his waistband, and climbed expeditiously in the dark. Eventually, his head was level with the deer stand. He peered over the edge, peeked inside the lighted stand, and saw Leila tied with rope, hanging by her wrists from the ceiling, arms apart, fully clothed in a black sweater and jeans. Rope also bound her ankles together. Hailangelo stood in front of her, facing her, and holding his syringe near her chin. Her eyes were shut.

Casey aimed Nell's gun at Hailangelo, squinting down the barrel to align the sight with the kidnapper's back.

The sculptor startled and shouted, "I'll kill her! Drop your weapon or I'll make her my next masterpiece." He held the needle to her carotid artery.

Casey's shoulders and head slouched, his hands flopping to the floor of the deer stand.

Hailangelo relaxed and cackled. "Narcolepsy, the greatest sculptor of all. Bravo!"

Casey didn't move.

"You were so close," Hailangelo taunted, casually approaching Casey. "But your impotence is your defining feature. You know the only thing worse than kissing your sister? Thinking her statue is sexy."

Casey's head snapped up. "Psych!" he said, raising Nell's weapon and firing. *POP! POP! POP!*

Two of the three bullets from the Glock 22 ripped through Hailangelo's collarbone on his left side. He fell backwards to the floor, bleeding.

The kickback from the gun had messed with his aim, but Casey had been happy to hit him at all. Hailangelo scrambled for the hypodermic needle. Casey climbed into the deer stand.

Hailangelo grabbed the syringe with his right arm, stood up, and hastily stabbed backhanded at Leila's chest.

"No!" Casey shouted, reaching toward her in vain. Metal clinked on metal. The needle had hit her father's dog tags!

POP! POP!

Blood sprayed from the side of Hailangelo's head. He screamed, fell to the floor, dropped his needle, and rolled onto his back. He clutched his head wound and groaned, blood seeping through his hand.

Casey's heart thumped like a rabbit entrapped. Had he killed him? Casey kept the gun trained on the sculptor.

A moment later, a skinny Latino appeared on the ladder behind Casey. He aimed a pistol at the reporter. "FBI," he said. "Drop your weapon!"

Casey complied and raised his hands. "Don't shoot! He's the killer." He pointed at Hailangelo.

The agent climbed into the stand, hustled to Hailangelo and kicked the syringe away from him. He bound Hailangelo's wrists and ankles with plastic ties, then hog-tied them together. The agent turned and pointed the gun at Casey's chest. "I'm Special Agent Antonio Torres. Step away from the weapon."

Casey did, hands still in the air.

Agent Torres grabbed Nell's gun and looked at Casey. "Who are you?"

"Casey Thread, the reporter working with Special Agent Nell Jenner." Casey nodded toward Leila, still hanging by her wrists. "That's my sister." He took a deep breath and let it out slowly.

Agent Torres stared at Leila, seemingly half-sympathetic and half-incredulous. He muttered, *"Ay, Dios Mío."*

Casey strode toward his sister. "Let's cut her down."

Torres snapped back to reality. "Wait! We need photographic evidence." He holstered his weapon, grabbed his cell phone, and took pictures of Leila.

Casey hated leaving her tied for another second, but also didn't want another abuser to avoid prosecution for what he had done to Leila.

Hailangelo groaned and started to roll, trying to hurtle himself over the edge of the deer stand.

Torres ran to him, kicked him in the groin and grabbed his shirt.

Hailangelo moaned.

Torres opened his cell and pressed a speed-dial button. "We've got four agents down, one possibly DOA. Suspect is in custody with multiple GSW's." He closed his cell and said to Casey, "The helicopters should be here any second."

"What the hell took them so long?" Casey asked.

"They were already deployed on a separate sting operation in Milwaukee," Torres said. "It has been a tough night."

Nell! They had to help her. "Agent Jenner fell off the ladder," Casey said. "Hailangelo kicked her."

"She all right?"

"I don't know. She was okay a minute ago." Casey ran to the ladder. She hadn't moved since her fall. "Nell?"

No response.

He climbed down to her. "Hey gorgeous, you okay?"

She stirred. "My arm's on fire...the rest of me is a Nell-cream cone."

"Help is coming."

"Is Leila all right?"

"Unconscious."

"Go to her."

"I'll be right back," Casey said and climbed to the deer stand.

Torres used a combat knife to saw at the bindings holding Leila. She remained unconscious.

Casey grabbed a blanket, wrapped it around Leila, sat on the floor, and held her. "Leila, it's Casey. It's okay. You're safe now. I'm so, so, sorry." If she died now, she'd never get a chance to accept herself, find her passion, fall in love, experience contentment in her adult life. If that happened, he would never forgive himself. What would he tell Mother? She'd hold that damn kabob in every nightmare for the rest of his life. He hugged his little sister once more, then rose and marched to Hailangelo. "Why?"

Agent Torres held Casey back.

"Why did you do it?" Casey shouted.

"Calm down, sir," Torres said.

Hailangelo tittered in delirium.

Casey hadn't forgotten all the scientific facts Nell had shared, or her theories on why Hailangelo had committed his crimes. He figured Hailangelo might be aware of some of them, but probably not all. Still, for some reason, he wanted to hear an explanation from the man himself.

Hailangelo said nothing, cachinnating until his eyes rolled back.

A bald Caucasian FBI agent climbed into the deer stand and unzipped the tarp serving as the wall on one side of the blind. Cold air rushed in.

"Casey, this is Special Agent Anderson," Agent Torres said. Anderson nodded and went right to taking pictures with a high-powered camera on a strap around his neck.

A helicopter thundered in the distance. Casey watched it approach the deer stand. It swooshed overhead. The wind blew their hair and vibrated the sides of the stand. Casey broke into goose bumps. A searchlight from the chopper scanned the ground around the tree until it found Nell and the other fallen agents.

A man in black FBI gear and a Kevlar helmet hopped out of the chopper, clinging to a wire as they lowered him to the deer stand. Anderson released Hailangelo from the bindings that hogtied him and placed handcuffs on him, while the agent from the helicopter attached a harness around Hailangelo then linked it to his own harness. A cable lifted the men into the helicopter. Hailangelo winced and groaned at the compression of the harness on his wounds. The helicopter took off and Anderson returned to photographing the scene.

After the chopper got some distance away from the tree, Casey turned to Torres. "Why didn't they take Leila first?"

"There's another chopper coming."

"How do you know Leila's condition isn't more critical?"

"She's breathing."

"So is Hailangelo."

"Maybe not for long. He's critically wounded. We need to get as much information as possible out of him in case he goes into shock."

Incredulous, Casey shouted, "But Leila's the victim!" He curled his fingers like talons.

Torres looked at Casey as if snakes had popped out of his head singing "Mary Had a Little Lamb." The agent patted the air between them in a calming motion. "Your sister will be fine. They're coming, and we'll take good care of her."

"Hey T," Agent Anderson shouted. "Check this out." With a gloved hand, Anderson held up a vial.

Torres read the label. "Zolpidem."

"Ambien," Anderson said, looking at Casey. "These days, Z-drugs are the most common date rape drugs. Much more accessible than roofies."

Casey placed his hands on his head. "Oh no, no, no…"

"Calm down," Torres said. "There's no indication he got that far."

Casey dropped his hands to his side, nodded, and took a deep breath. "Will she be okay?"

"Assuming that's all he gave her?" Anderson said. "Yeah."

An identical FBI chopper landed in the field, near Nell. Two men from the chopper loaded Nell and Agent Agu onto stretchers and into the aircraft. They worked with the efficiency of a unit operating in enemy territory. The helicopter took off.

Casey saw a third chopper in the distance. When it hovered above the tree, an officer dropped to the deer stand on a wire and latched a harness around Leila. Groggy, she threw her arms around him. The winch in the chopper hoisted them up.

Torres turned to Casey. "Stay here. She's in good hands." The helicopter ascended.

"Leila!" Casey shouted in full throat, then broke into tears, more out of frustration and exhaustion than anything else. He glanced around the deer stand at the mural, allowing himself to be judged through the depicted binoculars. The agents shared a look and shook their heads.

Anderson said, "This is crazy."

Casey ran his hands through his pompadour. "This is nothing."

Both agents turned toward him, surprised.

"Wait 'til you see his basement."

41

Agent Torres drove Casey to Green Bay Hospital, where doctors treated Leila and Nell. As they entered the building, Torres glanced at Casey and said, "I have to admit, if someone had told me the narcoleptic reporter would be the one guy to walk away from this fiasco unscathed, I would have told him he was nuts."

"Yeah, well," Casey said, "I wouldn't say unscathed. I'm about to curl up into a ball in the corner and rock incessantly."

Torres chuckled.

Casey's phone played "Message in a Bottle." It was another text message, this time from Samantha Narziss. In it, she reported that she had discovered her husband's affair with Elena, taken the kids, and left Todd. While she didn't have proof that he had ordered a hit on Elena, she forwarded to Casey cryptic e-mail messages between her husband and Skeeto DeWillis. The notes alluded to a kidnapping plot. At one point in the messages, Todd Narziss solicited Skeeto to "put the fear of God in her." The frequency of the messages had intensified just before Elena had disappeared. Samantha wrote to Casey, "I tolerated a cheat for the benefit of my children. But I can't take it any more."

Casey figured Narziss had asked Skeeto to convince Elena to either eliminate their bastard child or to move back to Quito. But Hailangelo had either beaten them to it, or killed Skeeto so he could get Elena back. Either way, Casey envisioned a cover story. He couldn't help it; he had become trained to think that way. He had rent to pay, too.

Torres and Casey entered the hospital without any problems, thanks to Torres' FBI identification. Casey peeked into Leila's room. He turned back to Torres and thumbed in her direction. "I'm going to check on my sister."

Torres nodded. "I'll see how Agent Jenner is doing."

Leila turned away from the TV and smiled at her brother.

"You're awake!" Casey almost didn't recognize her in a white hospital gown. She appeared rather...angelic. "How are you?"

"I'm good." She smiled.

Good? "I'm sorry," Casey glanced over his shoulder and pointed at the hallway. "I must have the wrong room." He looked back at her. "I was looking for my sister, Leila Thread?"

"Can it. I'm still alive. That's good, right?"

"Yes. Yes, it is."

"Whatever he did to me, I was out nearly the whole time. I don't have many memories to compartmentalize."

"What do you remember?"

"I think he drugged me."

Casey nodded. "He did."

"But according to the nurse, the rape kit was negative."

Casey exhaled hard, leaned over, and gently hugged her. "That's great news." He stood back up. "Listen, Leila, I'm so, so, sorry."

"Hey, it was my decision to go off with him. You would think I'd have known better."

"Don't blame yourself. You're not the first woman to date a man who turned women into famous statues."

Leila raised her brows skeptically.

He snickered. "Okay, maybe you are. But you can't assume everyone is out to get you, or next thing you know your apartment will be lined with tinfoil."

"Ha, I'll stick to my paintings."

"Good call. Anything I can do?"

"Help the feds throw him in prison and melt the key. Then write an article so other people can avoid sludge like him. Think you can handle that?"

"I do." A smile gradually spread across his face. His next breaths were getting sweeter all the time.

Their mother entered the room. "Leila? Oh, my darling, sweet child."

Shantell bashfully curled inside the door, her finger in her mouth. Casey encouraged her to come stand next to him. "I won't bite," he said. Elzbieta shuffled toward Leila, arms outstretched dramatically, and embraced her daughter like never before.

"Ow, Mom, I have bruises," Leila said.

"Oh, sorry, dear. Are you okay?"

"I'm fine. I actually don't remember much."

"Oh, thank God you're all right," Elzbieta said.

"For the first time in years, I feel happy," Leila said. "I've dealt with the rape, and I finally gave that"—she glanced at Shantell—"clown his comeuppance."

Elzbieta looked at Casey for an explanation, and he shook his head as if to say, "Don't ask." She held her daughter's hand with both of her own. "You'll be back to work at Fixate Factory before you know it."

"That's not a big concern right now, Mother," Leila said.

"Well, a job is nothing to sneeze at, dear."

Leila changed the subject. "Ma, a man from the FBI said Casey saved my life."

Mother crossed herself.

"I had help from Nell and the other agents," Casey said.

"Where is that bastard, Football-angelo?" Elzbieta said. "If he's not dead I'll—"

"Ma, it's Hail-angelo," Casey said. "And it's okay. He's in FBI custody. The feds will handle him."

Elzbieta sat in a chair, deep in thought. "What if he escapes?"

"Casey shot him multiple times," Leila said.

"Oh my," Elzbieta said. "Is he dying?"

"They flew him to a hospital," Casey said. "He survived and is under tight security." Casey placed his hands on his mother's shoulders, leaned in, and whispered. "Hailangelo killed at least eleven people in four states, Ma. He abducted Lei; they're not going to let him get away with this."

"Thank God," Elzbieta said, placing her palm over her heart, as if trying to control how fast it pumped. She opened her purse, extracted knitting materials, and knitted feverishly. "I really wish we could smoke in here."

"It's a hospital, Mom," Leila said. "You know…the place where you're supposed to get healthier?"

"Yeah, well, my brain would feel much healthier with some nicotine."

Casey raised his brows and said gently, "They do have nicotine patches for that, Ma." Elzbieta scoffed at him. "Who died and made you Surgeon General Koop?"

"Elena Ortega," Casey said.

Shantell approached Leila. "Why are you wearing that funny dress?"

"It's a hospital gown," Leila said. "Standard issue."

Shantell wrinkled her nose. "What's standard issue?"

Casey whispered in his mother's ear. "Bad news, Ma. Shantell's mom didn't make it."

She stopped knitting. "Oh my. Where's the father?"

He shrugged. "Out of the picture, as far as I know. I'll ask Agent Torres to see if Shantell has family that can take care of her, okay?"

"Oh." Elzbieta nodded reluctantly and resumed knitting.

"What? I thought you'd be thrilled."

His mother cocked her head. "Well…I was sort of getting used to the little troublemaker. But, hell, I can barely manage myself. When you get to be my age, you pick your battles."

"You're doing fine, Ma. I'm going to check on Nell." As Casey opened the door to leave, his mother turned toward him.

"I could really use some grandchildren."

Casey froze in the doorway. "Easy, Ma, we met a little over a week ago."

"Yeah? Well, I've been waiting twenty-eight years."

42

Agent Torres sat bedside by Nell; they stopped talking when Casey entered the room.

Torres turned to him. "Well, well, well. It's the Caped Columnist."

"Hey, he does have super powers," Nell said. "I mean, faking narcolepsy; are you kidding me?"

Casey raised a hand and bowed his head. "Hold your applause." Torres must have filled her in. He approached Nell's bed. "You two know each other?"

"We were in the academy together," Torres said.

Casey felt a pang of jealousy. He nodded at Torres and looked at Nell. "How are you, gorgeous?"

Nell glanced down at her arm. "It's just a little broken."

"Better than a little dead," Casey said.

"Don't let her fool you." Torres pointed at her arm. "Those are stitches from the stabbing."

Casey winced. "Seems like she'll live."

"Don't be too disappointed," Nell said.

"They're running a few more tests," Torres said, "but the X-rays on her back were negative, other than some nasty contusions."

"Ten feet is a long fall," Casey said.

Nell tried to downplay it. "Eh, it's like a basketball player falling after a dunk. Not a big deal."

"She'll be out of here by the end of the day," Torres said, glancing up at the ceiling. "Lord help us."

"Rats," Casey said, "and here I was going to ask your mother to see your head carved in cheese before you got released from the hospital."

Torres raised his brows at her. "Your mother has your head carved in cheese?"

Nell smirked. "It's a long story. One far more excruciating than broken bones or stitches."

"You know what they say, the apple doesn't fall…" Torres noticed Casey and Nell staring at each other, so he trailed off, cleared his throat, and stood up. "Um, I could use a cup of coffee. Take care, NJ."

"Thanks, T," Nell said, "for everything."

"You bet. Mr. Thread?" Torres shook Casey's hand. "Thanks for your help out there."

Casey put a fist to his mouth to prevent a yawn. "Thank you."

"Well, if I can do anything for you…" Torres said.

Casey took out his business card and handed it to Torres.

"Actually, if you ever get a hot lead for a big story, I'd love to get an anonymous tip."

Torres read the card. "'Casey Thread: Freelance Journalist.' Nice." He nodded, put it in his pocket, and patted it. "I'll keep this in mind."

"Thanks."

Torres left.

Casey pulled a chair up to Nell's bed. "Nice digs you have here."

"I know, right? I was hoping for cashmere quilts, but you can't have it all."

"You're getting soft, Agent." He had missed her wit.

"I do have a soft spot…"

His face brightened. "For?"

"Chocolate martinis."

"Oh." Casey blushed and glanced away.

"You didn't think I was referring to you, did you?"

He said reluctantly, "That would have been nice."

"Come on, you're a Green Bay boy and I'm a Windy City girl. Long-distance relationships are doomed from the start."

"That's true. You'd have to get a lot sicker for me to wear a Chicago jersey for you."

"I'll work on that."

"But seriously, I travel so much it doesn't matter where I live."

"That's a lie," she said. "I travel, too, for cases. But home is still where you return, it's your center, your base, where your body recharges and your soul finds peace. How could it work if we're constantly coming and going?"

He stared for a moment at her IV. "I'd buy a day planner?"

Nell used the remote to turn off her TV. "Come on, Case, you'd miss the Hail, and Bay Beach."

"I don't have to live in Green Bay. Sure I'll miss Bay Beach, but Chicago has Navy Pier—where they filmed The Dark Knight."

Nell pursed her lips and raised her brows. "Checkmate, you win. When are you moving?"

Casey beamed. "Well, I should go back and get my things, but all I'd need is a place to stay."

She squinted at him. "You're not implying you want to live with me, are you?"

Someone knocked on the door to Nell's hospital room. It was a woman in her fifties. "Agent Jenner?"

"Yes," Nell said.

"I'm Susan Bachowski. From Galesburg?" She had the hulky bone structure of a discus thrower.

Nell said, "Yes, of course, Jenny's mother. Please, come in. I'd give you a hug except for my arm."

"And your stitches," Casey reminded her. Good grief, he hadn't even moved in with her yet and they already sounded like an old married couple.

"I just came to thank you for catching him." Susan entered the room carrying a glass vase of colorful flowers. Casey guessed her height to be six-foot-three.

"You heard?" Nell said.

"Yes, your bureau chief called with the good news. I couldn't cope with Jenny's death—even begin to heal—until her killer was in jail or dead. I know it sounds harsh, but there's a visceral impulse for a parent that's just so...to think more mothers and daughters could have gone through the same ordeal! I'm just so relieved."

"That's over now," Nell said. "We caught him. I can't believe you came all this way. You're so sweet."

"The worst feeling is waiting for something—that you know will have a major impact on your life—but over which you have no control," Susan said. "You ended that wait, that helpless feeling. I didn't know how to repay you, so I came to tell you in person how much it means to me." She set the flowers on the counter near Nell's bed. "I left right after I got the call."

"That's very kind of you, Mrs. Bachowski," Nell said. "But really, you should thank Casey."

"Casey?"

"Oh, I'm just a reporter, ma'am." He stood and shook her huge hand.

Susan sneered down at him. "I hate reporters."

Casey instinctively leaned back.

"They'd call me all the time to ask if the police had made any progress, or if I'd hired an investigator. I wish they'd just leave me alone."

That created awkward silence.

"Casey's the reporter who tracked down the killer," Nell said.

"You found him?"

Casey hunched. "With Agent Jenner's help."

Susan bear-hugged Casey...a little too tightly, lifting him off the ground as if he were her long-lost child.

Her grip on his chest squished him and restricted his voice. "Okay...thank you, thank you."

Susan let him go.

Casey gasped.

Nell chuckled. "We make a great team."

Susan's countenance darkened. "That monster ruined my life, and the lives of God-knows-how-many others." Then she glanced at Nell. "If there's anything I can do to help make sure he doesn't hurt anyone else—"

"I'll let you know," Nell said. "We may want you to testify, or speak at sentencing."

Susan nodded. "Absolutely."

"You could help me with my article," Casey said. "If that's okay with you, Agent Jenner."

"It's up to Mrs. Bachowski."

Casey interviewed Susan Bachowski about the night her daughter disappeared. She said Jenny had gone to a movie with Alyssa, Jenny's best friend from next door. Alyssa said they were in line for popcorn when a man with short-brown hair approached Jenny and asked if she were a model.

"Jenny, of course, was flattered," Susan said. "Who wouldn't be? I mean, a dark, handsome, older man says that to you? Come on. Every girl wants to be picked from a crowd. Jenny had my height and her dad's slender frame. Hailangelo told Jenny he was a sculptor, and that his work had been in galleries in Manhattan."

"Had they?" Casey said.

"I checked." Susan said. "He does in fact have an exhibit there. He fooled so many young women. It's every mother's nightmare. I just can't believe you caught him. This is really happening. My daughter really is dead." She fanned herself with her hand and held back tears.

Casey tried to focus on the moment and not allow his mind to wander back to that basement or those statues. Susan broke down and cried.

Casey fetched a tissue for her.

She blotted her eye liner and sniffled. "Do you have children, Casey?"

"No, ma'am."

"Someday you will and, when you do, you'll know why what you two have done here is a miracle granted by God."

Casey glanced at Nell. She shrugged as if to say, "Could be."

43

By lunch the next day, Nell and Leila were out of the hospital and Casey took them and Elzbieta out to eat at Fixate Factory.

Leila's boss, Frank, dried his hands with a towel. He had a full head of gray hair, a matching thick mustache, and a rotund figure. "Leila, by golly, great to see you in one piece. Your mom told me all about what happened. You eat free today." They ordered soup and cappuccinos to warm their bones, and beer bread to fill their rumbling stomachs.

Kenny walked in the door. "Case! What's up?"

"Hey Kenny, I'm just happy to be here. You ready for the big game?"

"I don't know, Case, it will be awfully tough for the Hail without Narziss or Cummings. Are you going to it?"

"Of course." A TV mounted to the wall behind the bar showed ESPN footage of Narziss leaving the hospital with his head bandaged. Casey's mother leaned toward him, pointing at the TV. "Why can't you be a nice boy like Narziss?"

Casey fell into a narcoleptic attack. Not now, he thought. How embarrassing.

AREA MAN'S MOTHER COMPARES HIM TO DRUGGIE JERK

Nell closed her eyes and laughed.

Words at the bottom of the TV screen scrolled from right to left and read, "Hail star Todd Narziss assaulted, ruled out for the season."

Elzbieta shook her son's shoulders. "Casey, snap out of it."

He came to. Kenny stood next to them, staring into his cupped hands, rocking slightly while gazing into his "box." Kenny said, "Casey takes me to Hail games."

Elzbieta looked confused. "Pardon me?"

Kenny leaned in, rocking slightly. "Casey is my friend." Kenny held up his cupped hands so she could see them. "He gave me this no-receipt gift."

"What gift?" She squinted and frowned. "I don't see anything."

"We're buddies who talk on the phone," Kenny said. "He takes me to Hail games. He never forgets."

Elzbieta hesitated. "I...see. But what do you mean, 'no-receipt gift'?"

Casey figured she would have to know or it would bother her.

Kenny stopped rocking and said, "It's a present you can't buy. And I like that kind best."

Casey winked at Kenny and pointed to him with approval. They made fists, bumped each other's knuckles, and pulled their hands away like squid in water.

Leila approached the table, holding a black Sharpie aloft. "Found one. Who wants to sign Nell's cast first?" She handed it to Casey.

Casey took it and drew a chocolate martini on the palm of her cast. Nell smiled. He kissed her forehead.

Leila frowned. "Get a room."

44

Nell and Casey packed belongings inside his Green Bay apartment to prepare for his move two hundred miles south to Chicago. She held up a recent issue of *Sports Scene* magazine. On the cover was a picture of New York celebrating its playoff victory over Green Bay, and the Hail players hanging their heads in defeat. "Look at this," she said, grinning as she read the headline. "'Sex, Drugs, and Murder: The Story Behind the Hail's Playoff Exit—cover story by Casey Thread.' Wow."

Casey taped a moving box shut and stood up, his back sore. "Even a narcoleptic squirrel finds a nut once in a while."

"Did they pay you more for the cover story?"

"It's funding my moving expenses." The magazine issue had set sales records. Casey's editors loved him. He had even gotten a congratulatory call from the publisher, whom Casey had never met. He wrote about Hailangelo a bit in the *Sports Scene* story, but saved most of the serial-killer saga for a prominent men's fashion magazine, well as an interview on a cable TV show. He detailed how Samantha Narziss had provided evidence in the form of email messages that her husband had plotted to have Skeeto make his bastard child disappear—all to prevent the stain of an affair from tainting the image of the Hail or their star player. But they were football men, not trained killers, so they were terrible at it. That allowed a true pro, Hailangelo, to beat them to her.

Now Nell draped her arms over Casey's shoulders. "I'm so proud of you."

"Couldn't have done it without you."

They kissed. Casey said, "There's one thing I still don't understand."

"What?" Nell said.

"Everyone else—even my mother to a degree—hasn't really accepted my narcolepsy."

"That still surprises you?"

"No, but the fact that you get it does."

"I like you for who you are, and what you do while you're awake."

"Huh," Casey said.

"What?"

"It's a coincidence, because I feel the same about you."

Nell smiled. They grabbed boxes and carried them to the moving truck, their muscles tightening against the cold.

45

Casey crawled out from bed and found Nell cooking at the stove in her Chicago apartment.

"Welcome to your first morning at La Maison de Nell. Hope you like scrambled eggs and slightly burnt toast." Her curly hair was up in a clip, and her black apron said in white letters, French Kiss the Cook.

Casey had never wanted her more. His stomach growled. "Considering I haven't had a decent breakfast in a week, that is gourmet." They had decided to take it slowly, simply cuddling his first night there. He knew most couples didn't approach it that way, but most couples hadn't recently been in Hailangelo's basement. Now Nell set Casey's plate on the table in front of him.

"Thank you for cooking." He took a bite of eggs. "Mmm." He chewed and swallowed. "I still can't believe Elena and Skeeto are gone."

Nell sighed. "I know. It sucks. How did Kurt Vonnegut put it?"

"'So it goes.'"

"So it goes."

"Despite what Skeeto did, I miss him, his voice, his jokes, his overzealous conga playing."

"I know, and I miss Elena. But she would be rolling her eyes at us moping. She'd crack a joke to lighten the mood."

"Or text us something witty," Casey said. They had grieved Elena at her memorial, and Nell was right that their friend would want them to heal. Casey felt fortunate he had Nell to understand what he had been through and to make happier memories with. Life—with or without narcolepsy—would never be perfect. But with someone to share it with, he could cope.

He felt inspired to tell her how he felt. "You are the shores of Pasadena, fair and contoured, like gentle caresses, with the intelligence of a witness to years of missed steps and holding hands, of playful splashing and aching laughter. And I, I am the ocean who encompasses, surrounds you and holds you, washes and secures you without a thought, without doubt and with confidence forever. I am on your horizon even when I recede. And we are both enriched when again we meet."

She kissed him. "Did you just make that up?"

He shrugged. "I've been thinking about it for awhile."

She removed her clip, shook out her hair, and sat on his lap. "I'm ready."

"Ready ready?"

Nell smiled and nodded. "The bigger question is, are you ready, sleepyhead? You know you can't fall asleep on a girl."

Casey grinned as they stood. "You keep me wide awake." He picked her up and carried her into the bedroom.

Their breakfast cooled.

§

Hailangelo lay in a hospital bed in the medical ward of a high-security prison in central Wisconsin. A tall male nurse, strong as a steed, dressed in all white, brought him his mail, a solitary letter postmarked from Seattle. Interesting, Hailangelo thought. He knew a few people in the art scene there. Did they want his work in their galleries? The envelope had been addressed to the correctional facility. But how did an artist in Seattle know how to reach him in prison? The phrase correctional facility made Hailangelo chortle; as if locking him up would somehow "correct" him. He opened the letter.

> *Dear Hailangelo:*
>
> *Greetings from the great Northwest. It's terrible to see any genius struck down in his prime, and so it is with a melancholy spirit that I write to you today. Your statues are resplendent, your talents brilliant, and I met the news of your arrest with extreme dismay.*
>
> *Do you hear it too—the reverberations of the music, dissonant chords and bass vibrations? I experience it whenever someone passes me on the sidewalk and I say "hello" and they walk past*

without acknowledgement, as if I do not exist. I feel it every time I ask someone to hang out and they contrive an excuse. You see, I think I exist but, if nobody acknowledges me, do I really? I suppose I might as well not. The solution then, as you know, is to make them notice. You've done that so artistically, leaving your work on college campuses. I'm sure that was hard for you, to part with such radiance, but I understand. It was the only way to get the attention you deserved.

The music, for me, is the same my mother used to play on the piano in our living room. She wasn't a "kid person," she'd say. I have no siblings, so I'd play alone in my bedroom, listening to her perform concerti, feeling the piano strings vibrate through the walls and in the floor. I feel the music right now, in fact. My hands shake.

I write this with confidence that we are of a kindred spirit, that you can sympathize with me, and detect my exuberance to become your protégé. Most artists aren't appreciated while they're alive—but I appreciate my contemporaries. I know I have much to learn from you. I also realize that most phenomena opt not to teach because, why would you, when you can simply...do? But now, what with your incapacitation, I summon the courage to ask. Will you be my mentor?

I promise not to let you down. I'll follow your directions precisely. I won't hesitate. I'm punctual. Together, we can turn our solo music into symphonies. Your work will carry on. I anticipate your response.

In sound,
The Savior

Hailangelo thought to himself, "The Savior?" How humble of him, how eager to "learn." Give me a break. He crumpled up the paper and shot it into the garbage can across the room.

What the sculptor wouldn't know until much later was that the "Savior" would act, with or without his correspondence.

THE END

ACKNOWLEDGMENTS

Thank you to Tracy Ertl of Title Town Publishing for her belief in me and this story. To Joel Gotler, for sharing his immense talents, and to Christopher Ming for all his support. To Megan Trank and Michael Short of Beaufort Books for all their support. To J.J. Hollenback, for his brilliant ideas, wit, and efforts to help make this tale worth telling. To Kara Corwin, for her assistance, advice, and steady guidance. To my beta readers: Sandy Keller, Sandra Eugster, Jill Muehrcke, Katherine Perreth, Richard Chamberlin, Dan Bertalan, Michael Roeschlein, and Dinorah Cortes-Velez, for your tireless help and positive outlook. To Michael Roeschlein, for sharing the song he wrote, "Zombie Girl," and for being the best half of the real Filing Cabinets. To Hilarie Mukavitz, for her cheering, commiseration, and historical perspective. To David Bowman and Caroline DeLuca for their editing talents. To Erika Block for her design work. To Andy Moore and Aaron Popkey, for the opportunities that changed my life for the better. To Professor of Philosophy Patrick Riley, for his wisdom, kindness, and encouragement. To Bob Bendt and Tom Stewart for their insights and anecdotes. You are all talented and terrific people.

To my entire family, especially my parents, for their support and love. To Jaimie, for her sense of humor, support, love, and eternal optimism. To Belle and John for their enthusiasm, belief, and cheering.

To everyone who ever supported this book, you have my affection and gratitude. Thank you. Here's to more to come.